"You don't have to be lonely, Rina," James said. **"If you need someone to listen, a shoulder to cry on, you can always come to me."**

She frowned, glancing back at him. "How can you make that promise to someone you barely know?"

She seemed sincerely confused, her honey-colored brows drawn down, her pert nose pulled up. He supposed it was a sweeping statement. But he'd made it, and he meant it, and he wasn't sure why she was so determined to doubt him.

"That's how friends behave," he said.

"And you consider us friends?" she asked, frown deepening.

With her looking all soft and serious, friendship seemed the least of what he wanted. "I certainly hope we're not enemies,

Still she watched him, as if waiting for something more. He felt himself slipping

Then he was leaning closer, and she was leaning toward him. It was only natural for their lips to meet, brush.

He pulled her close, anchoring himself in her touch, wanting never to let go.

She pulled back and stared at him, eyes wide and lips parted.

Not only had he found a way to convince the schoolmarm to stay in the wilderness, but he'd managed to let her wedge her way into his heart.

Regina Scott has always wanted to be a writer. Since her first book was published in 1998, her stories have traveled the globe, with translations in many languages. Fascinated by history, she learned to fence and sail a tall ship. She and her husband reside in Washington state with their overactive Irish terrier. You can find her online blogging at nineteenteen.com. Learn more about her at reginascott.com or connect with her on Facebook at facebook.com/authorreginascott.

Books by Regina Scott

Love Inspired Historical

Frontier Bachelors

The Bride Ship
Would-Be Wilderness Wife
Frontier Engagement

The Master Matchmakers

The Courting Campaign
The Wife Campaign
The Husband Campaign

The Everard Legacy

The Rogue's Reform
The Captain's Courtship
The Rake's Redemption
The Heiress's Homecoming

Visit the Author Profile page at Harlequin.com for more titles.

REGINA SCOTT

Frontier Engagement

*Read by
Geoff Hill
march, 2020*

⬧ HARLEQUIN® LOVE INSPIRED® HISTORICAL

Recycling programs
for this product may
not exist in your area.

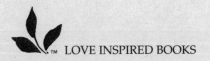

™ LOVE INSPIRED BOOKS

ISBN-13: 978-0-373-28322-4

Frontier Engagement

Copyright © 2015 by Regina Lundgren

www.Harlequin.com

Printed in U.S.A.

Charm is deceptive and beauty is fleeting;
but a woman who fears the Lord is to be praised.
Give her the reward she has earned, and let her
works bring her praise at the city gate.
—*Proverbs* 31:30–31

To my nieces Sarah and Linda—
no *Dr. Who* and no dogs and cats,
but all my love just the same; and to the Lord,
who loves me no matter who I am today.

Chapter One

◆

Seattle, Washington Territory
June 1866

Alexandrina Eugenia Fosgrave clasped her hands
tightly together, one up, one down, as she walked along
the carpeted corridor of the boardinghouse for the formal parlor. Though her white organza gown floated
about her slippers like a cloud, her heart was hammer-
ing against her ribs and her legs felt rubbery. None of
that now! She was not going to let her nerves affect
the outcome of this interview.

A gentleman wished to hire a schoolteacher, the girl
who had come for her had said. He'd already spoken to
two others and rejected them out of hand, even though
he had few choices. Alexandrina was one of the last
teachers among the Mercer expedition who had yet to
be whisked away to the wilderness since their arrival
in Seattle nearly two months ago.

She knew why the women who had traveled with
her from the East Coast had been hired first. They
had more experience and stellar references. She had

only the written word of the sheriff near Framingham, Massachusetts, that she was of good character, a statement grudgingly given. She was fairly certain he had wished he could have locked her up as easily as he had the other members of the Fosgrave family.

But lacking a position, her financial situation grew more dire each day. She very much feared that she might be forced out into that wilderness, not as the teacher she'd hoped to become, but as a penniless waif.

Please, Lord, let this job be mine! You have been with me through it all. You're the only one I can rely on.

She paused outside the closed door of the parlor and drew in a deep breath. Mrs. Elliott's pristine boardinghouse always smelled of roses, the scent matching the pink papered walls and flowered carpeting. It was a suitable lodging for ladies, but she doubted a gentleman would appreciate it.

She tried to imagine the gentleman waiting for her beyond the door now. He'd be an older man, established in his profession, the head of his community. He'd ask about her skills, her experience, her eagerness to mold young minds, the values her family had instilled in her. She'd have to be both honest and circumspect in her answers, for her skills were untested, her experience nonexistent and her eagerness waning with each rejection.

And as for her family, the less said the better.

At least her past had prepared her to exude a certain presence. She felt it slipping over her now. Her head came up, her breath evened out and one hand slipped to her side as she reached for the iron doorknob with the other. She knew every honey-colored hair was in place, her hazel eyes bright and confident even though she quaked inside. She allowed herself a pleasant smile as she walked into the parlor.

And then she very nearly missed her step.

Standing by the cold hearth was a fine figure of a man, tall, lean, with straight golden-brown hair neatly trimmed to the collar of his brown wool suit coat. His broad shoulders were damp with rain, as if he'd ridden far.

But he couldn't be the head of his community. He looked only a year or two older than her two and twenty years. And other than the warm color of his skin, he didn't appear as if he lived out in the wilderness and worked out of doors. Those men came to town in flannel shirts, rough trousers and thick-soled boots. With his tailored suit, elegantly patterned waistcoat and bow tie at his throat, he was easily the best-dressed man she'd seen here.

But the man she'd called father had cut a fine figure as well, and look what a scoundrel he'd turned out to be.

Hat in hands that looked strong enough to wield an ax, he nodded a greeting. "Miss Fosgrave, thank you for meeting with me."

She nodded, as well. He made no move to sit, and she wasn't sure whether he expected her to perch on one of the hard-backed wooden chairs that dotted the space. With its single shuttered window overlooking Puget Sound, Mrs. Elliott's parlor resembled a meeting room more than a retreat.

As if he meant to set her at her ease, he offered her a smile. It broadened his lean face, lit his eyes and caused her quaking to cease. Yet something told her he knew exactly how potent that smile could be.

"I came to Seattle on a mission, Miss Fosgrave,"

he explained. "We're about to open a new school in our area, and we have very high expectations for our teacher."

That was more like it. Every school that had requested a teacher had also sent a list of expectations. She'd rehearsed how to respond. "I was tutored in mathematics, science, geography, history and literature," she told him. "And I'm fluent in two other languages besides English."

"Excellent, excellent," he said, giving his hat a twirl as if he couldn't contain his delight at her answer. "What we really need is a teacher who is refined, polished and poised. I think you'll do nicely."

His gaze swept from her toes to her top, and she felt her blush growing along with his smile. She'd attempted to impress, but how could he know she was the right one for the job just by looking at her? She realized her recent experiences had made her too prone to suspicion, but she could not shake the feeling that there was more here than met the eye.

"You will want to see my credentials," she said.

"Certainly," he agreed. "But I have complete confidence in you."

Arguing with him was like refusing a gift, but she couldn't accept such an offer without questioning it. She'd seen too many people hurt by blind faith.

"Why would you have confidence in me?" she asked with a frown. "You have no proof of my skills, training or experience."

He blinked. "I know you have sufficient training— you told me so yourself, and Mr. Mercer would not have listed you as a candidate if you did not meet my criteria. He recommended you in glowing terms."

He obviously had a much higher opinion of the head of their expedition than she did. She'd grasped Asa Mercer's lifeline of an offer to travel around the continent to Seattle and teach, but the trip had proved to her that the fellow was too shrewd in his dealings. He had accepted money from a number of men to bring them brides, but he hadn't told the women someone had helped pay their passage or why. There was mounting evidence that he'd sold some of the women's belongings without their permission so he could pay for unexpected costs for travel. This man's connection to Seattle's so-called emigration agent only raised her concerns.

"How much did you pay Mr. Mercer for that recommendation?" she demanded.

His brows shot up. "Nothing, ma'am. He was happy to oblige an upstanding fellow like myself."

An upstanding fellow he might be, but she smelled deceit. "If you are one of those men who paid Mr. Mercer to bring him a bride, you can leave right now," she informed him.

That look was all innocence. "A bride, ma'am? I assure you, I'm here for a schoolteacher."

Alexandrina shook her head. "I know your game. You intend to carry off some unsuspecting lady with promises. By the time she realizes the error of her ways, her reputation will be compromised and she'll be forced to marry you. You should be ashamed of yourself for offering false promises to those in need! I will go nowhere with you and neither will any of the ladies in this house."

She thought he might back away, offer apologies. Certainly men had scrambled to oblige when the woman she'd known as Mother had used such a tone. Instead, his reaction to her set down proved his determination. He approached her and took one of her hands in his, holding it reverently and gazing at her beseechingly. He had the eyes of the deepest blue. They pulled her closer more surely than his grip.

"Miss Fosgrave, please don't dismiss my offer," he urged. "Nothing I said was false. We need someone of your intelligence and sophistication to bring culture to our youth. Who else but a lady of your refinement could adequately guide them into the future?"

As fulsome compliments went, his weren't bad and neither was the earnestness of his manner. Under other circumstances, her resolve might have even wavered. But he couldn't know that she'd heard far better from veteran charlatans who had pulled the wool over the eyes of hundreds of townspeople. His considerable charm paled in comparison.

She drew back. "Unless you have someone to vouch for your purpose, sir, I must ask you to leave."

He frowned as if he wasn't used to being refused. A gamin-like grin, a well-worded tease and copious amounts of compliments had probably won the day for him more times than he could count. But he would find she was made of stronger stuff.

"Do you know Miss Madeleine O'Rourke?" he asked.

Now Alexandrina frowned. "Yes. We share a room."

His brow cleared. "Then she can vouch for me." He grabbed her hand again and attempted to tug her toward the door.

She dug in her feet, the soles of her slippers dragging against the carpet. "Release me this instant!"

He complied immediately. "Forgive me, ma'am." He nodded toward the door. "It's just that Miss O'Rourke was out on the porch when I arrived."

Did he think her so dim that she'd venture out of doors with him? "How very convenient. We must ask her back inside."

"If you wish." He clapped his hat on his head and strode out of the room for the front door. She followed cautiously. She let him open the door and step out onto the wide front porch, where wooden chairs sat sheltered from a misty rain. Sure enough, the redheaded Maddie was leaning against one of the porch supports, looking out toward a waiting wagon. Yet it wasn't her friend but the team of black horses on the street that drew Alexandrina's gaze.

"Oh, what beauties!" Just as the man beside her was one of the most prepossessing gentlemen in Seattle, his team was one of the best she'd ever seen. Those strong haunches, those alert ears, all those fine lines. She hadn't seen their like since the sheriff had confiscated her team. Before she knew it, she was out on the porch.

"Do you race them?" she asked the man beside her.

He cocked his head as if he could not have heard her correctly, and too late she realized prim and proper schoolteachers should not know about racing horses. But he merely straightened and adjusted his bow tie. "Certainly not. I'm a serious horseman."

That she could not believe. Even now she could see the gleam in those deep blue eyes, daring her to laugh with him. Going back inside was no doubt her best option short of ordering him out of her sight.

But she'd challenged his word, and the least she

could do was follow through. She turned to her irrepressible roommate. "Do you know this man, Miss O'Rourke?"

Alexandrina had met Maddie O'Rourke aboard ship. Her short stature belied the force of her personality. Alexandrina might have had cause to doubt many people, including herself, but experience had taught her that Maddie would always speak her mind.

The Irishwoman pushed away from the porch support now with a nod. "I've had the misfortune of meeting him," she said, brown eyes twinkling over her russet gown. "This rogue is James Wallin, brother to the man who wed our dear Catherine."

Oh, no. Alexandrina had attended Catherine Stanway's wedding, but she'd sat at the back to allow closer friends to sit near the bride. She hadn't paid much attention to the men who'd ranged alongside the groom, but she'd heard from several of her traveling companions that they'd been an impressive group. If this man had been one of them, she had indeed misjudged him and cost herself a position in the process. She'd destroyed her future by focusing on her past. She wanted to sink into the rough boards of the porch.

Yet James Wallin seemed to bear her no grudge. He went so far as to bow to her as if they had been introduced at a formal ball. "Miss Fosgrave, a pleasure."

She nodded, unable to meet his gaze. "Mr. Wallin. Forgive me for doubting you. I truly did suspect you were here for a bride."

"And how could you not?" Maddie asked with a tsk. "Mr. Mercer must have collected bride prices from more than a dozen men, all of whom have had call to visit. But you needn't worry about James here. Catherine tells me he's a sworn bachelor."

She could only feel relief at that statement. Unlike some of the women who had journeyed west on the good ship *Continental*, she hadn't planned to marry. So many of the things she'd grown up believing had proved false, yet she still felt that marriage meant two people giving themselves to each other. They shared dreams, hopes, feelings. They benefited from the association. They became one. She wasn't sure she could ever trust another person to that extent again. At times, she didn't even trust her own judgments.

"I hope you'll hear me out now, ma'am," James Wallin said, standing taller as if about to address a congregation. "We really do need a teacher. And I believe we have a great deal to offer—a new schoolhouse that can seat as many as thirty students. A large room to yourself. A salary of forty-five dollars per quarter. All the wood you could want, chopped and stacked just outside your door, with a spring an easy walk away for water. Plus a tithe of the produce raised within a two-mile radius."

Bounty indeed. She knew women who'd left Seattle for promises half as great. Some of the women back East had been earning no more than thirty dollars a quarter and lucky to have board with a local farming family.

"How many students now?" she asked, heart starting to pound hard again with hope.

"Just a few," he admitted, "but more and more folks are settling out our way. The school will only grow."

Just like her dreams. This was exactly the sort of situation she'd promised herself when she'd left Framingham. She'd find some place she could make something good out of the tatters of her life, where she could make a difference.

"They're a lovely family," Maddie put in. "Sure-n you won't be sorry to help them. I'd be happy to take the position, only I've no experience, and I wouldn't want all the children to learn to speak like me."

James Wallin spread his hands. "And what would be wrong with the way you're a-speaking, me darling girl?"

She laughed at the way he'd mimicked her brogue. "You've just proven my point."

How easily they chatted. She wanted a life like that. Somewhere there must be people who would laugh with her, talk to her as if she was one of them, families she could help, young minds she could challenge to think.

You give beauty for ashes and joy for mourning, Lord. Help me to see this as an opportunity.

But try as she might, doubts circled her like ravens. What if the Wallins didn't like her? What if she didn't like them? What if they saw right through her to the scared little mouse inside?

What if he wasn't telling the truth?

She drew in a breath. A good offer had two sides. Mr. Wallin had stated his requirements. She had every right to state her own.

"I would prefer to visit the school first," she informed him. "I expect to be interviewed properly and hired by those who will have children in the school."

He nodded. "Anything you want."

Anything? That she could not believe. "And if I decide that the position and I do not suit, you will return me to Seattle immediately."

He spread his hands even as his smile widened. "If you decide you don't want the best schoolhouse and most dedicated students in the territory, ma'am, I'll personally escort you wherever you want to go, at my own expense. That's a promise."

He said it so firmly, as if he expected her to take him at his word. And she realized if she truly wanted this position, her only choice was to do just that.

At least for the moment.

She held out her hand. "Very well, Mr. Wallin. I will go with you."

She'd agreed to come, if only to look at the place. James wasn't sure why he was so relieved when Miss Fosgrave gave him her hand in pledge. Yet one look at that solemn face, and he wanted to dance around his team and crow for joy.

Which would likely have frightened both his team and Miss Fosgrave.

So, he merely clasped her hand and gave it a shake. "Thank you, ma'am. I'll wait while you pack."

She pulled away quickly, as she'd done the other times he'd touched her hand, which was a shame. She had soft, warm skin and a gentle grip that felt good in his.

In fact, she was the prettiest schoolmarm it had been his privilege to know. Her figure in that soft, white dress was admirable. Her hair was a warm sunny brown, combed back from a face that could only be called sweet. The eyes gazing at him from less than six inches below his own were liberally lashed, clear and open and a whimsical color that wasn't quite brown and wasn't really green but made him want to lean closer.

And presence? Oh, but she had that. She moved like a dancer he'd seen at one of Mr. Yesler's cultural events—fluid and controlled at the same time. She spoke with an authority even the renowned Reverend Bagley would have envied. She was poised, she was polished, and she was exactly the sort of teacher they needed. And he'd managed to convince her to come to Wallin Landing.

Even as his chest swelled with pride, she took a step back as if already regretting her decision. "Pack? Nonsense. I cannot possibly be ready on such short notice."

"We've only the things we brought with us on the ship," Maddie pointed out. James had nearly forgotten she was there, so focused had he been on Miss Fosgrave. "It can't take all that long to pack. I'll lend a hand if you like."

"No," she said, then quickly softened the word with "thank you. I prefer to pack my own things."

She certainly knew her own mind. Very likely that had been a requisite for joining the Mercer expedition. It couldn't have been easy traveling all the way around the country and starting over. He was willing to grant her anything, so long as she came.

James glanced at the sky, where the sun was trying to burn through the remaining clouds. "I've a few commissions to complete while I'm in town, but I'll need to start back in the next hour or so to reach home before dark. Will that give you enough time?"

"I suppose it must suffice," she said. "I shall endeavor to be ready when you return, Mr. Wallin." She inclined her head and turned to precede them through the door with ladylike tread.

Maddie, who had been watching Miss Fosgrave, shook her head. "Sure-n she has finer manners than the queen of England. But sometimes, if you catch her unawares, she'll be having the saddest look in her eyes. Someone's hurt her, that's certain sure." She shook a finger at James. "Don't you be going and adding to her troubles."

James held up his hands. "Me? I wouldn't hurt a fly."

"A fly, maybe," Maddie acknowledged. "But I'm thinking you've broken a few hearts in your time."

"Not intentionally," he assured her, lowering his hands. "I've never promised undying devotion to any woman."

"Yet," Maddie said with her usual twinkle.

"Ever," James corrected her. "Life can change in a heartbeat, Maddie. Best not to take it too seriously."

"So you say," Maddie replied, heading for the door. "But *I* say you'll be changing your tune for the right woman, James Wallin."

James shook his head as she left. He'd liked Maddie from the first moment he'd met her at Catherine's marriage to his oldest brother Drew. The feisty redhead generally gave as good as she got. Like him, she'd laughed off Catherine and Drew's threat to match them all up with sweethearts.

Oh, he knew most men reached a point in their lives where marriage seemed the best course. But those men hadn't watched their father die. He'd seen the light fade from Pa's eyes, and then he'd seen the pain flare in Ma's when Drew had delivered the news. And he'd known it was all his fault.

That was why he'd jumped at the chance to do his family a service when Catherine had entrusted him with this commission. His sister-in-law had been firm in her expectations.

"The women of the Mercer expedition are a determined lot," the lovely blonde had explained over coffee that morning at the main house of Wallin Landing, the forested area to the north end of Lake Union where James's family had staked their claims. "Many of them have already secured positions, and the remaining ones may balk at settling so far out."

"Fear not, fair maiden," James had assured her. "I will overcome every objection."

Catherine's cool blue eyes could look remarkably warm when she was set on a goal. "See that you do and that you don't raise any reason to object in the first place. We must have a schoolteacher if we're to achieve your father's dream."

James had nodded. Ever since marrying Drew a month ago, Catherine had been obsessed with honoring Pa's dream of building his own town along the lakeshore. James wasn't sure why she was so determined. She had never met Pa; he'd been dead more than ten years now.

His father's accident—felled by a widow-maker from a tree they were clearing—had affected everyone in the family. James was fairly sure Drew's overprotective nature stemmed from the fact that Pa had entrusted the family to his care. And sometimes he wondered whether the cool detachment of his next oldest brother, Simon, wasn't a result of watching Pa die.

He was glad neither had berated him for his role in the tragedy. He'd been only fourteen at the time, and it had been his job to look out for potential problems. He hadn't noticed the loose branch then, but he could see problems aplenty with the town they were trying to build.

Catherine, Drew and Simon knew the challenge, but they were undaunted. They'd drawn up plots, laying out the streets and placing key buildings. Drew had wanted to construct a hospital first because many people needed Catherine's skills as a nurse, but she'd insisted that the school was more important.

"A hospital tends their bodies for the moment," she'd said. "A school tends their minds for the future."

None of them could argue with that. Even now his family, including his younger brothers John and Levi, were back putting the finishing touches on a schoolhouse and attached room for the teacher.

And it was James's job to convince a teacher to fill it.

He took that commission as seriously as Miss Fosgrave apparently took her profession. This was his chance to make a difference in the family. Nothing would bring Pa back, but building the town he'd always dreamed of was the next best thing. And it had been a long time since his family has asked him to undertake something so important.

So, James had done all he could to make a good impression on the schoolteacher. He'd dressed in his best suit, tailored by a fellow from San Francisco no less. He'd shaved and washed his hair with the lavender-scented soap his sister Beth enthused about, making his hair look almost gold. More than one lady had glanced his way as he'd driven first to the territorial university to consult with Asa Mercer, its president, and then to the boardinghouse.

But who would have thought his horses would be the thing to convince Miss Fosgrave to take a chance on him? He'd seen the way she'd looked at the team, as if they were somehow an answer to a prayer.

"Always said you boys were the finest animals in the territory," he told them as they turned the corner for the merchant his mother favored. The flick of their ears and the height of their steps told him they agreed.

But as he finished his commissions in town— picking up a paper of needles for Ma and a new sketchpad for Beth, checking at the post office for any mail—he felt unaccountably fidgety. Did he doubt the outcome of his task? He might not have Drew's brawn, Simon's brain, John's knowledge or Levi's determination, but he knew how to turn a phrase to his will.

That's one skill You gave me, Lord. The least I can do is to put it to good use. You've given me a chance to atone. I won't let You down.

He took a deep breath as he guided the horses back toward the boardinghouse. Miss Fosgrave might have reservations about the position, but he had none about her. Her presence was her best quality. It would win the day at the school Catherine had planned. So, like it or not, that schoolmarm had an engagement with the frontier.

She just didn't know it yet.

Chapter Two

She was waiting on the porch with several other ladies when James drew the horses to a stop in front of the boardinghouse. Despite the fact that she had said she would only come to visit, standing beside her was a trunk that would all but fill the bed of his wagon. James tried not to cringe.

She'd also changed clothes for the journey. This gown was purple, the bodice fitted to her form, with bands of white satin sculpting the collar, shoulders and waist. Triple bands of the stuff followed the curves of her wide skirts. A straw bonnet with velvet ribbons covered her shiny curls. How could his family possibly find fault?

Determined to match her formality, he wiped the smile from his face, stepped down from the bench and marched up the walk. Stopping at the edge of the porch, he tipped his hat.

"Ladies."

She stepped forward. "Mr. Wallin. Shall we?"

The others were watching her so solemnly he might have been Death come to take her on her final journey. He offered his arm. "It would be my pleasure, Miss Fosgrave."

He thought he heard a sigh of envy from one of the other ladies.

If Miss Fosgrave heard it, she gave no indication. She merely accepted his arm, her touch light and sure. James walked her to the wagon as if escorting her to a dance. He couldn't deny there was something fine about strolling beside a lady in all her glory. His brothers might tease him unmercifully about his liking for fine clothing, calling him a dandy and far too citified, but he'd always appreciated the sheen of satin, the brush of fine wool. Women weren't the only ones who sometimes had a hankering to look good.

But looking good came at a price on the frontier, and he spied the problem with Miss Fosgrave's pretty gown the moment they reached the wagon. She couldn't possibly climb up onto the bench in those skirts. When she paused with a frown as if realizing the issue, he bent and scooped her up in his arms.

Her eyes, now on a level with his, were as clear as spring water. They widened as she cried, "Really, Mr. Wallin! What are you doing?"

"Just my duty, ma'am," he promised, setting her up into the bench.

Face turning pink, she arranged her skirts around her. "A little warning would have been preferable."

He leaned against the wagon and grinned up at her. "Very well. I promise to warn you the next time I feel an urge to take you up in my arms."

The blush deepened, and she faced forward rather than look at him. "A warning that will end any such thoughts, I trust. Now, if you'd be so good as to fetch my trunk."

"Please?" he suggested.

Her mouth tightened. "Please."

James pushed off from the wagon and swept her a bow. "At once, your royal highness."

Her look speared back to him. "Don't call me that. Don't ever call me that."

Why had he thought her eyes as cool and refreshing as clean water? Now they positively boiled with emotions. What had he done to earn her wrath?

James kept his own face still, determined not to give her any reason to change her mind. "Forgive me, ma'am. I meant no offense. Wait here, and I'll get your things."

As he ventured back to the house, he shook his head. Why had she reacted that way to a simple tease? Did she think he was laughing at her expense? Nothing could be further from the truth. He'd only been trying to make her smile. It was obvious he'd have to work much harder to stay in her good graces. He nodded to the ladies still watching from the porch and put his hand to the trunk.

One tug, and he nearly groaned aloud. What had she packed—enough bricks to build a house? With the other ladies standing there, and her waiting on the bench, he wasn't about to admit it was too heavy. He seized the leather handle at either end and heaved it up into his arms. One of the ladies gave an "ooo" of appreciation at his demonstration of strength. It was all he could do not to stagger down the walk.

Miss Fosgrave didn't so much as look his way as he brought the trunk and shoved it into the bed of the wagon. Sweat trickled down his cheek as he made his way to the front once more.

"All set," he said, knowing a longer statement would likely come out breathless. He took up the reins and climbed onto the bench.

"Good luck, Alexandrina!" one of the women called, and they all waved or fluttered handkerchiefs as if she were taking off on a grand journey.

He could only hope the end of the trip would be more auspicious than the beginning and his family would find her as perfect as James did.

Alexandrina sat beside James Wallin, heartbeat slowly returning to normal. She hadn't expected such a reaction, but then she'd never been held like that before. None of the men who had showed interest in her would have dared put an arm about her for fear of offending her family. One did not mistreat Princess Alexandrina Eugenia Fosgrave of Battenburgia.

"Though of course we do not use our titles here," Mr. Fosgrave would always confide to the rapt listener in a hushed tone. "Our enemies are everywhere. But when we have been returned to our kingdom, you will be well rewarded for your kindness."

It had been a potent promise, recalling days of pomp and circumstance that made the average American surprisingly sentimental. So everyone had treated her with kindness, deference, humility. Until the truth had come out. And there had been nothing kind in it.

"Alexandrina," James said, guiding his magnificent horses up a muddy, rutted trail that hardly did them justice. "That's an unusual name. Does it run in your family?"

She couldn't tell him the fiction she'd grown up hearing, that it had been her great-grandmother's name. "I don't believe so. I'm not overly fond of it."

He nodded as if he accepted that. "Then why not shorten it? You could go by Alex."

She sniffed, ducking away from an encroaching branch on one of the towering firs that grew everywhere around Seattle. "Certainly not. Alex is far too masculine."

The branch swept his shoulder, sending a fresh shower of drops to darken the brown wool. "Ann, then."

She shook her head. "Too simple."

"Rina?" He glanced her way and smiled.

Yes, he definitely knew the power of that smile. She could learn to love it. No, no, not love it. She was not here to fall in love but to teach impressionable minds. And a smile did not make the man. She must look to character, convictions.

"Rina," she said testing the name on her tongue. She felt a smile forming. It had a nice sound to it, short, uncompromising. It fit the way she wanted to feel—certain of herself and her future. "I like it."

He shook his head. "And you blame me for failing to warn you. You should have warned me, ma'am."

Rina—yes, she was going to think of herself that way—felt her smile slipping. "Forgive me, Mr. Wallin. What have I done that would require a warning?"

"Your smile," he said with another shake of his head. "It could make a man go all weak at the knees."

His teasing nearly had the same effect, and she was afraid that was his intention. He seemed determined to make her like him, as if afraid she'd run back to Seattle otherwise. She refused to tell him she'd accepted his offer more from desperation than a desire to know him better. And she certainly had no intention of succumbing to his charm.

She clasped her hands together in her lap, one up, one down, fingers overlapping, and made herself look out over the horses. Sunlight through the trees dappled their black coats with gold.

"Nonsense," she said. "What about you? Why were you named James?"

"It's from the Bible," he said, shifting in his seat as one of the wheels hit a bump. His shoulder brushed hers, solid, strong. "Pa named us for the first apostles: Andrew, Simon, Levi, John and James. I suspect you'll like my brother John. He reads a lot."

He glanced her way as if expecting agreement. Most likely he thought she read a great deal as a schoolteacher. That had been true once. She'd loved reading stories of kings and queens and gallant knights, imagining they were like her own life. A shame their stories had proved more real than the one she'd lived.

"Reading is important," she acknowledged. "But putting what we read into practice is even more so."

He laughed. It came so easily, freely. She wasn't sure she'd ever laughed like that.

"Now that would depend on what you read, ma'am," he told her. "Pa left us epic poems and adventure novels. I'm not sure how well we've put those lessons into practice."

"Well," Rina pointed out, "you do live in the wilderness. That is considered romantic in some circles."

"No circle I belong to." He swatted at a branch that hung over the track. "But at least Wallin Landing is becoming more civilized all the time. We have four cabins, a good-sized barn and the schoolhouse. Next is Catherine's dispensary. Before you know it, we'll have a town."

A town. There was something fine about the idea of building for the future. But was it any more real than the stories Mr. and Mrs. Fosgrave had told?

The pattern had always been the same. The three of them would journey to a new town and seclude themselves, careful to hide the horses and carriage somewhere for easy access. This practice was for their safety, the woman she'd called mother had insisted, lovely blue eyes tearing up at the supposed memories. And Rina had learned not to ask too many questions about the past, for it had always upset the dear lady.

But somehow the story would slip out—how her father and mother had been deposed by a cruel tyrant, how even now their loyal subjects were massing to retake the throne. Bankers would extend credit, expecting to be repaid in gold. Society hostesses would vie with each other to fete them. The horses and carriage would come out of hiding, perhaps even join in a few races for which her father would be handsomely paid. Life would be wonderful, until her father would wake her in the night with news that they were no longer safe. And then away they'd go again.

She'd been as shocked as the inhabitants of the last town, Framingham, Massachusetts, when the Fosgraves had been unmasked. Someone had finally questioned her father's web of lies and discovered that there was no kingdom of Battenburgia, no king and queen with subjects eager to reinstate them, certainly no princess waiting for her prince to arrive. The reality was a long series of debts run up by two charlatans with no intention of ever paying anything back.

She'd been fortunate not to have been indicted with them.

"Don't blame Alexandrina," Mrs. Fosgrave had said from the stand the day the judge had pronounced sentence, those blue eyes brimming with tears. "She never knew the truth. She isn't even our daughter. We found her abandoned when she was about two, and we thought she'd make a nice addition to the story." Her gaze had pleaded with Rina for understanding. "We did become fond of her."

Rina's hands were fisting in her lap now just remembering the moments before the judge had sent the Fosgraves away to prison, allowing her to go with no more than an order not to follow in their footsteps. No one in Framingham had been willing to befriend her. Her darling horses had been sold to help pay the debts.

She'd managed to convince the judge to let her sell most of her clothing for living expenses rather than to pay off the Fosgraves's debts. The only other things she'd kept were Mr. Fosgrave's pocket watch and a miniature of the three of them, buried safely in her trunk. When she'd seen the advertisement in the paper about Asa Mercer's expedition to bring schoolteachers to Seattle, she'd known what she must do.

She might not be a princess, but she'd been raised with the education of one—having been tutored in every town by the very best instructors. Her education was the one thing they could not take from her. It was the one thing she could give to someone else.

She forced her fingers apart and pressed her hands into the smooth fabric of her gown. Everything she had believed had been a lie. That didn't mean she couldn't believe in something else, even if she hesitated to believe in *someone* else.

James Wallin was the perfect example of someone she should suspect of telling tales for his own profit. He was confident, and he was glib. He was relaxed behind the reins, as if nothing and no one could shake him. Didn't he realize that they were driving farther from the safety of Seattle every second? Shouldn't he be looking for catamounts, bears, savages? Was he even armed?

Catching her watching him, he grinned again, and despite all her thoughts, something inside her danced. Dangerous fellow. She refused to be taken in.

"Tell me about Wallin Landing," she said. "What prompted you to start a school?"

"It was Catherine's idea," he said. "You'd have to ask her."

A vague answer, but she supposed he might only be the messenger. He certainly talked as easily as he laughed, going on to tell her all about his widowed mother, four brothers and sister, the addition of Catherine to their group. But what impressed her more than his easy manner was his skill behind the reins.

Her father had taught her to drive early, on a lark, he'd said. Now she could only wonder whether he had been preparing her to help make a quick escape if needed. Either way, she'd learned to love the feel of the reins in her grip, knowing that all the power of the team was hers to control.

Sitting beside other gentlemen who pulled on the leather and sawed at the bits had been painful in the extreme. James Wallin gave the horses their heads, only correcting them if they strayed too far from the path. He guided them effortlessly, as if from long practice. And he seemed to trust them as she'd trusted her team.

"I haven't seen many steeldusts in Seattle," she ventured at one point.

"Steeldusts?" He gazed at his team. "Is that what they are?"

She'd never met a man who didn't know the sort of horse he owned. Her father had examined every aspect, from the size of their ears to the conformation of their hindquarters. He'd known breed and lineage, could gauge strength and stamina. Or at least so he'd claimed.

"I believe that's the name given them in Texas," she said, suddenly doubting. Had her father made up the name like he had everything else? Maybe she didn't know as much about horses as she thought. "I heard they are prized by cattlemen."

"Well, I'm hardly a rancher," James said with a laugh. "My family prefers oxen. I'd ridden with friends from time to time, but these are my first horses. I bought them off a fellow in town who was giving up his stake. They had a certain dash."

She smiled. "Oh, they have dash, all right. See those high haunches? All power. A steeldust can run a quarter mile on good track in a few seconds."

He glanced her way. "You seem to know a lot about horses."

His tone was admiring, but her stomach sank. When would she learn? She had to guard every word now, not to protect a so-called family secret but to prevent being tarred by it. "My…family owned a team much like yours," she told him. "They raced a few times. Not that I condone the practice."

"We can't control our families," he assured her as if he knew firsthand. "Though that doesn't keep us from trying."

Her breath came easier. He wasn't going to press her for details. "What are your team's names?" she asked.

To her surprise, he glanced ahead as if to estimate the distance to their destination. When he spoke, he lowered his voice. Did he fear the trees would overhear him?

"The fellow who sold them to me didn't think much of naming horses," he said, gaze more serious than she'd seen. "Neither do my brothers. Drew says you don't name your tools or your saw."

To her, horses were far more than tools. They were intelligent, caring creatures whose loyalty you were blessed to earn. Yet if he didn't believe in naming them, he probably wouldn't understand that.

He turned toward his team once more, and she could see their ears twitching back to listen to him as he spoke again.

"I disagree with Drew," he said as if making a confession. "My horses are more than bone and muscle, meant only for turning a field or tugging out a stump. I rely on them, and I know they rely on me. They believe in me when no one else does. I think of them as Sir Lancelot and Sir Percival. Lance is a little bigger and prouder, but Percy has the greater heart."

What beautiful sentiments! His look was soft, paternal even. Rina had to fight the urge to touch his shoulder, tell him she understood.

And he knew the legend of King Arthur? Perhaps

Le Morte D'Arthur had been one of the books his father had left him. She couldn't count the number of times she'd read it, believing that her parents' kingdom was as marvelous as Camelot.

Now it wasn't a kingdom awaiting her, but a frontier schoolhouse. After traveling thousands of miles and counting off the months, she was about to achieve her dream of teaching. She could hardly sit still as James guided his team out of the woods at last. A clearing opened up around her, wide pastures surrounded by curly-topped cedar and fir pointing to the darkening sky. A large, two-story log house sat across one end of the clearing, with a barn to the south of it. But what drew Rina's eye was the building at the back of the clearing, up against the hillside.

The newly peeled logs gleamed gold in the setting sun. The brass bell on a stand outside the planked door looked as if it would ring for miles. She could imagine children lining up outside, eager to come in for lessons. Her heart swelled. This could be her school.

This might be where she could make a difference, where her life would count for something.

Chapter Three

From far too close, a gun roared.

Rina gasped and ducked away from the sound, pulse racing.

"It's all right," James assured her, reaching out a hand. But the gun barked again.

"Are we under attack?" she cried.

"Not at the moment," James promised with a gentle smile as he reined in near the school. "That's just how we call folks to dinner."

Rina managed to catch her breath and nod. She had to remember she was far from the world into which she'd been born. But she'd hardly imagined she'd be fired on the moment she reached Wallin Landing!

"James!" The call came from the house, where Rina noticed a young woman with straight blond hair. She hung a gun on a hook near the door on the rear porch, lifted her pink gingham skirts and came running to meet the wagon. Her smile broadened her heart-shaped face as she gazed up at Rina.

"You're here! Thank you so much for coming! I can't wait to see what you'll teach us. I've read all of

Pa's books and any John could get, but I know there's so much out there to learn. I love history, but I'm not terribly good at math. John says I just need more practice."

"This is Beth," James said when the young woman paused for breath. "She'll be one of your students. She's enthusiastic. About everything."

Beth's full cheeks turned red, and Rina felt for her.

"Any student who enjoys learning will be a blessing to teach," she told the girl.

Beth beamed. "Thank you. I promise not to talk so much in class. Or at least I'll try. Dinner's nearly ready. Will you eat with us?"

Rina glanced at James for guidance. He'd said the teacher was to have her own place, but perhaps she should eat with the family nearest the school until they were all sure the position was hers.

James eyed his sister. "Who cooked tonight?"

She raised her head and stuck out her chin. "Levi, but I helped."

James nodded. "It's safe, then, Miss Fosgrave. Levi does a decent job, but I'd beware of John's cooking." He leaned closer and lowered his voice, eyebrows wiggling. "Far too creative with the sauce, and don't get me started on his use of cinnamon."

Beth giggled, but Rina felt herself slipping into those deep blue eyes. She forced herself to look away. "I'd be honored to join you for dinner, Miss Wallin. Give me a moment to change out of my travel dirt."

Beth's eyes widened as if Rina's propriety awed her, but James straightened.

"No need," he said. "We're all nice and dirty in our family."

With another giggle, Beth excused herself to hurry back to the house. Rina frowned at James. Why would he refuse her? The Fosgraves had changed clothes at least four times a day. She only wanted to look her best for the people who would hire her.

"I do not believe my choice of attire is any concern of yours, Mr. Wallin," she informed him.

"Oh, yes it is," he declared, hopping down. He came around the wagon to her side. "Until one of my brothers shows up, I'm the one who'd have to ferry that trunk of yours to the school so you could change." He bent and pressed a hand to his lower back with a groan. "'Bout near crippled me the first time."

Rina shook her head, fighting a smile. "You do not strike me as particularly feeble, sir."

He straightened. "Not in the least, but I'll admit to being lazy as the day is long. I'll let Drew carry your trunk. I'll take the more delightful task." He held up his arms. "Fair warning, ma'am, as I promised. I mean to take you in my arms. Only to help you down, of course."

The ground was a long ways below. She knew she needed his help to get off the bench, but she wasn't sure she was ready to feel those hands on her waist. She must have hesitated a moment too long, for his smile faded.

"I'm sorry, Miss Fosgrave," he said, lowering his arms. "I seem to keep offending you. It isn't intentional. I'm just used to teasing people I like."

He liked her? Why would he like her? She'd given him no reason, hadn't been particularly encouraging. She was no longer someone whose favor he needed to curry. Of course, as friendly as he seemed to be,

he probably liked everyone and they liked him in return. Yet she couldn't help feeling as if he'd given her
something precious.

"Forgive me, Mr. Wallin," she said, offering her
hands. "Of course you may assist me."

He slipped his arms up under hers and lifted her
down as carefully as if she were made of fine crystal.

"Certainly not feeble," she told him with a smile
as he released her.

"Thank you kindly, ma'am," he said, removing his
hat and waving toward the house. "After you."

Rina lifted her skirts and crossed the ground, where
close-cropped grass grew in tufts. The scent from the
Sound was softer here, tempered by something—
perhaps fresh water and new growth? The heels of her
shoes clacked against the boardwalk that surrounded
the house as he darted ahead to open the door for her.

Rina stepped inside and glanced around, not sure
what to expect. She'd only visited a few houses in Seattle, and those had been Spartan, especially compared
to the homes the Fosgraves had preferred to rent.

The Wallin cabin seemed designed for comfort.
The plain wood walls of the spacious room were made
warmer by the colorful rag rug in the center of the
plank floor, the pieced quilt draped over the bentwood
rocker by the stone hearth. Stairs set into the far wall
must have led up to the sleeping area. The openings on
either side of the hearth gave access to another room
that seemed to be used as a kitchen if the tangy smells
coming from that direction were any indication.

An older woman, curly reddish hair turning gray,
was standing by the fire, hands clutching her dark
green gown. Beth waited beside a long table flanked by

benches, with a hardwood chair at either end. Nearer to hand, a woman with pale blond hair neatly confined behind her head gazed at Rina and James, light blue eyes assessing. Even in the blue-flowered cotton gown and with an apron tied around her waist, Catherine Wallin looked elegant to Rina.

Her old traveling companion came forward with a smile. "Miss Fosgrave, isn't it?"

Rina returned her smile. "Yes, thank you. How kind of you to remember me, Mrs. Wallin. I can only hope we find that we suit each other."

Catherine frowned as if she wasn't sure of Rina's meaning. She glanced around Rina for the door, where James stood. He crossed to Rina's side.

"You know how I am, Catherine," he said. "I have on occasion exaggerated to make a point. Can you blame Miss Fosgrave if she wanted to make sure I was telling the truth before committing to being our teacher? She graciously agreed to come here for her interview so you wouldn't have to travel all the way into town."

He was coloring the facts, even now. Her list of requirements had not been given all that graciously.

"Oh, I see," Catherine said, but by the look on her face, Rina thought she saw more than James intended. "That was very considerate of you, Miss Fosgrave. We can talk more after dinner."

James took a step back. "Good. I'll just go see to the horses." With an encouraging nod to Rina, he left.

The room seemed somehow darker once the door closed behind him. She shook herself. She was here to teach, not to hang on every word from a certain gentleman's mouth. Particularly when the words coming out of that gentleman's mouth were nonsense more often than not.

"Thank you for inviting me to dine with you," she said to Catherine.

Catherine's smile returned. "Of course! You'll find this table is always open. Let me introduce you to everyone. My husband and most of his brothers are expected any moment, but the others are here. You've already met Beth."

Rina nodded to the girl, who was now setting pink-and-white patterned dishes on the table. "Yes, and I understand I shall have the pleasure of instructing her." She could imagine the older girl helping beside her, teaching the little ones their letters.

"Indeed." Catherine led her over to the other woman, a tall lady, her eyes were a vibrant shade of green in a face shaped like Beth's.

"This is Mrs. Wallin, Beth's mother," Catherine explained.

"So glad you could join us, Miss Fosgrave," the elder Mrs. Wallin said with a ready smile. "If there's anything you need, just let me know."

Something pounded on the boardwalk then, and the door opened to admit the rest of the Wallin men. They were all dressed in rough trousers and cotton shirts open at the neck and rolled up at the sleeves to reveal flannel beneath. Rina recognized the largest as Drew, Catherine's husband, and he confirmed the fact by crossing to their sides and kissing Catherine on the cheek.

The more slender brother, who was as tall as him with hair the color of James's, was introduced as Simon, and the younger one with red-gold hair and green eyes as John. The youngest yet, who must have been Levi, poked his curly-haired head from the back room and ordered John to help him serve. The rest started moving toward the table.

She knew she should join them, but she suddenly felt alone, uncertain. They were so eager, so helpful. Would they still want her to teach if they knew about how she'd been raised, by whom she'd been raised?

James was the last through the door. His brothers hailed him, and his mother called his name in greeting. He offered them a smile before crossing to her side and holding out his arm.

"May I have the honor of escorting you to the table, Miss Fosgrave?"

This time it was easy to place her hand on his arm, to lean on that strength. "The honor is all mine, Mr. Wallin."

He led her to the table, then pulled out one of the benches to allow her to sit. She didn't realize until he moved away that everyone in his family was staring at him, Beth with mouth open wide.

James went to hold out the chair at the foot of the table for his mother. "Manners?" he suggested to his brothers with an arched look.

"Well, la-di-da, as Miss Maddie would say," Levi retorted, carrying a steaming cast-iron tureen to the table. "What are we, the queen of France?"

Rina's face felt hot, but Mrs. Wallin pointed a finger at her youngest son. "There is nothing wrong with treating others with respect, Levi Aloysius Wallin."

Catherine turned to her brother-in-law. "Aloysius?"

Now Levi was coloring. "Pa said it was from the old country."

Rina could not bear to see the boy teased. "It's a fine name," she said. "Far better than being called Alexandrina Eugenia. I have had to live with that most of my life."

He shook his head. "You surely have me beat, ma'am."

"Welcome to Wallin Landing, Alexandrina Eugenia Fosgrave," Mrs. Wallin said.

"Rina, please, Mrs. Wallin," Rina said. "A recent change." She couldn't help glancing at James, who was, of course, grinning.

The rest of them sat then, and Drew said the blessing from the head of the table. Head bowed, Rina listened to his deep voice thank God for what they were about to receive. She was thankful, as well. They'd arrived safely, and the family seemed kind and considerate. But she had yet to see if the school was as James had described it. She could only pray she had been right to trust him.

James munched on one of his brother's famous biscuits slathered in honey butter and watched Rina pick at her food from across the table. At first, each laugh had made her flinch, and she'd glanced around as if waiting for someone to order them to cease their nonsense.

Of course his older brother Simon had been nearly as bad. He kept narrowing his light green eyes at her as if something about her simply didn't add up. That was Simon—analyzing every situation and spotting the problems just as James spotted the potential. James would never admit it to his strong-willed brother, but he admired Simon's ability to get things done, to stay on track. Still he wasn't about to let Simon pick on Rina.

He couldn't help remembering what Maddie had said, that someone had hurt her. Part of him wanted to hold her close, shelter her from whatever had sapped her joy. The other part wanted to tease her unmercifully until she smiled again.

He must have restrained himself sufficiently, for his family noticed.

"Are you feeling sick?" Beth asked as he helped her clear the table. Catherine and Ma had taken Rina aside, most likely to talk about their hopes for the school.

"Never felt better," James said, carrying the empty tureen to the washtub in the back room. He peered over his shoulder through the opening by the hearth in time to see Rina frown. Didn't she like what they were saying? Was she even now thinking about leaving? He'd worked too hard to coax her into coming!

"No, there's something wrong," John said, following them with a stack of cups. "Otherwise he would have answered your question with a joke."

James shook his head. "Not everything has to be a joke."

Beth clutched her chest. "What! Where is the James Wallin we know and love?"

"He perished under the weight of Miss Fosgrave's trunk," James answered, and his sister and brother laughed.

He was smiling as he returned to the front room. He liked making people laugh. Something about the light in their eyes raised his own spirits. For a moment, he felt worthwhile, like he could do something his more talented brothers couldn't.

Why couldn't he make Rina laugh?

He'd seen hints of it, a twitch of those pink lips that suggested she wasn't immune to his charm. But he wanted to hear her laugh. He wanted to see her eyes brighten, her smile broaden. That, he thought, would be a glorious sight.

He'd simply have to think of another strategy.

As he began gathering up the remaining dishes, Catherine moved to his side.

"I must ask, James," she murmured. "Why did you choose Miss Fosgrave?"

James glanced to where his mother was showing Rina one of her colorful quilts. "Look at her, Catherine. Nothing rattles her. That's what we need in our schoolteacher. You know how some of those women would react when they discovered they'll have three students for the moment, two of which should have graduated the schoolroom years ago."

Catherine shook her head, pale hair gleaming in the lamplight. "I know our school is unique, and I can see Miss Fosgrave has a presence, James. But she's quite pretty."

James eyed her. "It doesn't require a hatchet-faced spinster to teach a fellow, ma'am."

"It doesn't take a beauty, either," she retorted. "At the moment, however, I'm more concerned with her skills. I want you to join us on this interview. There's a great deal we must know about Miss Fosgrave before we grant her this position."

Was she determined to make it difficult? Or was it that she could not trust his decision? "We never asked to see your credentials when you came to take care of

Ma," he pointed out. "You said you were a nurse, and that was good enough for us."

She blinked. "James Wallin, there are moments when you are positively brilliant."

James raised a brow. "Mere moments, ma'am?"

She laughed. "Take the victory I'm giving you, sir. I'll ask her some questions, but I'll see whether her actions confirm her abilities. It may be that she has a great deal to teach her students." She eyed James. "And you."

"Me?" Only the dishes in his arms kept him from raising his hands. "I don't need schooling."

"About some things," Catherine insisted. She turned to motion Rina over, but James felt as if the plates had tripled in his grip. Although he appreciated the light in a woman's eyes, the gleam in Catherine's just then had been positively terrifying. Her smile to Rina was even more so.

He was very much afraid his sister-in-law intended to follow through on the threat she'd made at her wedding to match them all up with brides. And she meant Rina for him.

That plan had to be chopped down faster than an ailing cedar. His father's death had taught him that life was uncertain, unpredictable. The more you clutched close, the more could be taken from you. He had no intention of marrying, leaving behind a wife in sorrow or living with the pain of watching her die. He shoved the dishes at John and tugged down on his waistcoat, preparing for a fight.

Catherine was all encouragement as she invited Rina and Ma to the table, then sat and placed her hands on the worn wood surface. The light from the lamp highlighted the planes of her face. James was glad Simon had excused himself after dinner to tend to chores at his cabin or this interview could have turned into an inquisition. James positioned himself now where he could see Rina. Her color was high, but at his presence or the upcoming questioning, he couldn't be sure.

"Now, then, Miss Fosgrave," Catherine said, "you were going to tell us why you wished to become a teacher."

James leaned closer, eager for the answer. He could almost see Rina's confidence slide over her like a royal robe. She sat taller, raised her chin and met their gazes in turn. Her gaze only wavered when it touched his.

"I consider it an honor to help children prepare for a better future," she said.

James nodded, smile hitching up. That's what they wanted for the school, as well. He glanced at Catherine, who offered Rina a smile.

"And how did you prepare for this honor?" she asked. "Where did you attend school?"

"I received the finest education from personal tutors," Rina told her. "I am well versed in mathematics, geography, history, literature and science, and I am fluent in French and Italian."

How could anyone not be impressed with her? He looked to his mother this time.

"A good education," Ma agreed with a smile, "though I'm not sure what call my children will ever have to speak French."

"Please don't teach Beth," James couldn't help teasing Rina. "We barely understand her as it is."

His mother swatted his hand. A smile lifted at one corner of Rina's pretty pink lips.

Catherine remained relentlessly on topic. "What about references?"

Rina inclined her head. "I have a character reference in my trunk. I can show it to you once I unpack."

"But no references from previous positions?" Catherine asked with a frown.

Now his mother looked concerned as well. "Have you ever taught school?"

Rina took a deep breath, the satin at her shoulders bunching with the movement. "No, Mrs. Wallin. But I believe I have the skills and determination necessary to make a good teacher. You will find no one more dedicated to her profession."

James could believe that. Her fervor shone from her eyes. But she couldn't know how important this school was to his family and to him. This was his chance to make up for what had happened to his father. He still thought Rina had the backbone for the job, but for the first time, he began to doubt he'd made the right choice.

Rina had all but accused him of picking her for her looks, and Catherine seemed to fear as much. Could it be that Rina wasn't the right teacher for them after all?

Had he made as grave an error in judgment as the day he'd looked away from the tree and missed the branch that had killed his father?

Chapter Four

They were going to send her packing. Rina refused
to shiver at the thought. She'd already given Catherine
and Mrs. Wallin doubts about her abilities. She could
see it in their frowns, the way they leaned back from
her, Catherine's cotton gown crinkling. She didn't want
them to think she also had no confidence in her skills.

Even if she did doubt herself on occasion.

"Dedication is all well and good," Catherine said.
"But ours is a somewhat unusual school, Miss Fosgrave. I wonder that someone without experience will
know how to deal with the problems."

"Problems?" Rina couldn't help glancing at James.
He seemed to be examining the lowest button on his
waistcoat. Did he doubt her now, as well? Somehow,
that made her feel all the more shaky.

Mrs. Wallin rose. "Perhaps it would be best if we
showed her the school, Catherine. We can explain better there."

Catherine stood, too. "Very well. James, if you'd be
so good as to light the way."

He shuddered as if it were a difficult task, and Rina

waited for some joke to pop out of his mouth. But he merely lifted the brass-based lamp from the table and went to open the door for the ladies.

"Wait for us!" Beth cried, grabbing Levi's hand and tugging him with her from where they'd been playing chess near the fire. Simon and John had already retired for the evening, but Drew also pushed off from the wall to join them.

They made quite a procession in the moonlight, James at the head with the lantern, Catherine on one side of Rina and Mrs. Wallin on the other with Beth and Levi tailing behind and Drew bringing up the rear. The light pushed back the darkness and cocooned them in warmth. Yet still Rina felt chilled.

"It's a wonderful school," Beth was bubbling. "I know you'll approve of it, Miss Fosgrave. Everyone worked so hard to make it perfect."

Her excitement should have been contagious, but it only served to make Rina all the more aware of the tension in James. He strode along, one hand fisted at his side as if trying to hold something in. She realized she'd only known him a few hours, but his attitude seemed off-kilter. Was it only her lack of experience that troubled him, or something more?

Her concerns gnawed at the edges of her confidence. Was she about to discover the dark side of these seemingly bright and happy people?

James stopped in front of the door, where someone had painted "Lake Union School" in white letters. Below, a blank space had been left for the teacher's name. A tingle shot through her. Her name could go right there, if only she could prove herself to the Wallins. She clasped her hands tightly together in front of her gown, one up, one down, as James threw open the door.

She followed him inside, gazing about. The single room was long, with a window on either side to let in light and air and a hearth at the back for warmth. A fire glowed in it now. Next to the hearth stood a door that must lead to the teacher's quarters.

Beth's claim that they'd all worked hard was evident everywhere Rina looked. The logs making up the walls had been squared off, smoothed and chinked, the floor planked tightly together to keep things snug in cold weather. Benches made from shaved logs, carefully sanded and dotted by several small slates that lay waiting for their students, ran in rows down the center. A proper desk with ink well and tilted surface sat near the front with a hard-backed chair covered in a quilted cushion for the teacher.

But not everyone apparently was as pleased with the school as Beth. Written on the broad blackboard on the front wall in large, crooked chalk letters were the words, "We don't need no stoopit school. Go away now else you might get hurt."

Rina gasped.

Catherine's reaction was more visible. "Levi Wallin!" she cried, whirling to face her youngest brother-in-law. "Shame on you!"

"You know better than to behave like this," his mother scolded him, rounding on the boy.

Levi stepped back from their fury and raised his hands, face red. "I didn't do it!"

Rina didn't know what to believe. His protests seemed genuine, but then so had every word from the Fosgraves' mouths. The letters made it plain that someone didn't want her here. But whether she taught at Wallin Landing was Catherine and Mrs. Wallin's choice.

And hers.

Rina lifted her skirts and swept to the board. "I certainly hope a student in my school would realize the impropriety of using a double negative. And stupid—" she picked up the chalk and marked through the word "—will never be applied to this school or any of its students."

A sharp sound startled her. Turning, she found James applauding, his grin growing with each movement. He looked as if his marvelous horses had just birthed a prize foal. The cold she'd been feeling evaporated to be replaced with a warmth that went straight to her heart.

"Well said, Miss Fosgrave," Mrs. Wallin declared with a nod of satisfaction. "I do believe we've found our teacher."

"So it would seem," Catherine replied with a smile to Rina and a look to her husband. "Let me show you the teacher's quarters, Miss Fosgrave. Beth took special care to make them welcoming." She glanced over her shoulder at James and Levi as if daring them to misbehave.

"Why don't you go check on the horses?" James said to Levi. "You know I can't mix Lance's grain to his liking."

Levi rolled his eyes. "You get it wrong on purpose so I'll do the work for you."

James put a hand to his heart. "Never!"

Drew chuckled, then lay a large hand that could not be denied on Levi's shoulder. Eyes narrowed, the youth left the school with his oldest brother. Rina felt some of the tension leave with him.

She thought James might follow his brothers, but he insisted on carrying the lamp for the ladies. Indeed, he hung on Rina's heels like a loyal guard, as if determined to protect her. Did he think whoever had written those words was hiding in the other room, ready to make good on the threat? A chill ran through her at the idea.

"If Levi didn't write those words on the board," she said to Catherine as her hostess led her to the door beside the hearth, "who did?"

Catherine and Mrs. Wallin exchanged glances.

"I wouldn't be concerned," Mrs. Wallin said. "It was only a childish prank."

Rina wasn't so sure. She didn't know too many children who would dare to deface the schoolroom or threaten the teacher.

"Do the other families want this school as much as you do?" she asked Catherine as her former traveling companion pushed open the door.

Catherine's lips thinned. "Want it or not, the school is much needed."

Beth wiggled past them just then, snatching the lamp from James. "Oh, please, let me do the honors. I do so hope you like it, Miss Fosgrave. I chose the patterns out of *Godey's*."

"A magazine that is the end-all and be-all of Beth's existence," James murmured to Rina with a smile that brightened the room more than the lamp.

The teacher's quarters consisted of a single cozy room. Heat would radiate from the stones of the hearth, and the window overlooking the woods made the space seem larger. A wooden bedstead stood against one wall, covered with a blue-and-green quilt that matched the colors on the braided rug covering the floor. A real armchair—overstuffed and comfy looking, sat in the corner with a set of shelves beside it to hold her things. An oval mirror and porcelain-covered washbasin rested on a worktable, with a beautiful carved chest beside it.

Rina pressed her fingers to her lips, tears burning her eyes. She'd slept on feather beds, under swansdown-filled comforters covered in velvet. But this, this was real and truly hers.

"Oh, Beth," she said. "It's beautiful."

Beth's face turned a happy red.

James wandered to the wooden chest. "I see you're putting all your hope in education, Beth," he said, fingers touching the carved roses along the side.

Her color deepened as she raised her head. "Drew made it for me. I can do with it what I want."

Realization struck. "Beth, I can't accept your hope chest!" Rina cried. "I can make do with my trunk to store my clothing. We'll have someone return your chest to the house."

James pressed a hand to his lower back and groaned, earning him a laugh from Beth.

Rina couldn't help but be touched. They'd taken such pains to make the school and teacher's quarters lovely as well as functional. Who would find fault with the school or threaten the teacher?

"You were going to tell me about the students," she said to Catherine.

"Did you notice the quilt, Miss Fosgrave?" Beth

asked, hurrying to the bed. "Ma stitched it. You can see the school in the middle."

Rina could make out a shape that resembled a log cabin sewn into the fabric. But she had a feeling Beth was merely trying to divert her attention.

James evidently thought the same, for he straightened. "You don't have to posture, Beth. We may have decided that Miss Fosgrave is everything we could wish in a teacher, but she deserves to know everything about the position before making her decision." He turned to Catherine. "Tell her."

Catherine nodded as if accepting her fate. "We only have three students right now, Miss Fosgrave—Beth, Levi and a young fellow named Scout Rankin."

Rina frowned. "Forgive me, but I must have misunderstood you. Beth is nearly grown…"

"Thank you!" Beth cried with an eye to her mother, who shook her head.

"And Levi appears to be an adult," Rina finished.

"He's eighteen," his mother confessed. "Scout's seventeen." She eyed her daughter. "And despite any other hopes, Beth is still only fourteen."

Beth deflated with a sigh.

So did Rina's hopes. She could feel James watching her as she glanced at each of them in turn. "You have no need for a grammar school," she said. "You want a university."

Beth nodded eagerly, but Catherine held up a finger. "Not quite. For one thing, their skills aren't advanced enough for a true university setting. For another, the distance to Seattle is great enough that we cannot send them to the territorial university there, even if they had the proper underpinnings. Besides, I would never trust their education to that man."

That man. Rina knew she must mean Asa Mercer. Catherine and her friend Allegra Banks Howard had been some of the most vocal opponents of the emigration agent and university president aboard ship on the way to Seattle. Like Rina, they could not appreciate his high-handed ways and underhanded approach of accepting bride money from men without informing the prospective brides. Any teacher would be better than him.

But Rina hadn't come prepared to teach at the university level. At times she'd wondered whether she would be able to discipline an unruly child. How did one discipline men? She'd purchased primers with the last of her funds, prepared to teach rudimentary skills to young learners. These would be more determined students, ones with every ability to thwart her, try her patience, sap her strength.

Keep her from remembering all she'd lost.

"We know we're asking a lot," James said to her, gaze serious for once. "But this school is important. Beth and Levi are important. We want the best for them."

And he thought she was the best. Once more her heart swelled. He knew exactly the words to disarm and persuade her. She shouldn't trust him, yet she wanted to.

She turned to Catherine and Mrs. Wallin. "It would be my honor to accept the position of teacher at the Lake Union School. I will do everything in my power to provide my students with the education needed to take their places in the world."

James smiled as if he'd known all along this was the right decision. Rina felt it, as well.

Thank You, Lord.

Beth wasn't content to smile. She threw her arms around Rina and hugged her so tightly Rina's breath left in a rush. "Oh, thank you, thank you, Miss Fosgrave!"

James reached out and carefully disengaged his sister. "She doesn't come with a warning, either," he murmured to Rina.

She couldn't help her smile. There were many things to warn her away from Wallin Landing. Yet all she wanted to do was stay.

James followed Catherine, his mother and Beth out the door of the school, leaving Rina to settle herself in her new home. After that note on the board and Catherine's explanation of their unorthodox arrangement, he'd half expected Rina to demand that he return her to Seattle immediately. But she'd heard about the school and accepted their terms. He ought to be overjoyed.

Still something nagged at him. He didn't believe his brother's protests for a second. Levi had no interest in schooling. It would be just like him to leave that note on the blackboard. James had made sure to erase it before exiting the schoolhouse, but by the look on Rina's face where she'd stood in the doorway to the teacher's quarters watching him, she wouldn't be able to forget it.

And James couldn't forget Catherine's concern that Rina didn't have the experience to handle a student like his brother. Would she stay long if Levi kept up his pattern of harassment? He knew from experience that threats and punishments had little effect on the boy. James had been much the same way, until Pa had died.

"You go on," he told Catherine, who was walking beside him as Ma and Beth hurried for the house, chatting about what Beth intended to wear the first day of school. "I just want to make sure there's enough wood for the fire."

Catherine paused to eye him. With the night so clear, he could see her smile in the moonlight. "A very wise precaution. I think we should do all we can to make Miss Fosgrave comfortable, particularly after what Scout wrote on the blackboard."

"You're sure it was Scout?" James asked with a frown.

"Who else?" Catherine sighed. "He's had a difficult time of it. We have to help him. His father clearly won't."

Scout was another of Catherine's projects. His father, Benjamin Rankin, lived in a run-down cabin on the lake to the south of Wallin Landing. The man's high-stakes card games and homemade gin drew a certain crowd to his door. James had to agree it couldn't have been a good situation in which to raise a child.

"Still, that doesn't mean the task should fall to Rina," he protested. "Between Scout and Levi, she may well hightail it back to Seattle."

Her smile inched up. "I know I can rely on you to convince her to stay, James."

She knew nothing of the kind. "Your confidence in my abilities is inspiring," James quipped. "But I can tell what you're trying to do, Catherine, and it won't work. You and Drew may be blissfully happy, but that doesn't mean marriage will have the same effect on the rest of us."

"And it doesn't mean it won't," she countered.

"That sounds like one of those improper double negatives," James teased. "Rina was pretty set against them."

Catherine gave his arm a squeeze. "But she isn't set against you. I see how she looks to you for support."

To him? That wasn't possible. Ever since Pa had died, everyone looked to Drew or Simon, and with good reason. His older brothers were stable, reliable. He normally preferred to live each moment as it came, without a great deal of fuss about the future.

"She'll learn," he told Catherine. "She's a teacher. She'll see who she can count on, and it isn't me."

Catherine puffed up as if prepared to argue, but he turned his back on her. This request to secure the teacher had been the first time she'd ever asked anything of him. He was fairly sure if he hadn't had this glib tongue, she'd have been focused on convincing another of his brothers to do the job.

Still he was thankful for his brothers as he gathered up an armload of wood from the pile leaning against the side of the barn. They each took turns filling the crib, so he wouldn't have to chop tonight. He carried the fuel to the schoolhouse, stamping his feet on the porch to make sure Rina knew he was coming. Balancing the wood in one arm, he opened the door with the other.

"Just delivering some firewood, ma'am," he called.

She rushed out of her room and jerked to a stop beside the last bench, chest heaving and eyes wild.

"Close the door!" she cried, finger pointing behind him.

Did she consider it improper to leave the door ajar? Beth always seemed to think doors should be left open when a young lady and gentleman were together, but maybe that rule didn't apply to schoolmarms. For all he knew, it was something that editor at *Godey's* had dreamed up. James kicked back with one foot to slam the door, then went to drop his load in the wood box near the hearth.

Rina paid him no attention. She ran to the window and peered out, head turning from one side to the other as if trying to take in every inch of the darkness.

"Thank the Lord you made it here safely," she said before turning to look at him. She blinked. "Why aren't you armed?"

She was obviously terrified to be out in the wilderness. He should have thought of that, but then, he hadn't considered Seattle all that much more civilized. Best to keep things light. He made a show of raising his arms and glancing at each in turn. "I thought I was armed."

"Will you be serious? Help me with these." She whirled to tug at one of the shutters beside the window. James crossed to her side and helped her close them. He could hear her breath coming quickly. How could he ease her concerns?

"There you go, Rina," he said, stepping back as if to admire their handiwork. "All shut in, safe and sound. Probably a good idea considering the treasure this schoolhouse is guarding."

She frowned at him, the pink of exertion darkening her cheeks. "Treasure? What treasure?"

"Why, the prettiest schoolmarm west of the Mississippi," he told her, adding a smile for good measure.

She stiffened. "Nonsense. Really, Mr. Wallin, I wish you would attend to the problem for once."

James threw up his hands. "And I wish you'd realize there *is* no problem!"

From outside came the howl of a wolf.

Rina grabbed his arm, eyes wide. "Did you hear that?"

"Hush, now," James answered, listening. The call came again, close to the schoolhouse, yet he could hear no whinnies of terror from the barn, no worried lows from the oxen or squeals from the pigs.

"Can it get in?" she whispered.

James touched her hand. "You're safe, Rina. I won't let anything happen to you."

She gazed up at him, face pinched. She wanted to believe him—he could see it in those clear eyes. Yet she couldn't. Had Catherine told her how he'd failed the family in the past? No, of course not. Catherine wanted Rina to fall in love with him. She wouldn't point out his faults. Perhaps it had been Ma. Or maybe Rina had just noticed that he was the least talented of his brothers. She was clever enough to have figured out she couldn't afford to believe in him.

Another call sounded, and something scratched at the door of the schoolhouse. Rina clung to James, trembling. He felt for her—alone, vulnerable and with only him to lean on.

He straightened and set her back from him. "Stay here. I'll deal with this."

She shook her head, hair falling from her bun to

brush her shoulders with gold. "No, James, please! It's too dangerous!"

James touched the silk of her cheek. "What is it you always say to me? Nonsense. I'll be right back, Rina. I promised to protect you, and I mean to keep that promise."

Chapter Five

Rina's fingers felt numb as James pulled away and headed for the door. She hadn't been able to catch her breath since she'd heard noises outside. First had come a rattling sound outside her window, as if something was shaking the bushes. Then those hideous cries had pierced the night. She might have been raised in civilization, but she'd read about the mournful call of the wolf. How was James to defend himself against an entire ravenous pack?

"Please, stay inside," she begged, following him to the door. "If anything happens to you…" She couldn't make herself finish the sentence.

His smile was sad. "Life would go on. I'm not that important in the scheme of things. But you are. Now, stand back."

She scuttled away from the door. *Lord, please protect him! Send those creatures away before they harm any of these kind people!*

He edged out the door and shut it behind him.

Rina ran to the panel and pressed her ear against it. How many were out there? Would they jump on him?

They certainly sounded too fierce to run away. Why, oh, why had she agreed to travel all the way to Seattle, to come out into the wilderness with him? This chance for a school was beyond wonderful, but nothing was worth the loss of a man's life.

From outside came a crack and a yelp. Was he hurt? Should she go help? Her hand was on the latch, fingers trembling, when she heard footsteps crossing the porch. Wolves did not wear shoes. She backed away, hands pressed to her chest, as the door opened.

James stood there, fir needles speckling his hair, smile on his face, all limbs accounted for and not a scratch on him. "Problem solved."

Rina peered around him, unable to believe things had been settled so easily. "Have they gone?"

"Not exactly." He raised his voice. "Levi, Scout— inside. Now."

His younger brother slunk through the door, curly-haired head bowed. A slighter boy with a misshapen nose followed him.

"Miss Fosgrave is your teacher," James said, his look more severe than any of her tutors had ever given her. "And she deserves your respect. But I think you have something to teach her at the moment. She seems to think we have wolves besieging the schoolhouse."

Levi snickered, and his friend smiled. Why was that funny? Did they know some way to subdue the beasts?

James focused on the smaller boy. "Is there a wolf pack in this area, Scout?"

So this was her other student. His brown hair was as thick and wild as a crow's nest, sticking out in all directions, and his clothing appeared to be several sizes too big and several days past a washing. At James's question, he visibly swallowed and shoved his hands into the pockets of his tattered trousers. "No."

The word came out reluctantly, sullen. She would not allow James to be so disrespected.

"No, sir," Rina corrected the boy.

James looked surprised. So did Scout.

"Why?" he asked, glancing at James. "It's just James Wallin."

"Listen to your teacher," James ordered him.

Scout bowed his head. "All right. Sir."

James nodded. "And do we occasionally see a rogue wolf in the area, Levi?"

His brother jumped as if he hadn't thought he'd be questioned too. "Yes, but don't expect me to call you, sir."

More disrespect. It simply wasn't right. James was their elder, a man who, it seemed, had earned a certain stature if his charter to bring them a schoolteacher was any indication. They had every reason to treat him with deference.

"A simple yes or no will do, Mr. Wallin," Rina said.

Levi colored.

"When was the last time we saw wolf tracks, Levi?" James persisted.

Levi scratched his head. "I don't know. Maybe two years ago now?"

"Two years ago?" Rina glanced at James, truth dawning. "So, those noises…"

"Were most likely not made by wolves," James concluded. "At least, not the four-footed variety." His gaze returned to the youths. "Anything you'd like to say to Miss Fosgrave, gents?"

Scout wiped his nose with the back of one hand. "Too bad you came all this way fer nothing."

Levi nodded. "Maybe you could teach Beth how to talk all fancy-like so she can attract a rich husband, but I don't reckon you got anything to teach us."

Something pricked at her. Like her so-called father, Levi Wallin was so certain he knew more than anyone else that he was somehow above the petty rules that others obeyed. She might not be able to reach such a closed mind. But then again...

"Tell me, Mr. Wallin," she said, raising her chin. "What do you hope to do with your life now that you're a man?"

James shook his head as if afraid she'd given his brother too much credit. Levi straightened with a sneer to James. "I'm moving into town first chance I get."

James's gaze drifted to the ceiling as if trying to look anywhere else but at his brother.

"And what will you do there?" she pressed.

Levi grinned at Scout. "Anything I want."

Scout grinned back.

"What a delightful life," Rina said. "How do you intend to pay for your frivolity?"

Levi's grin faded. "Frivol-what?"

"All the fun you'll be having," James explained with a smile to Rina.

"I assume you want to have fun, Mr. Wallin," Rina confirmed.

His grin returned. "Yes, ma'am!"

Rina took a step closer, gaze drilling into his. "How will you pay for it? Fine clothes and food must be purchased, sir. Money doesn't grow on trees, even here in

Seattle. So what will you do? Labor for Mr. Yesler at the mill? Work in a shop?"

Levi's chest swelled. "I don't need another person telling me what to do all day. I'll open my own shop."

James chuckled and turned the noise into a cough when Levi glared at him.

"And how will you do that?" Rina asked. "Do you understand the language of a warranty deed? Can you calculate the interest on a loan? Do you know how to amortize payments? How much will you need to earn from your goods to turn a profit? How much profit will you need to invest so that you can continue to expand your business?"

With each question, Levi's color fled a little more. Before he could answer her, she turned to Scout. "And what of you, Mr. Rankin? Do you intend to move to town and have fun like Levi?"

"No, ma'am," he said, gaze dropping to where his bare toes were pressed into the floor. "Makes no sense, as most folks in town wouldn't give me the time of day. I'd like to homestead. Don't reckon you know how to do that."

His voice held more despair than defiance. There was a story behind this boy. She wondered if it was anything like her own—abandoned, lied to, left to fend for herself. Still, she had clean clothes, food, the hope of a future. She wasn't so sure Scout Rankin had any of those things.

"I know nothing about homesteading, Mr. Rankin," she admitted. "But I know about the *Farmer's Almanac*. I can teach you to understand it, and from there you can learn how to calculate crop yields, determine the best times to plant and harvest and even predict the weather."

His head came up, and his eyes widened. Like his hair, they were a muddy brown, but she could see the light of intelligence in them, the flicker of hope. "That would be right helpful, ma'am."

Levi narrowed his eyes as if he thought his friend was giving in too easily.

Rina refused to be daunted. "Good," she said. "Then I expect to see you both tomorrow morning at eight when I ring the bell."

"Yes, ma'am," Scout said, though Levi merely snapped a nod.

"And I expect," James added, "that Miss Fosgrave will hear no more wolves outside her window or find threats on the blackboard."

"Yes, sir," they chorused. James pointed to the door, and they shuffled out.

Rina shook her head. "You knew all along it wasn't a wolf pack, didn't you?"

"I suspected," James said with a shrug. "But I thought it best to make sure. I'm sorry they frightened you, Rina."

She sighed. "They terrified me. Nothing in my life prepared me to fight off vicious predators."

He wrinkled his nose. "I don't imagine too many people have that preparation. Beth, Ma and Catherine can handle a rifle if needed. I suppose we better teach you how to shoot, just in case."

She raised her brows. "Just in case of what? Do you expect more wild beasts, real ones, to come calling?"

He laughed. "No. Once in a rare while, something wanders a little too close to the barn, but normally the wild animals give us a wide berth. They've learned humans can be dangerous."

So had she. "Then I doubt I must carry a gun."

"Maybe just a whip and chair for your wild students," he joked.

Rina shook her head. Levi and Scout were going to be a handful, but she supposed she couldn't blame them for resenting the school. They were both at an age where sitting around learning had to sound tedious and tiresome. She'd have to find ways to make the lessons relevant for them.

But for all her fine arguments, what did she know about opening a shop or understanding the *Farmer's Almanac*?

Her concerns must have been written on her face, for James put a hand to her elbow as if to steady her. "You dealt with them brilliantly. You're going to be a great teacher."

She drew in a breath, feeling as if she drew in strength as well. "It will be a challenge. Thank you, for the encouragement and for routing my wolves."

He dropped his hold and saluted her. "Any time, ma'am. James Wallin, wilderness scout, at your service."

She smiled. "I hope this is as close to the wilderness as I ever come."

He cocked his head. "It's not so bad, you know. Come on. I'll show you."

He held out his hand, but Rina couldn't make herself accept it. "Where do you intend to take me, Mr. Wallin?"

He grinned. "Into the wild."

* * *

James thought she would refuse. Those clear eyes were crinkling at the corners from doubt. When her fingers slipped into his hand, he felt as if she'd entrusted him with her life.

He led her out onto the porch. Between the trees and the usual cloud cover, it wasn't always easy to see the sky in Seattle. Now thousands of stars set the darkness to shimmering, bathing the clearing with silver. The light from the main house and Drew's and Simon's cabins offered a golden counterpoint.

She sighed as if she saw the beauty too. Down by the lake, frogs chirped a chorus and something splashed in the water. The breeze touched their cheeks with gentle fingers.

"There now," James said. "Not so very scary."

"Only because I have an escort," she said. "And the cabins remind me that there are others just across the way. It was another matter when I was alone in my room."

"And a strange room at that," James commiserated. "Though, mind you, I think my sister's designs are always a little strange. Those wide skirts and puffy sleeves." He shivered as if the very idea was unthinkable.

She didn't laugh. "Your sister is a dear. I just feel a trifle unsettled."

"I know what you need," James said. "Horses."

He'd been trying for a smile or at least one of her scoldings that he was talking nonsense again. Instead, she straightened, squeezing his hand. "Oh, yes. That would be wonderful!"

Bemused, James escorted her to the barn.

The cool of the night had yet to penetrate the log structure. Earthy smells and familiar calls greeted them as James pulled open the door. He lit a lamp and led Rina toward the back of the barn, where Lance and Percy had their stalls.

The pair were standing, heads down and backs toward the aisle, their dark coats gleaming in the lamplight. Both turned to greet him, hanging their heads over the door of the stalls and nickering. James stroked each velvety nose in turn. Lance's dark eyes were stern.

"Yes, I know it's after bedtime," he told the horse. "But you'd never been properly introduced to the lady. Rina Fosgrave, meet Sir Lancelot and Sir Percival."

Rina spread her skirts and curtsied like a grand lady greeting the president. "A pleasure to make your acquaintance, my fine sirs."

Lance raised his head as if he were above such things. Percy craned his neck to demand her attention.

Rina reached out and touched his cheek. "Such a bold fellow. I bet you are your master's favorite."

James pressed his hands to Lance's ears. "Shh! Not so loud. He'll hear you."

Lance shook away from his touch and turned in the stall to put his back to James.

"There," James declared. "Now you're done it. I'm going to have to bring apples for a month to make it up to him."

Rina giggled. It was a soft, silvery sound, brightening the barn, lifting his heart. A man would do almost anything to hear that laugh again and know he'd been the cause of such joy.

"Why don't we go for a drive?" he asked, reaching for the stall door.

She dropped her hand from Percy, and the horse nudged her shoulder to urge her to continue. Instead, she stepped away with a frown. "I would never take them out after dark for fear they would fall into a hole and break a leg."

There was that. He never had been all that good about thinking through consequences. "Of course," he said. "You just looked so happy with them."

Her frown eased. "They are impressive fellows. And if we have an opportunity after school some time, I would be glad to go for a ride." She raised her voice. "Especially with you, proud Sir Lancelot."

Lance snorted as if he couldn't care less, but James saw his ears tip back to listen.

They stayed a while longer, then James walked Rina back to the school. The farther the barn lay behind, the more he felt her stiffen. Was she still worried about teaching?

"You'll be fine tomorrow," he assured her as he opened the door for her and the light from the teacher's quarters spilled across the boards of the porch.

Her stiff smile told him she didn't believe him.

"I imagine every teacher is nervous her first day of school," he tried again. He nudged her with his elbow. "Just think how nervous your students must be. They've never been in school before. At least you've been a student."

She blinked, golden lashes fluttering. "I never thought about it that way. I suppose I do have more experience in a schoolroom than your sister or brother." This time her smile warmed him.

"Sleep well, Rina," James said, backing off the

porch. With another smile, she closed the door behind him.

James knew he ought to turn in as well, but he had one more task to ensure Rina had a good first day at the school. Surely if things went well tomorrow, she'd feel more comfortable staying on. That's why he returned to the main house and cornered Levi.

The boy had holed up in half of the upper room, where he normally slept. He and Scout, who was staying the night, were lounging on the straw ticks that had once held all the Wallin brothers, Ma's quilts piled around them. Both sat up as James paused in the archway that led into the space.

"That was a sorry show," he said, "trying to scare a lady."

Scout scratched under his arm. "It was just a prank."

James shook his head. "She might have left."

"Good," Levi said. "Best thing that could happen if you ask me."

James had hoped Rina's talk might have opened his brother's eyes to the possibilities of a good education, but that didn't seem to be the case. "No one asked you."

"I noticed." Levi lay back and put his arms behind his head. "So I thought I'd put in my own say, my way."

"By writing all over the blackboard like a coward," James accused him.

Levi sat bolt upright. "I'm no coward."

But he didn't deny writing the words. "Are you going to behave, then?" James challenged him.

"Maybe," Levi said, eyeing him. "But don't think it's on account of you. I'm not afraid of you."

"Neither am I," Scout agreed, but his voice cracked on the last word.

James leaned against the stone fireplace that separated the room from the one his mother and sister shared and crossed his arms over his chest. "Never asked you to fear me. But I know a higher power who might have something to say about your attitude."

Scout glanced at Levi, who shrugged again. "I can handle Ma."

He could indeed. Their mother had always had a soft spot for her youngest son. James straightened. "I wasn't talking about Ma."

Levi rose, blanching. "Don't tell Catherine."

Scout shuddered. "She'll dose us with something awful, just like she did Pa when he misbehaved last month."

Though Scout's father refused to admit it, James and his brothers were fairly certain he'd been behind a string of fires and other harassment in the neighborhood recently. He had a harsh way of dealing with anyone who owed him money, and even Levi had fallen in debt to him for a short while before his brothers had bailed him out. Only Catherine's medical care had won them a grudging peace with the man.

"Catherine might do more than dose you," James told them, keeping his face stern. "You know that look of hers can peel the skin right off your back."

Levi nodded as if he knew the look all too well.

Scout scrambled to his feet. "We'll be good. Promise."

"You'll be respectful of Miss Fosgrave," James told them.

Scout nodded. Levi shrugged again.

"You'll attend to your lessons," he continued.

"Yes, sir," Scout said, as if he'd already learned something from Rina.

"If they're interesting," Levi allowed.

"And no more threats on that board," James insisted, watching them.

"I told you, I didn't do it," Levi protested.

"Neither did I," Scout said.

James frowned. With their eyes open and skin neither red nor pale, they both seemed sincere. But if they hadn't ridiculed the school and threatened Rina, who had?

The concern remained on his mind as he retired for the night in his own cabin beyond the woods. When his mother and father had first staked their claims fifteen years ago, they had laid out narrow strips running from the lake over the hill toward the Sound. Since then, every Wallin son who had reached his majority had lined up his claim along theirs.

Simon's lands lay to the north; Drew's was to the south. James's claim abutted Drew's, and he'd finished the cabin two years ago. It wasn't anything fancy—a single room with a sleeping loft overhead accessed by a wooden ladder. He'd constructed the hearth of stones from the field he'd help Drew clear on his brother's property. A spring on the hillside bubbled water past his door. He'd never gotten around to clearing his own fields, adding furniture other than a workbench below and the straw tick above or putting glass in his windows. Why work harder than he had to?

But as he lay on his bed, curled up under the quilt his mother had made for him when he'd turned eighteen, he couldn't help thinking about Rina. The idea that wolves might be at her door had frightened her.

Didn't she know every Wallin would come running if she called? He'd brought her all the way from Seattle. He wasn't about to abandon her now.

And then there'd been the way she'd fussed over his safety, as if he was someone important. That alone made him want to prove himself to her. But why? He needed her to appreciate the school, not him. He needed her to stay.

Which she wouldn't do if someone was intent on scaring her away.

No one in his family but Levi would have written those words on the blackboard. He didn't know anyone else in the area who bore them a grudge with the possible exception of Scout's father. Rina certainly didn't owe Benjamin Rankin money, and James couldn't see him caring otherwise.

So who else had been in the school? And why lash out against it or Rina? Had he brought his family a teacher only to lose her to some unknown threat?

Chapter Six

Rina stepped out of the schoolhouse at a quarter to eight, according to Mr. Fosgrave's pocket watch. A light rain was falling, a mist shrouding the clearing so that the top of the barn looked translucent. She drew in a deep breath of the cool air. Time to see what she could do.

She'd slept better than she'd expected after praying for strength and wisdom to be the teacher the Wallin siblings and Scout needed. This morning, she'd risen at dawn to set out the materials for the day, sweep the room and fetch water from the spring. Her first challenge had been to revive the fire in the hearth with the wood James had brought the previous night. She'd piled logs around it and backed away from the resulting smoke, but it seemed to settle down and start burning. She supposed she'd need to learn the best way to manage it.

Everything else seemed to be exactly as James had promised. She had a good schoolhouse and fine quarters. She'd been the one to set her expectations on little children rather than the youths she'd be instructing.

She took another deep breath. She could to this. *Please, Lord, help me do this!* She set her hand on the rope and pulled.

The iron bell rocked on its stand, the clang echoing against the hillside and rolling down the clearing. Once, twice, three times she pulled. Then she stood and waited.

Beth appeared first, running across the muddy ground so fast her feet didn't seem to graze the puddles. She was dressed in a blue gingham gown with an apron tied over the front. Shaking raindrops off her head, she hopped up on the porch beside Rina.

"Good morning, Miss Fosgrave," she said with a wide grin as she held out a bowl topped with a checkered cloth. "I brought you some apple bread. Ma thought you might like it."

It was all Rina could do not to pull off the cloth and dig in right then. Dinner last night seemed a long time ago, and she hadn't thought about what she'd eat this morning.

When she'd lived with the Fosgraves, food had always appeared on the table on a predictable schedule, prepared by a cook and served by a footman who likely never received their final wages. Less appetizing food had also been served aboard ship on the way here and at the boardinghouse. She'd have to add cooking to the list of skills she'd need to learn in her new life.

"Thank you, Beth," she said before directing the girl into the school to a seat near the front.

Levi and Scout came together, sauntering across the clearing as if neither the weather nor her presence could daunt them. Each wore trousers and a cotton shirt, though Levi's were in better condition than Scout's.

"Morning, ma'am," Levi said while Scout nodded. They started around her, but Rina moved to block their way. Although Scout's eyes were on a level with hers, he refused to meet her gaze. Levi looked down on her, both from height and attitude.

"I will brook no nonsense from either of you today," she warned, hoping they could not hear her pounding heart.

"We promised not to play any more pranks," Levi said, grudgingly she thought. "We'll keep that promise. Right, Scout?"

His friend nodded again. "And thank you for forgiving us, ma'am."

Levi glared at him before slouching into the schoolroom and taking a seat near the back. Scout followed him.

Rina sighed. Well, she'd expected a challenge. Now was the time to meet it. She turned from the door and squared her shoulders.

"Wait for me, teacher."

She blinked, glancing behind her. James was jogging out from under the trees. Gone was the fancy suit he'd worn to interview her. Today he looked like a frontiersman, with heavy black boots, dusty trousers and a blue-and-green plaid flannel shirt that made his eyes all the more blue as he landed on the ground beside her and doffed his knit cap.

"Good morning, Miss Fosgrave. I hope you have room for one more."

He knew her schoolroom was only ten percent

filled. "Certainly, Mr. Wallin," she said, willing her heart to slow. "Who else will be joining us?"

He grinned. "Me."

Him? She took a step back. "Nonsense, sir. What need have you for schooling?"

"More than you might think, according to Catherine," he said. Before she could argue with him, he ducked past her into the room.

"Good morning, Beth, Levi, Scout," he said before taking a seat in the final row behind his brother. Beth frowned at him, but Levi and Scout turned their backs to face the front of the room.

Why was he here? He couldn't need education. Catherine certainly hadn't mentioned him as one of the students. Was it that he felt he needed to lend a hand with his brother? Or had Catherine or Mrs. Wallin sent him to report on her?

Either way, her hands shook as she walked to the front of the room and took her place at the blackboard. She'd dressed in her most severe gown that morning—black matte satin with blue dividing the skirt and edging the sleeves and placket of her short jacket. She had been particularly thankful that she'd adopted the short stays she could maneuver herself, as schoolteachers, unlike princesses, could not boast a lady's maid to help them dress. But the ensemble didn't feel nearly as impressive as she'd hoped as four pairs of eyes gazed up at her.

"Good morning, class," she said. No, no, that sounded far too breathless. She cleared her throat and raised her chin. "Good morning. I am delighted to see you all today."

"I'll bet you are," Levi muttered.

"As you are aware," she said without acknowledging him, "I am Miss Fosgrave. I believe you all know each other."

Levi started, then stared at Scout. "Who are you and how did you get in this school?"

Scout laughed.

James frowned. Was she being too lenient? She'd thought ignoring bad behavior might be her best choice, but if James knew a better way to deal with his brother, she wished he'd share it.

"We will start with an assessment of your current skills," she continued, "so I know where to begin with the instruction. Please write your full name on your slate."

Beth picked up her chalk and set to work. Scout waited for Levi to start writing before bending his head over his own slate. James picked up the slate beside him and toyed with the chalk. Those long fingers looked so strong.

Perhaps it would be best if she ignored him, as well.

"When you have finished," she said, "hold up your slate for me to see."

Beth whipped hers upright. *Elizabeth Ann Wallin* was written in neat white letters.

Levi held his up as well. *Bumpkiss J. Whoosits*.

Rina refused to react. She eyed Scout, whose head and slate remained down. "Mr. Rankin?"

His gaze met hers, haunted. "I don't know my full name, ma'am. Pa just calls me Scout, and so does everyone else."

His pain brushed against hers. She knew that feeling of confusion, of trying to determine who she was, where she fit in the world. "Well, then, Mr. Rankin," she said, "you are in a very fortunate position. You can choose any name you want. I suggest you can do far better than Bumpkiss."

Levi colored.

Scout nodded. "Thomas, then. Always liked that name. Not sure how to spell it, though."

Rina spelled it out for him. As he wrote it on the slate in large, shaky letters, she couldn't help glancing at James. His slate was up, as well.

Your humble servant, he'd written. *Not that you need any help from me.*

She was amazing. James could only be pleased with how well Rina was handling his brother and Scout. From what he could tell, their unknown threat-maker hadn't returned or caused any trouble. Everything was going as well as he'd originally hoped.

Better, actually. Rina gave Levi minimal attention for bad behavior and lavished praise on Beth and Scout for their good work. By lunchtime, even Levi was busy calculating on his slate.

James stood when she escorted the others to the door. As Beth and the boys started across the clearing, he moved to Rina's side. She glanced up at him, paling.

"Well, Mr. Wallin?" she asked. "Will you make a good report of me?"

James frowned. "I wasn't aware the teacher required a grade, ma'am."

"Is that not why you attended, to grade my skills for Catherine and your mother?" she challenged, hands on the hips of her black gown. It was darker and made of finer material than nearly any gown Beth or Ma owned. The style outlined her figure to perfection, and the color brought out the gold in her hair.

"If you think I sat through a school session merely to please Catherine or Ma, you must not own a mirror," James told her.

She blushed. Beth and Ma tended to redden at his teasing, but Rina's skin turned the shade of pink that sometimes colored the sky at sunset. He wanted to feather his fingers across her cheeks to touch the warmth.

"And if you think I would suspect any other reason for your visit, you must find me conceited in the extreme," she countered.

"You have more reason to suspect me of conceit, ma'am," he assured her. "And you wouldn't be wrong." He drew himself up with an arch look. "I'm a fine figure of a fellow if you ask me."

His teasing must have worked, for she seemed to be fighting a smile, lips twitching. They were as pink as her cheeks.

"So, if you did not attend to report on my teaching skills," she said, "why did you come to school today?"

He had a feeling she'd be no less pleased if he admitted that he'd been concerned for her safety. "Why, to inspect the building, of course." He turned and gazed up at the ceiling. "Good strong beams." He reached out and rapped on the chinking. "Walls well put together." He thumped his foot against the planks. "Solid flooring."

Rina shook her head. "You knew that before you even brought me to Wallin Landing. Come now, Mr. Wallin, why are you here?"

He met her gaze. "Maybe I just like spending time with you, Miss Fosgrave."

She dropped her gaze. "That is very kind of you to say. But you must know that it is far more difficult to teach with you in the room."

And here he'd thought he'd been unobtrusive. "I don't think I distracted your students," he protested. "Levi and Scout never looked my way, and Beth's eyes were all for you."

"You did not distract my students," she allowed, voice growing quieter. "You distracted me."

Now, there was a fine thought. Nothing he liked better than an attentive audience. He offered her his arm. "In that case, ma'am, allow me to distract you a bit more. I believe even the teacher is allowed some lunch. I'd be pleased to eat it with you."

As if in agreement, a rumble came from the vicinity of her stomach. She glanced up at him. "I failed to plan for lunch. I was unsure of the eating arrangements."

And likely hadn't had a thing to eat since dinner. James shook his head as he lowered his arm. "I should have told you. My brothers and I generally eat before dawn and head out for the woods or whatever claim we're working. We may take something with us to eat when we can, but we don't sit down to another meal until work is done for the day. That schedule doesn't apply to you. I'll ask Beth to bring you some victuals, and you can cook whenever it pleases you."

Her smile didn't look the least bit pleased. "Thank you. I should be able to manage something."

Why the hesitation? Did she think they were low on supplies?

"Well, there's always something on the stove in the

main house," he offered. "I can go fetch you something now if you'd like."

She smiled at him, and he felt as if he was the cleverest fellow in the territory. With a nod, he opened the door. The rain had stopped, and blue sky dotted the gray like patches on one of his mother's quilts. It wasn't nearly as pretty as the look in Rina's eyes as she sent him on his way.

At the main house, his sister was gushing to Ma about the morning's lesson as Beth, Levi and Scout ate fresh-baked bread slathered in honey butter at the table. Catherine rose from her seat beside them to meet him.

"I must congratulate you," she said, blue eyes intent. "From what Beth is reporting, it very much sounds as if Miss Fosgrave is as good a teacher as you thought she would be. We must do all we can to keep her."

He was in total agreement there. "I saw no signs of her planning to hightail it for the hills," James said, moving around her for the back room.

Catherine followed him. "But was she pleased with her students' behavior, happy with the accommodations?"

James took up a knife and sliced off a hunk of the loaf set out to cool. "Happy as anyone can be with Levi and Scout as pupils. I wouldn't worry, Catherine."

"Even you would worry if you knew what came in the mail today," she argued.

Reaching for a pint of his mother's apple preserves, James paused. "What about the mail?"

"John went into town this morning," she said, hands clutching the skirts of her flowered cotton gown. "He brought back a letter for Miss Fosgrave, stamped by the superintendent of the school at the White River settlement. It's another offer. I know it." She gazed up at James. "Can't you convince her to ignore it?"

He had to. There might still be an experienced teacher or two in that boardinghouse, but none of them would be able to deal with his brother the way Rina had.

"Give me some ham and a piece of Ma's rhubarb pie, and consider the matter done," James promised.

Armed with the best sustenance Wallin Landing could afford, he set off back across the clearing. Rina was already pleased with the arrangements—he'd seen how she'd looked at her room last night, as if it were the finest place she could imagine. Levi was difficult, but she'd proved herself able. It shouldn't take much to encourage her to stay.

But he'd barely crossed the threshold of the schoolhouse before he questioned his conclusions. She was standing by the far window, face turned to the light, and something sparkled on her cheeks.

She was crying.

He wanted to take her in his arms, promise her the moon to stop the tears from flowing, but he rather thought she'd be more embarrassed than calmed by such behavior. So he made a show of carrying the food to her desk and laying it out as if he'd brought a feast, all the while pretending he didn't notice that she was wiping at her cheeks.

"There you are, ma'am," he said, pulling out her chair for her. "Fit for a queen."

She raised her chin as she approached the makeshift dinner table. "I appreciate your efforts, Mr. Wallin, but you must not coddle me."

"Coddle, ma'am?" He grabbed one of the benches

and pulled it closer so he could sit beside her. "The way I look at it, you just gave me the perfect opportunity to eat lunch with a pretty lady. If anyone's being coddled, it's me."

Her lips twitched as she spread her skirts to sit. "I suspect that smile wins you a great amount of coddling from your family, sir."

If only it were that easy. "As much as I can manage, ma'am." He directed her attention to the food and tore off a piece of the bread to munch on while she ate. He'd brought a plate and utensils, and she used the latter with dainty fingers.

"That was a fine display of teaching," he offered when she was quiet. "Makes me wish Pa had started a school when I was a lad."

She cast him a glance over the apple preserves. "Where did you and your brothers attend school?"

"Ma taught us—reading, writing and figuring mostly," he admitted, flicking a crumb off his shirt. "What science we learned we picked up through experience. And as for history, Pa always said we were too busy making it to study it."

Her smile appeared at last, like the sun burning away the clouds. "Your father sounds like a very wise man."

James felt his own smile slipping. "Not wise enough, or he would have seen that loose branch before it fell and killed him."

She put a hand to his arm, brow puckering. "I'm very sorry."

"Everyone was," James replied, unable to look anywhere but at that hand draped over his sleeve. She had delicate hands, with longer nails than Beth or Ma,

hands that had never had to pull out weeds or scrub laundry for seven. "Everyone liked Pa."

"Just as everyone likes you," she said with conviction.

He wished that were the truth. "Not everyone likes me."

She raised her brow even as she pulled back her hand. "Name one person you failed to impress."

"You."

She dropped her gaze to the waiting slice of rhubarb pie as if unwilling to admit it. "I suspect I do not impress easily."

"And why is that?" James angled his head to see up under her hooded gaze. "Met lots of impressive fellows back East, did you?"

"A few," she allowed, fork crumbling at the crust. "And a few who thought they were impressive because they knew how to turn a phrase and a lady's head."

That sounded a bit too familiar. "I wouldn't blame them, ma'am. You have a mighty pretty head to turn."

She sighed. "But I do blame them. They were among those who taught me that flowery phrases seldom have substance behind them."

"Then you were talking to the wrong gentlemen," James told her, straightening. "If you mean to truly compliment someone, there has to be truth behind the compliment, or they won't believe you. And the compliment has to be about something that's important to them. Beth wouldn't be much pleased if I told her she has hands big enough to swing an ax, for all it's true."

"Probably not," she agreed. "But I suspect John would find it a compliment."

"John would find me odd for offering it," James

corrected her. "I'm not sure any of my brothers would take well to me calling their hands manly."

She giggled, and he knew he'd won the day. Perhaps enough to discover what was really troubling her?

"So why were you crying?" he asked, keeping his gaze on his bread as if it concerned him more than her answer. "If Levi left a snake in your desk, I'll have him on bread and water for a week."

She started. "Levi leaves snakes?"

James set down the bread and met her gaze. "Forget I mentioned it. But if my pesky little brother isn't the cause of your tears, who is?"

He could see her swallow as she looked away. "I just found myself unaccountably...lonely."

Lonely. How his family would chuckle at the thought of anyone feeling alone at Wallin Landing. With five brothers and a sister, there was always someone about. But he knew how she felt. At times, even with his entire family surrounding him, he felt alone.

"You don't have to be lonely, Rina," he said. "If you need someone to listen, a shoulder to cry on, you can always come to me."

She frowned, glancing back at him. "How can you make that promise to someone you barely know?"

She seemed sincerely confused, her honey-colored brows drawn down, her pert nose pulled up. He supposed it was a sweeping statement. But he'd made it, and he meant it, and he wasn't sure why she was so determined to doubt him.

"That's how friends behave," he said.

"And you consider us friends?" she asked, frown deepening.

With her looking all soft and serious, friendship

seemed the least of what he wanted. "I certainly hope we're not enemies, ma'am."

Still she watched him, as if waiting for something more. He felt himself slipping into those clear eyes. Then he was leaning closer, and she was leaning toward him. It was only natural for their lips to meet, brush.

Hold.

And he was falling, effortlessly, like a leaf dancing on the breeze. The world reeled around him, and he pulled her close, anchoring himself in her touch, wanting never to let go.

She pulled back and stared at him, eyes wide and lips parted. And he knew Catherine would be very pleased.

Not only had he found a way to convince the schoolmarm to stay in the wilderness, but he'd managed to let her wedge her way into his heart.

Chapter Seven

Rina could scarcely catch her breath. He'd kissed her, and she'd felt the wonder of it to her toes. Every part of her was tingling. She wanted to laugh and cry at the same time.

But more, she wanted to understand why. They'd barely known each other a day. A kiss so soon was not the behavior of a gentleman. Gentlemen courted ladies with consideration, with thoughtful conversation, touching fingers, kissing hands. What was he thinking?

"Why did you do that?" she demanded.

He leaned back from her, and she thought she saw a tremor in his hands. "It seemed like the right thing to do," he said.

Always the joker. "Nonsense," she said, trying to gather the shreds of her dignity. "You will have to do better than that, Mr. Wallin."

He raised a brow. "Complaining now is a bit like shutting the barn door once the horse is out, Rina."

Oh, but he could be maddening. "I did not give you permission to use my first name!"

He stood, and she leaned back to meet his gaze. "You didn't give me permission to kiss you, either," he pointed out.

"Indeed, I did not." She rose as well and shook out her skirts.

He frowned. "Why are you so angry? It was just a kiss."

Just a kiss. Just the casual meeting of two pairs of lips. Oh, but it had felt like so much more! That he didn't understand made her angrier. One did not steal kisses from a schoolteacher! They were held to far higher standards. Did he want to ruin her reputation?

"I think you had better go," she said.

"I think you're right." He nodded toward the remaining food on her desk. "Enjoy the rest of your lunch, and good luck this afternoon." He turned and strode out the door, closing it behind him.

Rina sagged on her chair. What was he doing? He couldn't have grown that fond of her so quickly. He knew little about her. She realized that there were times here on the frontier when things were more casual than where she'd been raised, but she was fairly sure that, even here, such a kiss was meant for something important, something deep, something permanent. It wasn't "just a kiss."

Unless you were the never-serious James Wallin.

She blew out her breath. At least she'd stood her ground, let him know she wouldn't condone such behavior. He wasn't likely to try kissing her again.

Worse luck.

She managed only a few bites of the rhubarb pie he'd brought before Beth, Levi and Scout returned. Putting the food away in her room for later, she took up her place at the front of the class. The mulish set to Levi's face told her it was going to be a long afternoon.

Indeed, the second half of the day was worse than the first. Levi and Scout must have felt more comfortable acting out without James present, or perhaps they sensed her rattled state. Either way, they questioned her on every topic and tried her least command. Then they insisted on leaving early with the excuse that there were chores that must be done. They seemed to know she would hesitate to argue with that.

"You just have to ignore them," Beth told her as the girl gathered up her things to leave. "They'll get tired of plaguing you eventually."

Though Rina hoped Beth was right, she didn't think it was a good sign that her student already thought she needed advice on how to teach.

"Oh!" Beth cried, whirling from the door and hurrying back to Rina's side. "I almost forgot. A letter came for you." She fished a battered piece of paper from her primer and handed it to Rina. "It looks important."

It didn't look that important to Rina. Indeed, dirt had darkened the folded paper, rain had made the address run, and the seal was cracked. But it was clearly made out to her from the superintendent of the White River school.

Another offer of employment?

Something inside her leaped at the thought. No more trying to pretend she could teach disrespectful older students. No more distracting handsome gentleman lounging in her classroom. No one stealing a kiss that nearly broke her heart. She wanted to tear the letter open immediately, but she was all too aware of Beth watching her, lips pinched as if she was afraid to utter a peep.

"Thank you, Beth," Rina said. "I shall see you tomorrow."

Beth brightened as if she'd doubted it. "See you tomorrow, Miss Fosgrave." She all but skipped out of the room.

Rina went to sit at the desk, then opened the letter and smoothed it out on her skirts. Every school had its challenges, she was sure. This offer, if that was what it was, would not cure all ills. She should probably stay here, work through any difficulties. But though she thought with hard work she might become the teacher Levi and Scout needed, she wasn't sure what to do about James. Just sitting across the dinner table tonight would be difficult. Every time she noticed his lips, she'd remember how they'd felt against hers. So much for promising herself she wouldn't fall for his charm!

Enough. This supervisor deserved an answer. She lifted the paper and began to read.

Dear Miss Fosgrave, he had written. *Mr. Asa Mercer has given us to understand that you meet our high standards for a teacher. We are pleased to offer you an assignment as assistant teacher at the White River school.*

Assistant teacher? Why, that could be perfect. She'd have another teacher to learn from, a mentor, until she was ready to take on a classroom by herself.

Term will not start until October, the letter continued. *However, travel during that time could be problematic. You will need to arrange passage at your earliest convenience to the White River Crossing. Mr. Hiram Buckhorn stops there every Saturday after-*

noon and will be glad to bring you the rest of the way with him.

She'd heard the Crossing mentioned in town. It lay nearly thirty miles to the south of Seattle, a couple days' journey through untamed wilderness. And she was fairly sure there was a wolf pack or two in the area.

Below you will find a list of our expectations for your behavior. We offer twenty-five dollars per quarter, your own cabin with a pump near the school and the gratitude of your young students and their parents. It was signed Mr. Josiah Montebank.

He certainly seemed sure of her answer! Had Mr. Mercer told him she was desperate? It would have been rather gratifying to write to their former leader and inform him she had another position, with better pay and closer to town.

But did she want to tell him that?

She fanned herself with the letter, thinking, and the list of requirements fluttered down to the floor. She retrieved it, and her eyes widened. My word, but what a paragon their teacher had to be!

She shook her head as she rose and set the letter aside. She'd have to write and refuse. Considering their requirements and her agreement with the Wallins, it was probably best that she stay here. That is, if the Wallins still wanted her. All Catherine and Mrs. Wallin would have to do is quiz Beth to learn that today had not been the best of days. They might be glad to see the last of her.

Footsteps alerted her to a visitor a moment before the door banged open. A man squeezed inside her schoolhouse. Folds of flesh hung from his bull neck, and his belly flopped over his dirty trousers. What was even more alarming was the glint of anger in his close-set eyes.

Rina stood a little taller. "May I help you, sir?"

He pointed a pudgy finger at her. "You can stop filling my boy's head with nonsense."

She knew the Wallin father was dead, so there could only be one boy he meant. "You must be Scout's father."

"That's right," he said, chest swelling so that it threatened the buttons already straining there. "And that's his name, Scout. I don't need any of you mealy-mouthed do-gooders changing his name or anything else about him."

Scout must have told him about his first day of school. "I doubt he meant any disrespect by choosing a different name," she told him. "I certainly meant no disrespect by suggesting it."

"I'll just bet you didn't," he sneered. His footsteps thudded against the planks as he strode toward her, and Rina backed up despite herself.

"He was content enough with his lot until you all started making him wish for more," Mr. Rankin said, coming to a stop less than a yard away from her. The bitter stench of alcohol and tobacco rolled off him in waves.

She refused to recoil. "And should he not wish for more?" she countered. "I believe we all want something better. Education can open doors for his future."

"He has the only future he needs, helping me." He thumped his chest. "Every minute he's away is time he could be working. You don't expect me to sweep out the place or do the cooking, do you?"

By the bulk of him, a little physical exercise would

not have been remiss, but she could hardly tell him that. "I released Scout from class early today precisely because he said he needed to do chores."

"And weren't that nice of you?" This close, she could see the spittle come out with his sneer. She could not bear to look at him and fixed her gaze on the wall behind him instead.

"I was being practical," she said. "Many children have attended school and still managed to finish their chores."

"Children?" His laugh was rougher than the bark of a tree as he took another step closer. "Scout ain't no child. And he never showed the least bit of interest in book learning until a pretty little schoolmarm showed up." He reached out a finger and flicked at the trim of her collar.

He made it sound as if the boy came merely to ogle her. Scout's father certainly didn't hide his attentions as his gaze flickered over her. She felt as if she'd been splashed with mud. This was worse than when the townspeople had turned on her in Framingham. She tried to back away, and her foot caught on the chair. Down she went with a thud onto the seat.

He leered at her.

Rina pushed herself to her feet, determined not to let him see her fear. "I assure you, Mr. Rankin, that your son has the makings of a fine student. His education could even be an asset to you."

His tiny eyes narrowed. "How?"

Rina clasped her hands together to keep them from shaking, fingers locking properly in front her as Mrs. Fosgrave had always said was appropriate for a princess. "He could calculate crop yields, determine likely weather patterns."

He snorted. "Don't care a thing about crops, and no one but God knows the weather."

She had to convince this man, for Scout's sake and hers. "If you tell me what you do for a living, sir, I can explain how education can help."

He bristled and took a step back at last. She wanted to feel relieved, but she couldn't like the way his beefy hands were fisting at his sides.

"What I do is none of your affair," he all but growled. "I make a good living, and I never went to no stupid school."

Stupid school. Perhaps misspelled in his mind the way it had been on the wall. Here was the person who had threatened her with words on a blackboard. She'd thought that person must be a coward to hide. Now she realized he'd simply been building up to something worse.

Why had she thought she could manage all this? She'd been raised to deal with civil, cultured people who used words, not physical violence, to state their cases. This was no place for her.

Yet even as the doubts assailed her, she knew Scout needed an advocate. He had no one but her.

"If you could be a success with no education," she told his father, "think what more your son could accomplish with one."

He drew himself up, towering over her. "You just don't listen, do you? Maybe it's time someone taught the teacher a lesson." He raised one fist.

Rina ducked, bringing up her arms to protect her face. *Father, help me!*

From beyond him came the sound of a rifle cocking. "Step away from the lady, Rankin," James said.

Rankin turned, and Rina could breathe again.

"Figures a Wallin would come to the rescue," he said. "Whichever one of you plans to marry this woman better watch himself." He cast a contemptuous glance back at Rina. "She talks too much."

"So do you and look how popular you are." James advanced into the room, rifle at the ready as Rina lowered her arms. "In fact, I can hear your friends calling you. Time to go."

He shrugged in a ripple of fat. "I've said my piece. Step aside."

James raised the gun higher. Would she witness a gunfight? What if James were hurt? *Father, please, help us!*

"One thing before you go," James said. "Apologize to Miss Fosgrave."

Rankin swelled up like a sick toad. "Apologize? She ought to apologize to me for filling my boy's head full of nonsense."

"Oh, you did a good enough job before she ever came along," James replied. He advanced again, until the gun was a few feet away from her tormentor. "Apologize."

"It's all right, Mr. Wallin," Rina said, wanting only to see the man gone. "Let him go."

She could hear the oily smile in Rankin's voice. "There, you see? The lady's learned her place already."

Something hot flashed through her. Oh, but she would not let him believe that! She pushed around him until she was standing next to James. "You are not welcome in my school, sir. I think you should leave."

He laughed. "You can think all you like, missy. I'll go when it pleases me and not before." He strutted past James and out the door.

James followed him as if to make sure he left. Rina sagged against the nearest bench. What had she been thinking? She had no business confronting a ruffian!

And what sort of place was this, where parents felt free to physically threaten the teacher? Where she had to teach protected by a gun? Where her buried heart tried to rise at a kiss? Everywhere she looked, she saw challenges—to her dreams of passing on her knowledge, to her person, to her convictions. There was only one solution.

James must have been satisfied that the fellow was gone, for he came back inside and left the gun on the last bench to hurry up to Rina. "Are you all right?"

Rina swallowed. "No. I want to leave. Immediately. Just as you promised."

James stared at her. "Now?"

"Now," she insisted, turning for her room. "It will only take me a few moments to gather my things."

It had taken her far longer on the way out, but perhaps she hadn't unpacked last night. Now she was in such an all-fired hurry that he might have thought a bear was chasing her.

Given Rankin's size, she wasn't far off.

He could have throttled Rankin. James had been thinking about returning to the school and apologizing for kissing her that afternoon for all he couldn't make himself regret his actions. Then he'd spotted the troublemaker entering the school, and he'd gone for his rifle.

"Rankin is nothing but a bully," he told Rina now as he followed her. "He runs a gambling outfit that's just this side of the law. He picks on those he deems too weak to fight back. He's gone after Levi, and you can imagine how he treats Scout. I won't let him trouble you again."

"You can scarcely stand guard on the schoolhouse," she informed him, gathering up various items and dropping them in her trunk without so much as folding them.

"I will if I have to," James promised.

"Nonsense," she insisted. "Besides, Mr. Rankin's visit is only one of the things that proved to me that this position will never suit me." She paused as if considering the matter. "Or rather, I will never suit this position."

James sighed. "I'll have Catherine talk to him about Scout. She seems to be the only one he listens to."

Her head came up. "A teacher who must appeal to the school board for help over every little problem is not worth her pay, sir."

"This isn't a little problem," he replied. "It's Benjamin Rankin. He's so big he can barely fit through the door!"

She didn't so much as smile at his wit. "He is only one of the difficulties associated with this position. I am a new teacher. I was barely confident of my abilities to instruct young children. I lack the experience to deal with mature students who challenge everything I say."

James frowned. "We knew all that going in, and you were determined to take the position anyway. What changed your mind?"

"Today," she said, avoiding his gaze. "Reality. I am ill-prepared to take on this position. You can do better."

Perhaps, but he was starting to believe that Rina had a lot to give Wallin Landing, and they had a lot to give her, if she'd allow it.

He scratched his head. "Not so sure about that, ma'am. You did come highly recommended."

"By a man who is a well-known liar," she reminded him.

"And you have a certain presence."

"With insufficient knowledge and experience to back it up." She stopped her packing and dropped her arms, face scrunching. "I've been pretending even to myself I can do this. I'm no better than Asa Mercer!"

James couldn't allow such a statement to stand. "None of that now. It's obvious to anyone with eyes that you have the dedication to be a good teacher. That's what Wallin Landing needs."

She sniffed as if fighting tears. "I beg to differ, sir."

"You can beg all you like," he replied. "We need you. Besides, there aren't many more teachers to choose from."

She stiffened. "Is that why you offered me the position? For shame, Mr. Wallin!"

James held up his hands. "It was a joke! I knew you were the right one for the job the moment we met. You have the airs of royalty, madam, and that's what it will take to get through to my arrogant brother."

Her lips were so tight he thought her teeth must be grating together. "I am not royalty, sir. You must find yourself another teacher. I intend to take a position on the White River."

That letter! Catherine had been right. James raised

his head. "Whatever they're offering you, we'll double it."

"Nonsense," she replied. "They offer a school with young students, grateful parents and the chance to work beside a more seasoned teacher." She bent and closed the lid on her trunk, fastening the clasps with brisk efficiency before glancing up at him. "Which of your brothers will be driving me to the White River Crossing?"

At least that gave him an opportunity to slow her down, give her time to think about all this. "Well, everyone but Levi is out logging today," James acknowledged. "I could send you with him, but I don't allow him to take the reins."

She opened her mouth as if to argue, then closed it again. She must not have liked the idea of his volatile brother driving Lance and Percy any more than James did. "What about your mother or Beth?"

"It's a powerful long way to the Crossing," James said. "It could take days, especially if the river's up. I couldn't live with myself if something happened to Ma or Beth between here and there."

She blew out a breath, sounding a bit like Percy when he was miffed. "I suppose it will have to be you, then."

He'd never heard such reluctance, even from his family. "You could always wait a day or two for one of my brothers."

She shook her head. "No. I must go now. Will you carry this to the wagon for me?"

He ought to refuse. He didn't want her to go. In fact, it scared him how much he wanted her to stay.

He pressed a hand to the small of his back. "I'm not sure I can, ma'am."

Lightning flashed in those clear eyes as she straightened. "Nonsense. We have established that you are quite strong, sir."

"And lazy. Don't forget that. I'll wait until Drew gets back." He turned for the door, but she swept around him to block his way.

"But that could be hours," she protested. "And then it may well be too late to start out."

That was the general idea. "I'm afraid so. And I'll be needed in the woods tomorrow. Drew only let me off today so I could help you get settled. It might be a while before I'm free to take you."

She put her hands on her hips. "James Wallin. I cannot believe you are the sort of man to go back on his word."

Guilt tugged at him. "My word, ma'am?"

"Did you or did you not promise me that if this position did not work out you would take me anywhere I wanted to go?"

He grinned at her. "There, you see? That was your first mistake—believing anything I say."

She flushed darker than the sunset. "A mistake I will not make again. If you will not help me, I will appeal to Mrs. Wallin."

He didn't think she meant his mother. A shiver went through him that was no part charade. "Now, then, no need to be hasty. I'm sure we can come to some agreement."

"I am certain we can." She turned her back on him, lifted her skirts and marched out into the schoolroom. She snatched her cloak off one of the pegs by the door, and a snake dropped out onto the planks to slither for the shelter of a bench.

She eyed it. "What a fitting ending to my time here. I shall leave your brother to deal with his friend." She shook out the cloak as if to be certain nothing else hid in its folds, then swung it about her shoulders. As she tied the ribbons at her collar, she raised her chin and aimed her gaze at him. "Well, Mr. Wallin? What will it be?"

He was doomed either way. If he let her go, Catherine would be furious, and he'd have to live with the fact that he'd failed his family yet again. If Rina stayed, his own growing feelings and Catherine's matchmaking could easily see him wed by the next full moon. And that would be a mistake he and Rina might both live to regret. He wasn't willing to take on a wife only to lose her to illness or injury. And he certainly didn't want to leave a widow behind if something happened to him. Besides, she could do better than him for a husband.

Surely he could master his feelings toward her. He'd been hiding his guilt about Pa's death for years, masking it with a ready quip and an easy manner. He just needed time, both to convince her to stay and to convince himself he was better off without her.

Perhaps the time it took to travel to the White River.

"I'll take you wherever you want to go, Rina," he said, joining her at the door. And use every weapon in his arsenal to get her to stay.

Chapter Eight

Rina could tell that although James had given in to her demands to leave, he wasn't willing to go down without a fight. He was smiling too sweetly as he retrieved his gun, opened the door for her to leave the schoolhouse and escorted her toward the barn where his horses waited in the nearest pasture. He took the rifle into the barn and laid it in the wagon, leaving Rina waiting by the horses. She couldn't help the sigh that escaped her at the sight of them.

"They'll miss you," James said, going to open the gate. He put two fingers in his mouth and whistled.

"They haven't had time to form an attachment," she replied, fighting the longing to touch the horses, talk to them, as they trotted closer.

Sir Lancelot butted James's shoulder with his head, and James obligingly scratched behind the black horse's ears. Sir Percival, however, turned in a circle in front of Rina as if to show off his coat.

"Oh, but you are a fine fellow," she assured him as he blew a breath in her face.

"See?" James said, taking their halters and leading

them toward the barn. "I told you they'd be sorry to see you go. They didn't expect the drive you promised them to be taking you away."

She would not feel guilty. She was doing the right thing, for everyone. "It cannot be helped."

"And they won't be the worst of it," he warned. "You'll have to explain to Catherine and Ma."

Rina swallowed, following him. "Perhaps you could give them my resignation."

"No." James maneuvered Sir Lancelot into the traces. "They'll both have my hide, expecting I did something to cause you to leave."

She could not put him in that position. This was her decision. "Very well," she allowed. "I shall go speak to them now."

"And don't forget Beth," James said as she turned for the house. "She'll be sorely disappointed."

The thought of facing her most enthusiastic student nearly made her run back to the school. But she couldn't give in—not for Beth, not for anyone.

"Your sister is a dear girl," she told James. "She will surely thrive under the next teacher."

"For all we know, the next teacher will be a man," James pointed out, now buckling Percival in place. "There are few enough females in this part of the country."

"A male teacher might be more effective with Levi and Scout," Rina answered, guilt once more beckoning.

"But a male teacher won't be able to talk to Beth like you do," James argued. He came around his team to face her. "Doesn't she deserve a good teacher, too? She cares the most about the school."

"We are in agreement that your sister deserves a fine teacher," Rina said, backing away from him. "We simply disagree on whether I am that teacher."

"We disagree on a number of topics," James replied. "Such as how I'm supposed to take you to the White River without risking your reputation."

She'd been so determined to escape that she'd forgotten the issue of her reputation. She knew it could take a few days to reach the Crossing. She could hardly spend the nights alone with James.

"We must find a chaperone," she said. "Your mother, Catherine or Beth."

"I'm not ferrying Beth all the way to the White River and back," James said, standing so firmly she thought he'd leave an impression in the packed dirt of the barn floor. "My ears would fall off from the chatter before I reached Seattle. Besides, it can be dangerous where you're going. We may have to contend with wild animals or outlaws. Roads can suddenly disappear under rock slides. I won't put my family in such situations."

Rina could not argue with him on that point; she had no wish to endanger those kind ladies or Beth. But neither could she stay in Wallin Landing.

"There must be something we can do," she protested. "Ladies travel any number of places with escorts, though I suppose most are married and traveling with their husbands."

"Or are betrothed," he agreed, heading for the front of the wagon. He glanced back at her with a grin. "Guess we might as well get engaged."

She stared at him. "We most certainly should not!"

She must have sounded sufficiently appalled by the

idea, for he came back to her side and held up one hand, leaving Lance and Percy muttering in the traces at the delay.

"Actually, it's the perfect solution, now that I think on it," he said. "If we were to become engaged, Catherine would stop her matchmaking, thinking her job done. We won't have to risk anyone else on the journey. And your reputation would be safe on the way and at the White River settlement."

He seemed so pleased with himself, but she could not see the logic. "We would be lying," she pointed out.

"Not really," he said. When she bristled, he hurried on. "We'd agree to an engagement to last until you're safely settled at your new school. After that, either of us can break the arrangement. The engagement will be real so long as it lasts." He stuck out his hand. "Do we have an agreement?"

Still she hesitated. "You would not hold me to the promise of marrying?"

He shook his head. "Not in the slightest. Believe me, Rina, I have no wish to marry."

Though she felt the same way, she could not help wondering at his reasons. Her experiences had made it difficult for her to believe, to trust. He had no such background. Why refuse love?

He wiggled his fingers as if to remind her of his hand waiting for hers. "Come now, Rina. Am I so hideous you'd refuse to be considered my betrothed, even for a few days?"

"Certainly not," Rina said. Truly, she was probably letting her concerns get the better of her. His solution made sense for their circumstances. They both intended to behave with propriety. She wasn't promising forever, merely a few days.

She gave him her hand, and he shook it. Somehow, his grin eased the tightness in her chest.

But that tightness only returned as she went to the main house to say goodbye. She was relieved to find that Beth and Levi were out gathering greens from the woods, for Catherine's and Mrs. Wallin's dismay at her decision was enough to handle.

"If it's Levi who's made you change your mind," Mrs. Wallin said, green eyes narrowing, "I'll have words with him."

"I cannot blame Levi," Rina assured her, mindful that James had just entered the house and was returning the family rifle to the back room. "I simply realized that this is more than I am capable of handling. Please forgive me."

Catherine sighed. "You have every right to decide how you want to ply your trade, Rina. I take it James is going to return you to Seattle?"

James popped out of the back room as if he'd been waiting for such a cue. "I've almost got the wagon ready to go. But I'm not taking Miss Fosgrave to Seattle. I promised to carry her to the White River."

"The White River?" Mrs. Wallin frowned. "That's a terrible long way. What's taking you there?"

Oh, but she wasn't going to survive this. "I have been offered a position there to be an assistant teacher," Rina told her. "I thought it would help me learn my craft."

Mrs. Wallin nodded, frown easing. "I suppose it will at that, but I'm sorry to hear you'll be so isolated.

Folks only get to town a few times a year from that area."

She could not think about what that would mean to her. Most of the outlying settlements could say the same, and her traveling companions had gone willingly enough to those schools. Not that she'd heard anything about how they'd fared.

"It sounds like a fine position," Catherine assured her. "Just know that you go with our love and prayers."

That brought a tear to her eye. She would gladly have escaped then, except James came in and put an arm about her shoulders. "We'll be off, then. Just know that you needn't worry. Miss Fosgrave and I have an understanding." He went so far as to wink at Rina.

So that was how he intended to tell his family about the agreement. His mother reacted before Rina could explain the temporary nature of the engagement.

"Oh, James, that's wonderful!" she cried, clasping her hands together.

"Indeed," Catherine said, beaming. "I'm quite pleased to hear that. Congratulations."

"You don't understand," Rina started, but James reached out to take her hand and tuck it into his elbow.

"We should be going. I hope to make Seattle by nightfall and McKenzie's Corner by tomorrow night."

"But, why?" Mrs. Wallin asked as Rina tried without success to retrieve her hand. "If you and dear Rina are to be married, why must she leave?"

"Our engagement is on what you might call a trial basis," James said, towing Rina toward the door. "I have fields to clear and a cabin to furnish before I'm ready to bring home a bride."

He had an argument for every comment, just like

the Fosgraves had. She did not like it. She turned to Catherine, who with Mrs. Wallin had followed Rina and James out onto the porch.

"James and I agreed to a trial engagement until I reach the White River," Rina said, determination in every syllable. "I do not intend it to last longer than that."

Mrs. Wallin frowned. Catherine put her hand on her mother-in-law's arm as if to still any protests.

"I am unsure I believe you can have a trial engagement," Catherine said to Rina. "Engagements are rather like illnesses in this regard—either you are engaged or you are not. It appears that you, my dear, are engaged."

Put in that way, Rina could only shiver. As if Catherine saw her distress, she continued.

"You will be on well-populated roads, in an open wagon, where anyone might come upon you. You can likely spend the night in Seattle at the boardinghouse, and I've heard that McKenzie's Corner is rather civilized for a wilderness outpost. Besides, driving that far with your betrothed safeguards your reputation and could serve to fend off unwanted attentions from the many bachelors who still seek a wife."

There was that. Every time the ladies of the Mercer expedition had left the boardinghouse they had nearly caused a riot.

"And perhaps," Mrs. Wallin said, smile curving, "by the time all is said and done, your engagement will prove to be no temporary matter after all."

She and Catherine shared a look of satisfaction, proving that Catherine was still playing matchmaker, despite James's hopes to the contrary. Rina could not allow them to hope. "I have no intentions of marrying," she said. "My experiences have made me ill suited to the role of wife."

She thought Catherine might question her further, but the nurse merely inclined her head.

"That is, of course, your decision," she said. "All I ask is that you consider the possibility fully before rejecting it. I was determined not to marry before I met Drew. I do not regret changing my mind."

Mrs. Wallin's look said she thought Rina's chances of remaining unwed small indeed. She drew Rina close for a hug. "I can't wait for you to return so I can call you daughter," she said, beaming as widely as Beth generally did.

Rina was only glad James pulled the wagon up then, sparing her a response.

"Fair warning," he murmured a moment before he lifted her onto the bench. Her heart jerked in her chest, but she managed to return Catherine's wave of farewell as James drove the wagon out of the clearing.

The trees were closing in around them, thick and green and heavy with the resinous scent of fir, like sunlight in plant form. James cast her a smile as if well pleased with their plans.

It was so easy to return that smile, yet something inside her whispered a warning. Charm was deceitful, and beauty tended to fade. If only she could be certain there was more to James Wallin.

James had never thought to see the day he'd be engaged. He wasn't sure why the idea made him smile. Their agreement would last less than a week, and it was only for Rina's sake. It offered her far more protection than the reality that she was a single woman traveling alone. If she kept up the pretense, the idea that she was engaged to a powerful man might even offer her some protection from unwanted attentions out on the White River, if she truly did end up teaching there.

But she wouldn't keep up the pretense one moment longer than necessary. That was evident by the way she'd protested to Ma and Catherine, the way she'd argued with him when he'd first suggested it. She had a terrible aversion to anything even remotely related to tall tales.

Why? Had someone lied to her? Was that the source of the hurt Maddie had mentioned?

The clown in him only wanted to keep her smiling. He put a foot on the fender and eased up on the reins. Lance continued to walk along with insouciant majesty. Percy tugged a bit as if to confirm he couldn't escape.

"Easy now, boys," James called. "We're driving a lady today. Be on your best behavior, for she won't abide less."

Cloak loose about her shoulders, she folded her hands in the lap of her black gown. She wore the most severe colors to teach. He far preferred the floaty white confection she'd been wearing when they'd first met.

"I do not expect perfection, sir," she said. "But we must be careful in how we comport ourselves, engaged or no. You fail to understand the exemplary behavior required of a schoolteacher."

James rubbed a spot off his boot. He'd have preferred to have changed into one of his suits before going to town rather than wear his logging clothes, but he'd been afraid to delay any longer lest she head out alone on foot. Besides, if Drew or Simon had returned before he and Rina had left, James had no doubt he'd have more company than he wanted. Neither of his older brothers would have trusted him with the task. Simon hadn't approved of Catherine sending James after the schoolteacher to begin with.

"We didn't require so much of you," he pointed out to Rina now. "All we asked was that you do your best."

"The White River school board was much more explicit," she informed him, and he got the impression that wasn't necessarily to the good. "You should see the list of rules they supplied."

"Rules for the teacher?" He frowned as he nudged Lance and Percy around a bend in the road. "Like what?"

Her lips puckered as if she was trying to remember, and he suddenly recalled the feel of those lips against his. He forced his gaze out over the horses.

"I am to refrain from dressing in bright colors," she said, "dying my hair and smoking cigars."

He refused to crack a smile at the ridiculous rules. "I'll sneak you a box if you like."

He thought he heard a hint of a laugh. "No, thank you."

"What else?" he asked, encouraged. He chanced a glance to find she was tapping her chin with one finger.

"I am to be home between the hours of eight in the evening and six in the morning, unless at a school function," she said.

"So no moonlit strolls along the flooding river in cougar-infested territory," James mused. "Have they no sense of adventure?"

"My personal favorite," she said with a glance his

way, "is that I may not loiter in ice cream stores. Who knew they were such dens of iniquity?"

"Who knew the White River settlement even had an ice cream store?" He shook his head. "They must be coming up in the world."

"More likely they copied the rules from some other township back East," Rina told him. "They seem to take the matter of finding a teacher very seriously. That alone is commendable."

"Unlike us," he said. "We chose the first woman we liked."

She dropped her gaze and fiddled with her skirts. "While I am honored by your faith in me, Mr. Wallin, you need someone more skilled."

"So you say," James acknowledged, "but I still think attitude is a great deal more important than aptitude. You can learn most anything, if you've the will."

She sighed as if she feared she lacked that will. "I cannot argue that, Mr. Wallin."

Mr. Wallin. He'd hoped they'd reached the point where she'd feel comfortable using his first name. She'd already slipped a few times, though he knew she wouldn't admit it.

"You may get an argument from those White River folks, though," he said, keeping his tone light. "They sound mighty particular. What will you do when they find out about your past?"

She gasped, paling. "My past?"

What, had she robbed a bank back East? "Your lack of experience," he clarified, watching her. "The fact that this is your first school. We accepted your word that you could teach. Will they?"

She drew in a breath as if he'd given her a pardon.

"They must have been aware of my credentials before offering."

"Oh, no doubt." He forced his gaze out over the horses once more, all innocence. "Mr. Mercer being such a forthright person and all."

"You think Mr. Mercer inflated my skills to make the school offer me a position?"

She sounded so concerned he could not leave it at that. It was one thing to point out the possible flaws in her arguments. It was another to manufacture problems.

"I think it's more likely he wanted you to remain unemployed," he said, "so you'd be desperate enough to accept one of the men who paid him for a bride."

She nodded, drawing in a breath. "Besides, the position is for an assistant teacher, remember? The White River superintendent does not expect me to know everything like you did."

"We never expected you to know everything!" He shoved back his cap with one hand, and she raised her brows at him. He puffed out a breath. "Well, it might have seemed we expected that of you, but we were willing to compromise."

The way she shifted on the bench told him she wasn't so sure of that. "I expect every job has its challenges," she allowed.

That was more like it. "Of course they do. And what if this one is horrible? The children may be spoiled brats, the accommodations filled with mice."

"I certainly hope not!" Rina protested. "And even if they are, I would rather fight off mice than raving men."

James shook his head. "I knew Rankin had frightened you. I told you, I can handle him."

"I would prefer no one have to handle him," she replied, chin once more rising.

He had to keep trying. "What if there's a Rankin out at the White River? What if you decide you want to leave? There won't be a handsome fellow with a team of stunning horses ready to ride to the ends of the Earth for you."

She eyed him a moment, and James gave her his best smile. She shook her finger at him. "I know your game, James Wallin. You want to convince me to refuse the job."

Smart lady. He put a hand on his heart, reins pooled in the other. "You wound me, Miss Fosgrave. As if I would ever do something so underhanded. Of course, if you decide to refuse the other position, I'd be happy to turn the wagon around and carry you back to Wallin Landing immediately."

She faced forward, as if she could see the White River from there. "My mind is made up, so you can stop the what-ifs right now."

"If that's what you want," he said, facing forward, as well. She could protest all she liked. She was weakening. He could see it in the way her straight white teeth chewed on her lower lip, how her hands clenched and unclenched in the lap of her black gown. Either she was worried about her new position or feeling guilty about leaving the old one. Both could work in his favor.

And hers. If he'd truly thought that the White River was a better place for her, he would probably have let her go with his best wishes for a bright future. But the outpost was even farther from civilization than Wallin

Landing, and, by the sound of those rules, hopelessly demanding. She deserved to be somewhere she'd be appreciated and encouraged.

Like beside him at Wallin Landing. Now he just had to get her to see things his way, and he knew just how to go about it.

Chapter Nine

James had given Rina a great deal to consider, and she was fairly sure he knew it. Despite his protests to innocence, he was campaigning for her to return to Wallin Landing. She was not about to give in, but she thought she knew how to fight back.

"Have you ever shopped at Derango's?" he asked as they maneuvered among the other wagons and pedestrians past the Seattle mercantile with its windows crowded with goods.

"Several times," she said. "The manager there was very kind about extending credit to us."

"You better stock up while we're here," he warned. "As far as I know, there are no stores out White River way."

"How wonderful," she said. "Then I won't have to worry about spending my income on fripperies."

He frowned just the slightest as if he hadn't expected that response. But still he persisted as they passed Mr. Bagley's church, where Catherine and Drew had wed a month ago.

"Did you attend the White Church or the Brown

Church when you lived in Seattle?" he asked as if making idle conversation.

"The Brown church," she replied, wondering what he'd find to warn her about now. "Mr. Bagley is a fine speaker."

"Likely the best in the area," he agreed, guiding the team easily through the muddy streets. "Not that you'll find many other churches where you're going."

"People have worshipped without a building for generations," Rina said, keeping her voice and face pleasant. "There should be an opportunity on the White River."

He cocked his head as if considering the situation as he drew up in front of the boardinghouse. "I suppose you can even make new friends to replace the ones you're leaving behind."

She could find no easy quip to respond to that. "No one ever replaces a true friend, Mr. Wallin," she said. "But if we are very fortunate, we may add to their number."

That silenced him long enough to come around and help her down. His gaze softened as he set her on the ground next to him. "I hope you'll count me a friend when you look back, Rina."

She merely smiled. She could not count him a friend at the moment, but she was beginning to think he would be the one she'd miss most of all.

James waited until she was sure Mrs. Elliott was willing to allow her to spend the night in the boardinghouse, then headed to the Howard house where he thought to stay. Catherine and Allegra Howard were good friends, so Rina was sure Allegra would welcome Catherine's brother-in-law for the night. The members of the boardinghouse welcomed Rina back with smiles that were more than curious. Maddie, however, cried out in delight at the sight of Rina in the doorway of the room they had once shared and rushed to give her a hug as if Rina had been gone two years instead of two days.

"Oh, but it's good to see you," she declared, pushing Rina back to look at her. "I'd say teaching agrees with you."

Rina lips started to tremble. "Oh, Maddie, but I fear it doesn't!"

Maddie's face puckered in sympathy, and she took Rina's hand and led her to her bed. "Now, then, you just tell me who's been pulling out your heart."

So Rina perched on Maddie's quilt-covered bed and told her all about her experiences at Wallin Landing while Maddie drew out her extra pair of sheets and blanket to make up the other bed in the room, which apparently had yet to be filled with another tenant. The narrow room, with its two beds and window overlooking the Sound, had always felt a little foreign to Rina after the mansions in which she'd been raised, but she could not deny the warmth now as her friend listened to her problems.

"So off you'll be a-going," Maddie said, finishing tucking in the blanket. "With hopes this new school will be more to your liking."

Rina nodded, trying to relax now that the worst was over. Somehow her hands ended up clasped in front of her. "Exactly. Being an assistant to another teacher should help me gain some confidence."

"Confidence comes from different things, I find," Maddie said, sitting beside Rina on the bed. "It might arise from the experience of doing the same thing for many years. Or maybe from faith in the Almighty or faith in yourself. I'm thinking it's not so much the first you lack, me darling girl, but the last."

Rina could not raise her gaze above her interlocked fingers. "I fear you have the right of it, Maddie. You may not believe it, but I had complete confidence in myself once. I knew who I was, what I was meant to do. Now? Now, I have no idea!"

Maddie sighed, one hand reaching out to cover hers. "Sure-n, but I know how you're feeling. We've both had cause to doubt, I'm thinking."

Rina looked up at her friend. Maddie's head was down, her shoulders sagging, as if all the precious energy she generally shared with others had fled. "You doubt yourself, Maddie? Rarely have I met anyone so sure!"

Maddie's grin popped into view. "So, at least I've convinced one of us." Her smile faded as she met Rina's gaze. "No, Alexandrina, I doubt my choices, too. I thought I was doing the right thing to travel West, seek my fortune, but I had to leave family behind, a half sister and half brother as dear to me as my own life."

Maddie had rarely spoken of her past, any more so than Rina. That was one of the reasons it had been easy to become acquainted.

"How awful," Rina commiserated. "I always wanted siblings, so I can only imagine how terrible it must feel to have to leave them."

Maddie nodded, another sigh raising the chest of her gown. "I left them with a kindly lady who takes in orphan children. I told them I would send for them as soon as I could, but I'm only now scratching the pennies together from washing and cleaning. And I keep wondering. Wouldn't it be better if they found a mother and father instead of just me?"

The pain and bewilderment throbbed in her voice, touching Rina's hurting heart with familiar fingers. "Sometimes circumstances force families apart," she told her friend. "But there is nothing like the love that holds them together. Surely we could find a way for you all to become a family again."

Maddie twisted a strand of red hair around one finger. "So I've been thinking. I might have enough to bring them out to me, if I can find someone to watch over them along the way. I just don't know how to care for them when they arrive. It's not like I can afford a grand house like Mr. and Mrs. Howard."

Their friend Allegra had been reunited with her former sweetheart Clay Howard on the trip out west. They'd married shortly after arriving in Seattle, and Clay had built his bride a fine house high on the hill using money he'd earned from his entrepreneurial efforts.

"Few have a house as nice as the Howards," Rina said, thinking, "but you have friends who could help you make your own place. No one bakes as well as you do, Maddie. Why don't you ask Mr. Howard to invest in building you a bakery?"

Maddie stared at her. "A bakery?"

Rina nodded. "He loved what you baked aboard ship to convince him to teach us about Seattle. I've never had hot cross buns as good as yours. I would think you could impress the bachelors around here, as well."

Maddie leaped to her feet. "I'll do it! Sure-n but

I've calculated the costs often enough, to my despair. I can tell Clay Howard exactly what I'd be needing."

She seized Rina's hands. "Oh, me darling girl, you've no idea the hope you've given me. How can I ever repay you?"

"Bring your sister and brother out and make a family," Rina said, Maddie's excitement lifting her to her feet, as well. "Knowing you are happy is all the thanks I need."

"Ah, but how will you know, way out on the White River?" Maddie challenged. "I'm not liking you so far from us all. And it seems to me your heart isn't in it, either."

"My heart," Rina replied, raising her head, "has proven a very fickle organ. I'd much prefer to rely on my mind, and it says this is an excellent opportunity that I would be foolish to dismiss."

"Then I suppose you have your answer," Maddie said with a sigh as she released her.

"I suppose I do," Rina said with a nod. Now, if she could just convince her heart of the matter.

James returned to her the next morning.

"If you have to be journeying to the wild," Maddie told her, watching from the porch as he drew the wagon up in front of the boardinghouse, "at least you picked a fine escort."

Rina did not comment as James jumped down to help her up into the wagon. She was only glad Maddie had been understanding about their temporary engagement when Rina had explained it the night before.

Rina was also glad for a few moments that morning to write to the White River superintendent and accept his offer. The Seattle postmaster had assured her that he had a rider and a fast horse heading that way, so at least her news would arrive before she did.

"Next stop, McKenzie's Corner," James promised Rina, after he'd lifted her up and come around to take the reins. "That's the logical stopping spot between here and the Crossing. And I sure hope it meets with your approval."

"It will be fine," Rina said, turning to wave to Maddie, who waved back with her usual gusto as James urged the horses away from the boardinghouse. At least she knew her friend's future would be bright.

The overcast day was not nearly as bright. Heavy black clouds held on to their rain as the way led out of Seattle. A road, James called it. The term was far too kind. Trees had been cleared, but the horses had to step over stumps sticking out above the track, and several times Rina felt the wagon bottom scrape wood. The most she could see ahead and behind was the next bend.

At least this time they had company. Just as Catherine had predicted, they met plenty of farmers, loggers and tradesmen going to or coming from Seattle. Each one paused long enough to exchange news—the condition of the road, the favored hotels and eateries in town, sightings of bear, wolf and cougar.

The last discussion gave her chills, especially when a passing farmer warned James about the Rainier Valley.

"Never saw so many bears in one day," the older man complained, stopping to take off his straw hat and mop his brow with a red gingham handkerchief.

"Sows, boars, cubs. Must be plentiful food and water there."

"And who would pass that up?" James teased. When the farmer frowned at him, he tipped his hat. "Thank you for warning us. We'll be watchful."

"Do we travel through that area?" Rina couldn't help asking as he encouraged the horses on.

"Right through the center," James said cheerfully.

Did he want to get eaten? "Are we in danger?" she pressed.

"Most likely," James replied. "That's the way it is around here. The farther out you go, the more chances to make the acquaintance of wildlife. I reckon they must see a bear or two a day on the White River."

"There you go again," she complained. "Trying to make me change my mind by focusing on the negative."

James stuck out his lower lip. "Now, whether finding a bunch of bears is a good thing or a bad thing depends on your point of view. The more animals nearby, the better your chances at hunting. You can do a lot with a bear—smoke the meat, use the pelt for a rug, make the claws and teeth into a necklace." He grinned at her. "I'm surprised Beth's magazine hasn't printed a picture yet."

Rina shook her head. "I doubt even *Godey's* could make bear claws popular. And I have no interest in even seeing a bear, much less making use of its bodily parts."

"I don't know," James mused. "I hear bear grease puts a powerful shine in your hair. Not that you have any need for that."

"And stop resorting to compliments, too," Rina scolded him. "I am utterly immune."

James cast her a sidelong glance. "So if I said a fellow could melt right into your eyes, that wouldn't move you."

Rina adjusted her skirts in the foot well. "Certainly not."

"Or that your voice is sweeter than a chickadee's."

Rina made a face. "I do not recall chickadees having a particularly sweet singing voice."

James shook his head. "You're a mighty hard lady to please. But we have a ways to go yet. I'll think of something. After all, once you leave my company, it may be a long while before you find someone willing to take you back to Seattle through a territory full of bears."

He simply refused to give up. "And I imagine it rains on the White River every day, year round, as well," she said, eyeing him.

"Snows," he corrected her. "Drifts as big as a house. And don't forget the alligators."

Rina choked. "Alligators?"

"Alligators," he insisted. "Great scaly beasts the size of a man. They mostly eat the giant toads, if the toads don't pick you off first. And don't get me started on the killer pigeons."

Rina was having a hard time not giggling. "Killer pigeons? Really?"

James shivered as if just the thought chilled him. "Fearsome creatures, ma'am. Like to coo you to death."

Rina gave it up and laughed.

He continued on that vein for the next distance. Most of his claims were so far-fetched she had to smile, but she couldn't help remembering the farmer's warning. Was there really an abundance of dangerous animals along the White River? How would she protect herself, much less her students?

"What would you do," she asked James as the horses carried the wagon along a bubbling creek, "if you looked out the schoolroom window and saw a cougar outside?"

"You're assuming the White River school has glass in its windows," he replied. "I'm guessing it was too far to carry such breakable material. You might have openings in the walls, but you'd probably be safest to keep them shuttered. No, the soonest you'd know about a cougar nearby is opening the door and finding it on the other side."

Terrifying picture. "So, what would you do?"

"Shut the door."

Rina threw up her hands. "Well, of course I'd shut the door! I meant how would you make it go away. How would you protect the students?"

"If a cougar was intent on making you or one of your pupils its dinner, there's only one thing to do. Shoot it."

Rina felt ill. "I don't know whether I could."

"You need to learn to shoot," he said.

Rina shook her head. "I have no need for lessons."

"Course you do." James was so emphatic, he urged the horses to the side of the track and reined in. "I'll teach you." He hopped down and came around for her.

He didn't understand. "No, truly. Being able to shoot does not concern me."

"Good," he said, raising his arms to take her down from the bench. "I'm glad to hear you're not afraid of guns. But let's practice now. That way, you'll be ready

to protect yourself by the time we reach the Crossing."
He grinned up at her. "Though mind you, it will take
a while to be as good a shot as I am."

"Oh, will it?" She could not allow that statement to
stand. "In that case, Mr. Wallin," she said with a smile,
"we better start immediately."

James helped Rina down, trying not to revel in the
feel of her in his arms. He had to focus on his goal.
The longer it took to reach the White River, the more
chances he had to convince her not to go.

Her concern about the wild animals was a good
excuse to stop and rest the horses. Besides, she had
reason to fear. Seattle hadn't been settled for all that
long. Stories were still told of the king cougar, seven
foot from nose to tail, David Denny had shot five years
ago. James had seen the massive head of a bear Sheriff Boren had brought in last summer. If Rina was to
live anywhere in Washington Territory, she ought to
learn how to handle a gun.

He secured the horses where they had edibles to
graze on and drew her a little ways into the woods
where the noise would be less likely to frighten his
team. He found a small clearing, massive firs walling
in the sides and sunlight piercing through the green,
then motioned her closer.

"This is a rifle," he told her, holding out his gun
level on both palms.

"Indeed," she said, glancing at it. "A Spencer, isn't
it?"

James frowned. "Yes. How did you know?"

She pointed to the silver around the trigger. "It's
engraved right there."

James looked to the spot. "Huh. So it is. Well, this model is a lever-action." He pulled on the silver rod to show her. "And the cartridges go in the butt."

"Cartridges," she said. "Not powder and lead?"

"No indeed." He went on to explain the workings of the piece. It was a newer model, paid for by his logging. A man needed suitable tools to ply his trade and to protect himself and his family. And if he could look good in the process, so much the better. This model had a fine hickory stock with all the silver engraved with fanciful vines.

"Now, to shoot it," he said, coming around behind her and slipping the gun over her head and into her arms, "you start by positioning it like this." He brought the stock back against her shoulder and aimed the barrel out. Her hands came up to cradle the weapon.

"Very good," he told her. "Now, pick a target."

"That stump," she said, swiveling slowly and sighting down the barrel. Before he could advise her further, she pulled the trigger.

A piece of bark flew from the stump.

"It pulls to the left," she said.

James shook his head in admiration. "Yes, it does. To compensate…"

"I aim to the right," she finished. She spread her stance, cranked the lever to remove the spent cartridge and sighted again. The gun roared.

James waved a hand to dissipate the smoke and squinted at the stump. Sure enough, he could spot the bullet lodged in the wood.

"Pretty good," he admitted.

"Fairly tame, actually," she said, lowering the gun. "A Spencer repeater has a range of five hundred yards."

How did she know that? James had bought the gun, like his horses, because it appeared to be something stylish that would be useful to him. He'd shot it to make sure it worked, confirmed that the mercantile carried the cartridges it required. But he hadn't studied its capabilities. Had she?

"You didn't need lessons from me," he realized. "Who taught you to shoot?"

She snapped the lever to eject the cartridge. "I had a lady tutor once who was an avid sportswoman. She and my father failed to agree on the nature of my instruction. But after I won a few shooting matches, he changed his mind."

James smiled. "He must have been proud of you."

She held out the rifle to him as if tired of it. "I think rather he saw a benefit to my abilities. He wagered on the outcome, you see. Like you, a number of gentlemen found it difficult to believe a lady knew how to shoot that well."

James accepted the gun. "Well, you showed them. What else did the lady tutor teach you?"

She lifted her skirts to head back toward the wagon, and he followed. "I received lessons in archery and badminton," she said.

"Not sure what the second is," James admitted, "but I'm guessing you're good at it, too."

She ducked her head. "A bit. I fear I have a rather competitive spirit. I try not to encourage it."

"Why not?" he asked, shouldering the gun. "Whether you use a gun or a bow, hunting is an important skill out here."

She sighed as if she wished that were the case. "Not for a schoolteacher."

"For anyone," he insisted. "And I'd like to see you badminton some time. I might learn something."

She giggled. Oh, how he loved that sound. "It's not a particularly helpful sport," she told him, as he stowed the rifle then went to put Lance and Percy back in harness. "And forgive me for wasting your time to practice. I do hope you will listen in the future before assuming." She cocked her head as if waiting for him to agree.

"Oh, I won't promise that," James said, fastening the buckles. "It's too much fun jumping to conclusions."

She shook her head as he finished. Indeed, he could see the pensive mood slipping over her again and not because of her concerns for the future. No, Rina seemed more concerned about her past. But learning to shoot and fire a bow didn't sound like such bad things to him.

As he came to her side, he tried for a smile. "What can I do to get back in your good graces?" he asked, peering up under her brows.

She refused to meet his gaze as he lifted her into the wagon. "No need."

Not good enough. The urge to see her smile was like an itch he had to scratch. He could almost hear Catherine gloating that he must be following in love, but he knew the truth. That need to please wasn't love. He'd been making people smile or laugh since before Pa had died. Their laughter made him feel useful, worthwhile.

"I could recite you a poem," he offered as he took his place on the bench.

She shook her head again. "No, thank you."

"Spin you a yarn?" James suggested.

"I've had my fill of fanciful stories."

He puffed out a sigh. "What, then?"

She glanced to the front of the wagon, then laid a hand on his arm, smile hopeful. "You could let me drive."

Chapter Ten

Rina waited for James's reply. He was inordinately proud of those horses, and for good reason. She certainly would have balked if a near-stranger had asked to drive her team. She had struggled to sell them to a stranger as it was.

James cocked his head, blue eyes fixed on her. "Do you drive half as good as you shoot?"

"Better," Rina promised.

He grinned and waved a hand toward the team. "Then be my guest, ma'am."

A tingle shot through her. It seemed like forever since she'd sat in the driver's seat. And to drive a pair of steeldusts! She knew she must be trembling as he offered her the reins.

The supple leather warmed against her skin as she accepted them. Always before she'd worn gloves, either kid driving gloves or proper ladies' gloves. Now she fancied she could feel the horses' eagerness, matching her own, all the way along the strands.

The light in James's eyes told her he shared her

excitement. "Give them their heads, Miss Fosgrave," he said.

Rina threaded the reins through her fingers from long experience, pooling the excess leather in the foot well. Bracing her feet against the fender, she touched the reins to the horse's rears. "Gee-up!"

The team obligingly set off at a trot.

Time fell away. She felt buoyant, confident, the queen of all she surveyed. No, no, not the queen. She'd never be queen. But when she was driving, she ruled the road.

Muscles she hadn't used in months tensed, but she wiggled on the bench to shake them out.

"They're not difficult," James said, leaning against the backboard. "You just have to tell them to go, and they go."

He was right. His horses were well trained, though not, she thought, by him. Someone had taken great pains to teach them how to behave in harness. She could see differences in their personalities, though. Lancelot was the determined one, relentlessly pulling forward as if he couldn't wait to reach his destination. She had to rein him in a bit to keep him level with his teammate. Percival, on the other hand, was more play-ful, as wont to vie away as to stay the course. Only the confines of the harness and stocks kept him in tandem.

James put his feet up on the fender. "Nicely done. I'd like to see you take them on a smoother road. I imagine they could fly."

Rina smiled. "A shame the closest smooth road is likely in California."

"Kentucky," he corrected her. "But I think we could chance going a little faster if you'd like." He cast her a glance out of the corners of his eyes as if to gauge her reaction.

"Watch me," Rina said and called to the team.

Immediately they stepped up, drawing the wagon down the narrow road. Responsiveness and strength shouted with every movement. The trees whipped past, a curtain of green enclosing her, James and the horses. She wanted to laugh, to shout into the wind.

James didn't fight the feeling. "Yee-haw!" he hollered, slapping his hands down on his trousers.

Rina laughed and urged them faster.

With a bump, the wagon veered over a rut, skittering on the muddy track. The bench tilted, and she slid down next to James, who braced himself to keep both of them from falling. She pulled on the reins to slow the team.

"Forgive me," she said, edging farther away from his warmth.

He grinned at her. "Not a problem, ma'am. You can go that fast any time you like."

No, she really shouldn't. It wasn't fair to the horses to try to navigate this terrain at such a pace. She brought them back to a sedate walk with a sigh.

"You're as good as your word, Rina," James told her as if trying to encourage her. "You're an even finer driver than a marksman. Any other skills you care to share?"

"Nothing half so useful, I fear," Rina said.

James eyed her. "You might be surprised what I find useful."

She might at that. Something inside urged her to tell him more about her past, to share all her disappointments and fears. But she couldn't bear to see that grin fade from his handsome face.

"Very well," she said. "Since you asked, allow me to list all my useless skills. I can tell you how to seat important people at a dinner party so no one is offended."

He nodded, sticking out his lower lip as if impressed. "That's not useless. It ought to come in handy at Christmas."

She knew he was teasing her. "And I know the proper way to address the Queen of England and her children."

"Good," he said, settling on the seat. "We'll invite them over, too."

He was all too skilled at making her laugh. "I am also fluent in the language of flowers and can arrange a bouquet to send the appropriate message."

He tilted back to eye her. "Flowers have a language? I never heard a daisy shout."

"Certainly not," Rina said, struggling to keep her face and voice firm. "Daisies do their best to appear more refined than that, sir."

He raised a brow. "So, what do they say?"

"It depends on the daisy." Rina urged Percival back in line. "A wild daisy like the ones growing along there mean 'I will think of it.' A Michaelmas daisy means 'farewell,' and a colored daisy means 'beauty.'"

James shook his head. "Who knew? And you put these flowers together to send a message?"

"Exactly. I told you it was a ridiculous skill."

He scratched his chin as if he wasn't so sure of that. "I could see a use for it. What if I wanted to tell a lady how much I admire her?"

"She would have to know the language, too," Rina pointed out.

He grinned. "Oh, I have it on good authority she knows it well."

Her? Her hands tightened on the reins, and the horses slowed further. "You might try amethyst flower entwined with morning glory," she murmured. "The first speaks of admiration, the second of affection."

He leaned closer. "And if I wanted to tell her never to leave my side?"

Her mouth was suddenly dry. "You might gather jonquils, which mean 'I desire a return of my affections,' and forget-me-nots."

"I'm fresh out of jonquils," he said softly. "But I hope you won't forget me, Rina."

Forget him? Never. Believe his flattery? Not for a moment. She couldn't afford to rely on someone like that again. The results had hurt too much.

"Very likely my work will keep me too busy to think of much else," she said with a flick of the reins to set the team moving faster again.

He straightened with a sigh. "Very likely. Either that, or one of those fellows out White River way will win your affections with some talkative daisies."

She shook her head. "I hope you know by now that I am immune to such things, Mr. Wallin."

"And I'd think you'd realize by now that some gentlemen around Seattle are desperate," he countered. "What if they besiege you at the White River? Who's going to guard your door?"

She smiled. "You forget. I can shoot."

He sighed again. "Oh, but I pity the poor fellows."

Rina chuckled. "I don't."

"You're a hardhearted woman, Miss Alexandrina Eugenia Fosgrave," he said. "But you sure can drive a team."

Somehow, that praise warmed her more than any of his other compliments.

She drove all the way to their stop for the night. The rain had just begun to fall when he directed her off the main road into a clearing. A large well-tended log cabin sat along one side, with a smaller log shack opposite it near a wide barn. She could see smoke drifting from the chimney of the main house, and at least one horse shifted in the shadows of the barn.

As she brought the horses to a stop, she caught a good look inside the shack, where more smoke poured from open windows. Inside, a beefy fellow with the singed leather apron of a blacksmith straightened from his forge to eye her.

"Now, there's a sight you don't see every day," he declared, plunging the iron he had been working into the nearby vat of water. He exited through the steam and approached the wagon. He had a rough face, as if each feature had been carved with a blunt chisel, and silver like smoke drifted through his curly black hair and beard.

"How might I help you, pretty lady?" he asked.

Rina looked at James, unsure of protocol.

"This is Miss Fosgrave, destined for the White River school," James supplied. "I'm James Wallin, and I have the privilege of escorting her as her husband to be. We were hoping for a couple of beds for the night and shelter for the horses."

Their host wiped his soot-darkened hands on his apron. "Robert McKenzie. You're welcome to stay, two bits for bed and board, another bit for each horse. You'll need to bunk in the hayloft with my other guests, Mr. Wallin. I'll give the lady my room for the night so she can have a separate space."

So she'd be alone in a house, with James in the barn? She wasn't sure she liked the sound of that. As Mr. McKenzie moved toward the house, she leaned closer to James on the bench. "Are you certain there isn't another hostelry nearby?"

"Not for ten miles or more," James assured her, hopping down. "You take what you can get in the wilderness."

So it would seem.

Either their blacksmith host had sharp ears or he guessed her concern, for he nodded to her as James helped her down and she started for the house. "You'll be safe here, ma'am," he told her, holding the thick door open for her. "No harm ever befell a lady at my establishment."

His dark brown eyes gazed down at her with seeming sincerity under his thatch of tangled hair. She wished she could believe him. "How many ladies have visited your establishment in the last year?" she asked, pausing on the narrow stoop.

His brushy brows gathered as if he were remembering each face that had passed through his door. "Three, near as I recall. You'll be the fourth. And just so you know, I treat every guest in my home like family. We may be cantankerous or sweet natured, but we all rub together nicely. I'm sure you'll fit right in, Sister."

She could only hope he was right.

James couldn't be more pleased with the way things were going. He'd managed to make several points against the White River on the way here. Her pensive questions told him he'd given her food for thought. Now McKenzie's Corner was making his case for him. Rina had looked none too happy with the place, and he'd felt her stiffen at the description of the sleeping arrangements. Of course, he wasn't too keen on them himself. The barn seemed a far piece to run if she was in trouble.

So, he'd better make sure there was no trouble.

He settled Lance and Percy in stalls for the night, then hurried inside. With the windows shuttered, the main room of the cabin was a cozy place, furs hanging to dry from the well-chinked walls, hams smoking near the blazing fire. A counter ran along one wall, behind which were crowded anything a traveler might want, from wooden casks for fresh water to steel traps for catching vermin. Strings of dried peppers, red, yellow and green, draped bolts of calico and wool.

McKenzie presided over it all like a king in his castle, his tall frame squeezed behind the counter. And Rina was the queen. She'd perched on a stool across the worn wood planks from him, skirts draped about her, head cocked as if listening to a request to grant a boon. A small, older man with dark hair hanging to his shoulders and his lanky blond-haired friend were already bellied up to the counter beside her. By the skins they wore, James was fairly certain they were trappers.

"John Deerlund and Francis the Rock or some such," McKenzie introduced them, most likely mangling a French name. "Cousin Francis don't talk much, but Brother John's always up for a yarn. This here's Brother James Wallin."

Deerlund smiled, displaying crooked front teeth.

"A pleasure, sir. And it's an even greater pleasure to meet your lovely wife."

Rina glanced at James as if waiting for his reply.

"Miss Fosgrave and I aren't married yet," he explained.

The smaller man straightened and said something to his partner, who frowned.

Rina, however, beamed. *"Ah, vous êtes Français, monsieur!"*

The Frenchman beamed. *"Mais oui!"* He launched into a long story that had Rina exclaiming and James scratching his head.

"Do you speak the lingo?" he murmured to Deerlund.

The man shrugged. "Enough to follow along. He seems to be telling her about all the places we visited on our last trip. Either that, or he's proposing marriage."

That's what James feared.

Rina put her hand on James's arm. Turning to look at her, he found that her eyes were shining. "Monsieur LaRocque has invited us to dine with him. Shall we?"

He'd have much rather eaten dinner alone with her, but by the look of the cabin, that would be impossible. "I'd be delighted," he told her. "So long as you translate."

"Avec plaisir," she said, and he got the gist.

He had a feeling he'd be sitting by the fire and listening to a one-sided conversation all night, but as it turned out, dinner was a merry affair. They gathered on overturned bushels and piles of furs around the fire, wooden platters in their laps. Their host produced a brace of ducks roasted over the fire, plus fresh greens, tart blackberry preserves, and corn fritters that seemed to melt in James's mouth. The way Rina dug in, using a silver fork McKenzie had located for her, told James she was enjoying the simple food, too.

As for their host, McKenzie and Deerlund kept up a steady stream of stories, from the first time McKenzie had tried to catch a salmon and ended up floating downriver, to the day Deerlund had surprised a bear eating the last of his supplies and chased it off with a branch. Even the Frenchman contributed a story or two, with Rina translating. James had never seen her so animated, unless she'd been talking about his horses.

"So what about you, ma'am?" Deerlund asked, setting aside his empty platter at last. "Surely you have a story or two to share."

James perked up. She hadn't said a lot about her life before arriving in Seattle. From the way she'd been educated and the skills she'd acquired, he expected she'd been raised by a wealthy family. Even if she had been orphaned, why come West? Surely she'd had friends and other family who had wanted her by their sides.

"Oh, nothing as exciting as yours," she assured him, rising. James and LaRocque rose as well, but she waved everyone back to their seats as she went to carry her platter and tin cup that had held apple cider to the counter.

Deerlund watched her go, then jerked his head. "So, you tell us, Brother James. What do you know of her?"

James was watching her, as well. She set the platter down and carefully arranged the tin cup on top, but she didn't fool him. It wasn't organization but delay she was practicing.

"Not enough," James admitted. "But if she doesn't want to share her past, I wouldn't press her."

Deerlund seemed to accept that, for he turned to their host. "I don't suppose I could convince you to play a song on that squeezebox of yours, McKenzie."

The blacksmith stood, his shadow climbing the wall. "I might be so inclined, if I had willing hands to clean up."

Deerlund and LaRocque volunteered. As they gathered the remaining dishes, Rina returned to James's side. Her eyes looked dark in the firelight, heavy, and he didn't think it was the day that had worn her down.

"I should probably retire," she told him, smoothing out the wrinkles in her black skirt.

"And miss a good concert?" James teased. "It might be your last chance for music in a long while."

She shook her head. "They must have music out on the White River."

"Not like this, they won't," James promised.

He'd heard the tales in town about how Robert McKenzie entertained his guests with his concertina. Sure enough, as soon as the room had been set to rights, their host brought out a small box with buttons on either side and a hinge in the middle.

"What'll it be, gents?" he asked, opening the hinge to reveal thick leather folds between the two halves of the box that sighed as they opened. "Something sweet or something with a little kick to it?"

Deerlund, who had been leaning against the wall, straightened. "Something to make us tap our toes. I'm in the mood to dance." He turned and offered his hand to Rina. "What do you say, Miss Fosgrave? Will you be my partner?"

Rina dropped her gaze. "How kind of you to ask, Mr. Deerlund, but I fear my employer would frown on such frivolity."

Deerlund was the one to frown, but James wasn't sure whether he disliked the strict rules she lived under or whether, like Levi, he had no idea what frivolity meant.

James stood and offered Deerlund a bow. "Allow me to be your partner, good sir."

"Mais oui," LaRocque said. "This we did long ago." He slipped into French, and Rina translated.

"Apparently gentlemen danced with gentlemen back in the early days of the fur trade," she explained. "They had no other choice."

Deerlund chuckled. "Even fewer females back then, I warrant. All right, Wallin. I'll dance with you. But I lead."

James slipped into falsetto. "Why, certainly, kind sir. Just don't step on the toes of my dainty shoes." He clunked his solid boots against the floor.

McKenzie's box let out a squawk, and they all laughed.

Then he lit into a sprightly tune that set the dried peppers to rattling on their strings. LaRocque over-turned the wash tub on which he'd been seated and beat along in time. James clasped hands with Deer-lund, and they stomped around the floor, bumping into the counter, a pile of furs, each other. It was more fun than he'd had in ages.

"À présent moi," LaRocque declared, rising to push James aside. He and Deerlund spun around while James clapped in time. He glanced at Rina with a grin, then nearly faltered.

Her eyes were drawn down, her fingers pressed tightly together in her lap, her lower lip caught between her teeth. He'd never seen anyone yearn so hard.

"That tears it," he said, reaching down and pulling her to her feet. "You're dancing."

"But what if the school board hears of it?" she cried, resisting.

"Then you can come back and teach at Wallin Landing," he said. "We don't hold against having fun once in a while." And he pulled her out onto the floor with the dancing trappers.

Chapter Eleven

What was he doing? Was he determined to cost her her position? Rina nearly pulled away again as James spun her out onto the floor. Then Monsieur LaRocque flew past with a salute, and Mr. Deerlund patted her shoulder. Even if she could have stopped without interrupting them, the call of the music set her feet to skipping. Before she knew it, she was dancing along in time.

She had learned the waltz and the polka from a dance master, but she'd only performed them at balls and always with partners who kept the proper distance, sedate, accomplished. James and the trappers had a different way of dancing. It seemed to involve nothing more than the touch of hands and a great deal of stomping. She could feel the beat echoing up from the floor into her heart as they swirled around each other. Their movements weren't hard to follow, and she certainly didn't see any harm in the effort.

That is, until James put his hands on her waist.

"Mr. Wallin," she started, but anything else was

lost in the shriek of delight as he tossed her in the air and caught her again.

"My word, but that was fun!" She knew she must be grinning, and as widely as him for once. As if he appreciated it, he winked at her, took one of her hands and spun her around. The cabin became a blur of color, his touch her only anchor. But she couldn't care. She was a bird, soaring over valleys, a deer bounding up a mountain. For once in her life, she was free.

"Hand over hand!" Deerlund called, turning with her.

They all began passing back and forth among the group, left hands to left, right hands to right, around in a circle. She knew a few country dances that included such moves, but none went to this tune. Indeed, she suddenly had three partners instead of one, and they seemed to be making things up as they went along.

"Now promenade your partner," James called as his hand met hers, and she found herself marching along beside him down the room as LaRocque and Deerlund followed behind.

"Circle right," McKenzie shouted over the music.

Everyone joined hands, and around they went, moving with the notes. James's gaze carried her along, encouraged her, told her she was amazing. She didn't want to look anywhere else.

"Now left," McKenzie ordered, and her body bumped James's as they changed direction.

"Sorry," she murmured, but he just gave her hand a squeeze.

"Now thank your partner kindly," McKenzie finished, lowering his arms at last.

The concertina deflated with a mournful wail, and

Rina felt as if she might crumple as well without the music's support. LaRocque bowed to Deerlund, who clapped him on the shoulder, nearly oversetting him. James took Rina's hand and bowed over it. She didn't think the dance was the only reason she found herself breathless.

"Another," Deerlund demanded, rubbing his hands together gleefully.

"Fine by me," James said, giving Rina's hand a swing. "I have the only partner I need."

LaRocque stepped forward. *"Mais non,"* he said. "Such a flower belongs to no man."

Rina started to demur, but the trapper took up her other hand and switched to French. "Many years ago, I danced another way, a more courtly way. Dare I hope you know it as well, Mademoiselle Fosgrave? The minuet?"

Oddly enough, she did know the dance, though it had fallen out of favor years ago according to the dance master who had taught her. It was now only performed in court circles in Europe, favored by royalty for its impressive, controlled movements.

"I would be honored, Monsieur LaRocque," she said before turning to James and explaining the Frenchman's request in English. She wasn't sure how James would take the matter, but he released her into the trapper's grip.

The Frenchman requested a particular song from their host, who nodded and raised his concertina once more. Out came the strains of a slow, stately melody. Rina and LaRocque moved to the center of the room. One of his arms went about her waist as they stood side by side. Step-together-step, step-together-step.

She followed the trapper through the elegant forms. It was so prescriptive, so precise. She could not find the joy she'd felt earlier.

James tapped the trapper on the shoulder and said, *"À présent moi."*

She didn't think he knew the words meant "now me." He'd was merely copying what the Frenchman had done earlier. LaRocque obligingly released her with a bow, and James stepped into his place. At once, the room felt warmer, the music softer.

"Do you know the minuet?" she marveled.

"I never had the benefit of an education like yours," he admitted. "But I learn fast."

He proved to be right. In unison, they traipsed down the room. He performed the steps languidly, effortlessly, allowing her merely to react, to feel. He was the finest courtier at the king's command, and she was the princess he'd come to convince. Every defense she had was falling to the sweetness of his look.

The music stopped, and so did James. For a moment, they stood, gaze to gaze, breath coming as one. She didn't remember there was another person on the planet until Mr. Deerlund began applauding.

"Mighty fine dancing, ma'am," he said, coming forward from his place along the wall.

Rina curtsied. "Thank you, Mr. Deerlund."

"No," James murmured, bending closer to her ear. "Thank you."

She tucked a hair behind her ear as an excuse to step away from his warmth.

"That's enough for one night," McKenzie declared. "Best you gents finish the night with a nice game of checkers."

Deerlund grumbled, but LaRocque nodded toward the fire, and the two settled next to the glow.

James didn't seem disposed to release Rina's hand. "Care for a game?" he asked.

He was already playing a game she could not win. Her heart would only end up further bruised. "No. Now I really must retire if I'm to be ready to leave with you in the morning."

She thought he might argue, but he merely nodded. "Then may I see you to your room?"

She knew the others were watching them. They had to be wondering how highly she held James in her affections. Even with their temporary engagement, it was best not to give anyone the wrong impression. She pulled her hand gently from his.

"Mr. McKenzie showed me the way earlier. Good night, gentlemen, and thank you for a lovely evening."

They all climbed to their feet as she left. Even in the wild, it seemed, they knew how to honor a lady.

And she felt like a lady for the first time in a long time as she closed the door to the room Mr. McKenzie had given her and leaned against the planed wood. Oh, she'd never be a princess. But tonight, when James had held her hand and gazed at her, she'd felt as if she was the most important person in the room.

Perhaps the most important person in his life.

No, no. She couldn't dwell on that. She pushed off the door and went to see how she might settle for the night. Mr. McKenzie had a large bed, straw tick on ropes if the give of it as she sat was any indication. Its bounce made her think of the dance, how James had smiled, the way he'd held her. She knew why he was giving her his attentions; he'd told her so himself.

He wanted her to change her mind, return with him to Wallin Landing. Like her adopted parents, there seemed little he wouldn't try to meet his goal.

But why? The Fosgraves had been addicted to the trappings of wealth, going to extraordinary lengths to capture and keep them. With his horses, claim and logging income, James had more than many men on the frontier. And she certainly had no inheritance to interest a suitor.

Neither could she believe his claim that only she could teach at Wallin Landing. There must be other teachers in Seattle. And even if they all refused him, as he seemed to think, Mrs. Wallin could have taught Beth and Levi as she had taught her older sons. What was so important about having Rina as their teacher?

The questions nagged at her through the night, but she reached no conclusions by the time they set out the next morning, which was Saturday. Knowing that she was likely to meet Mr. Buckhorn at the Crossing today, she'd put on her best day dress, the purple satin belted at her waist and trimmed with triple rows of white satin banding along the sculpted skirt. Of course, her gray cloak with its voluminous hood hid most of the gown, but just wearing the dress made her feel regal, confident.

Mist shrouded the forest as she came out of the cabin. Voices echoed from the barn, James saying goodbye to Deerlund as he harnessed the horses.

"You stop by anytime, Sister Fosgrave," McKenzie told her as she paused in the doorway to wait for James to bring the wagon around. "You're part of our family, and you'll always be welcome."

He lay his hand on her shoulder, heavy, firm, and

she felt the conviction behind it. Tears stung her eyes, and she wrapped her arms as far as they would go around him and gave him a quick hug. "Thank you, for everything."

She thought she saw a tear in his own eye before she hurried to where James was waiting to help her up.

"Made another conquest, I see," he said as he guided the horses south.

"Made a friend," she countered, smile forming.

But her pleasure at the thought faded as they continued on their way. The track here seemed to grow narrower with each roll of the wheel, the road more rutted and overgrown. She could barely see the heavy sky through the overlacing branches. Everything hung wet and heavy, as if weighed down by her thoughts.

"I was under the impression that the way to the Crossing was widely used," she said, ducking under the limb of an encroaching fir that spilled raindrops down her cloak.

"This is a shortcut," James promised her. "We should reach the Black River soon. From there, it's straight on to the Crossing."

The Crossing. By tomorrow, she could be at her new school, surrounded by her new community, her future secured.

And James would be back at McKenzie's, kicking up his heels without her.

She should not care. What he did after depositing her was none of her concern. Yet she did care, far more than she should.

She heard the problem before she saw it. Ahead came a sound like a rushing wind, growing louder every moment. They rounded a bend, and James reined in. The road simply ended, the ground dropping away to where muddy brown waters boiled down a narrow draw.

"Shouldn't there be a bridge?" Rina asked. There was no other way he was getting her across that!

"No bridge," James answered, lowering the reins. "No one could afford to build it or maintain it clear out here. But normally this is an easy ford, the water no higher than a horse's hock. Something must have happened upstream, a mighty storm, a dam give way." He glanced at her. "Seems like somebody doesn't want you to reach the White River, Rina."

She didn't like the thought. James could tell by the way her brows gathered inside the hood of her cloak. Raindrops had spotted the wool with black, making it look as if she had been splashed with mud. Her look was nearly as dark.

"Be that as it may," she said, "what do we do now?"

"Well, we sure can't cross." James eyed the turbulent waters. He'd decided to take a different way to the Crossing, one that might give him a little more time with her, but he hadn't counted on the river rising. "That's likely to sweep away the wagon and us with it."

"I cannot like how it eats at the bank, either," she said.

James could see what she meant. The rushing waters were degrading the shore, chunks of ground disappearing into mud as he watched.

Though the way was tight, he could turn the team now. But heading back to the main road to the Crossing would cost him his opportunity to convince Rina to give up on the new school. There had to be something else he could do.

"Is there another road?" she asked, gaze turned to his.

"I spotted a side trail a ways back," James mused. "Looked like it might run parallel to the river. We can follow it for a time, see if the water widens lower down, cross over there. If we don't find a likely spot, we can backtrack to McKenzie's."

Rina stiffened. "Is that your game now? Trying to delay us?"

He wasn't about to admit it. "You have a high respect for my abilities, ma'am," he said, making sure to widen his eyes. Ma always said that made him look as innocent as a lamb when she knew he was a tiger. "I can't control the amount of water in a river."

"No, but you can control where we meet that river. I think you should take us back to McKenzie's immediately. Perhaps Mr. Deerlund or Monsieur LaRocque will be willing to escort me south."

He wasn't about to let her go with the trappers. They seemed fine fellows and all, but who knew when one would take it in his head to marry her? She'd have a horrid life as a trapper's wife—either she'd be dragged all over creation to follow the fur trade, or she'd spend all her time waiting for her husband to return.

"I'm not even sure they're still at McKenzie's," he told her. "Your best choice is to stick with me. I'll get you to the White River."

Perhaps just not quite as quickly as she'd hoped.

Rina raised her chin. "Very well. But whatever happens, I will not return to Wallin Landing."

"Whatever you say, ma'am," he replied, hanging on to the hope that she was wrong.

He managed to turn the wagon and team and go back the way they had come. Sure enough, a tiny trail, little more than the width of the wagon, led off the existing track. He clucked to the horses, who eased the wagon onto the trail. At least it had stopped raining. He could see the way clearly, past rocky hillsides and thick forest.

The lady beside him was stonier, face set and arms crossed over her chest. Surely he could make her smile again.

"Fine day for a drive," he ventured.

"Not from where I sit," she replied.

He leaned closer, gave her his best smile. "Not too late to turn back."

"I fail to see how you can even turn!" she protested.

"Oh, I'd figure something out," he said, straightening. "I always do. Just say the word."

"The word, Mr. Wallin," she grit out, "is onward."

So they were back to being prickly again. He sighed. "Is that one of the rules for a teacher—excessive formality? Otherwise I'm certain I'd be James by now."

"You didn't give me permission," she pointed out.

"I didn't ask it either, Rina," he replied.

Her lips tightened. "No, you did not, but I doubt my new employers would approve."

"A shame they aren't here, or to see you cavorting through the forest with an eligible bachelor." He wiggled his brows at her.

She regarded him coolly. "We are not cavorting," she informed him. "We are driving on a public road in full view of anyone who might drive by."

He glanced around at the trees, then back at her. "Very proper, unless you consider the fact that this is more a trail than a road, and we aren't likely to see another human being for miles."

"But we could," she insisted. "That is the point, Mr. Wallin."

"James," he corrected her.

"Fine," she said. "James. But I think it is clear by our actions that we are not attempting to be clandestine. Therefore, our behavior is completely aboveboard."

She had the cutest little nose. At the moment, it was high in the air, as if she had no doubt of her convictions.

"So, as long as it's done in the open, it's proper?" he asked her.

"Precisely."

"Good." He pulled on the reins to halt the horses.

Rina put a hand to the sideboard as the wagon jerked to a stop. "What are you doing?"

"Attempting to persuade you to come home with me," he said, and he bent and kissed her.

Emotions sparkled, brighter than sunlight through the trees. He wanted to pull her closer, hold her forever. Wherever she was going, he wanted to be beside her.

He reined in his emotions. He'd never wanted to get so close to another person, not after seeing how devastating losing someone you cared for could be. His engagement to Rina would only last another day. He couldn't afford to have his feelings last longer than that.

He had to remember his only goal was to bring her home to Wallin Landing to teach.

She leaned back, face flushed. "You must stop doing that. My reputation is at stake! If the good people of the White River feel ice cream parlors to be salacious, what do you think they'd consider a teacher who allows a strange gentleman to kiss her?"

There she went, looking at circumstances again. He put his hand on his heart, mouth drooping. "Why, Rina, you wound me. You consider me strange?"

She smacked his arm. "Stop that! This is serious!"

He took up the reins and clucked to his team, who obligingly started forward once more. "No, it isn't. Life is too short to worry about what other people think of you."

"This from a man who lives in the wild!" She threw up her hands. "You have only your family to be accountable to, sir. I might have a dozen parents, all concerned that I live as an example to their children."

He was glad the horses knew what they were doing, for his hands were still shaking from that kiss. "Children who, apparently, are never allowed inside an ice cream parlor," he reminded her.

She did not so much as chuckle. "Children who are impressionable. I must do nothing that would cause one to stray."

James shook his head at her obstinacy. "I imagine more than one little boy has stolen a kiss from a little girl in a quiet corner of the schoolyard."

"But his teacher did not." Rina sighed. "Forgive me, James, but I must take such matters seriously even if you do not. And I cannot think why you would believe a kiss would convince me to return to Wallin Landing. Surely you would not go so far as to play on my emotions that way."

Put in that manner, he sounded a bit like a scoundrel. "Certainly not."

She stared at him. "You did. You thought you could sweeten up the schoolteacher with some compliments and kisses. That is reprehensible!"

Though he was beginning to see her point, he had enough pride that he couldn't agree with her. "It most certainly is not," he protested. "At least, I don't think so, not knowing what reprehensible means. It was just a kiss!"

She held up her fingers. "Two kisses. Or are they so meaningless that you could forget?"

He would never forget either one. Even if she went to the White River, he knew those kisses would stay on his mind to his dying day. But he couldn't tell her that. He didn't want her to know how much she was coming to mean to him. Because those kinds of feelings demanded a commitment, one he wasn't sure either of them was willing to make. One he feared could destroy the carefully constructed walls he'd built around his heart.

He pulled in the reins once more, drawing the wagon to a stop. "The kisses weren't meaningless, Rina. But not every kiss is a heart-stopping experience."

"Yours are."

As soon as she said the words, she clapped both hands over her mouth, eyes wide over the top of them. She knew what she'd just admitted. She probably thought he'd laugh, call her naive. That was exactly the way he ought to behave if he wanted to keep his heart intact.

But she deserved better than that.

He sobered, turning to face her. "So are yours. But

we both agreed this engagement was merely tempo-rary, that we didn't want to marry. One kiss cannot change that."

The way she looked at him made him think she was no longer so sure of the matter.

"Good afternoon, friends," a chipper voice called. "Good of you to come out our way."

James jerked forward to see a large man with a grizzled beard, shotgun nestled in his burly arms. He stepped out of the woods in front of the team, who were shifting on their feet with unease.

Seeing he had James's attention, he leveled the gun at Rina. "Throw down your weapons and your valu-ables, and no one gets hurt."

Chapter Twelve

James's arm strayed over the backboard to his rifle. "Don't make the mistake of thinking us an easy target," he warned, pulling out the gun.

"You might not be, but your missus is," the would-be robber said, raising his gun as well. "For me and my partner. Right, Davy?"

"You bet," came a thick voice behind them. "That gray cape makes a mighty fine target."

Rina stiffened. James felt cold all over. He set the gun down carefully and raised his hands.

"All right, gents," he said, keeping his voice calm. "You got the drop on us. But I don't think you'll find much for your trouble."

"We'll start with your gun," the front man said, venturing closer. "Hand it over nice and easy like."

Oh, but he was going to miss that rifle. James offered the miscreant the Spencer, and the robber took it. Then he nodded to Rina.

"Open your cloak, now, ma'am. Let's see how well your husband has you decked out."

James thought she might protest, but she unhooked

the cloak and held it wide. Something sparkled deep in its folds.

The robber grinned. "That pocket watch will do nicely."

Rina's hand closed over the gold case. "It belonged to my...to someone once dear to me."

A chuckle came from the rear robber. "Heard that one afore."

That regal air was coming over Rina again, her spine straightening, her face stiffening. She'd get herself killed over a pocket watch!

James pressed his hand down on her free one in warning. "It's all right, dear," he said. "I'll buy you another on our anniversary."

He could only hope she'd understand why he was pretending in front of these fellows. It was safer for her if the robbers thought she was married and not an unattached female with no family to avenge her.

She pulled the watch all the way out of the inside pocket that had held it. James caught sight of a highly embossed case before she reached out and dropped the watch in the robber's outstretched hand.

He held it up. "Now, that's a lovely thing. You got anything else like this, missus?"

"No," she said, gaze out over the horses as if she were determined not to allow the thieves the least encouragement. "Everything was sold to pay off debts."

Perhaps she was just trying to throw them off the scent, but James thought she spoke the truth. Whose debts had she been forced to pay? Her own? A husband's? Was that where the watch had come from? He couldn't very well ask under the circumstances.

The robber tsked. "Shame, that. Davy, see if we can lighten the poor lady's load."

James swiveled in time to see the other robber approaching the back of the wagon. He was a small man with the short-cropped brown hair, tiny eyes and long nose of a rat. Robbing must not have paid well, for his clothes were worn and dirty, patches barely hanging together in places. As Rina turned, the fellow grabbed for her trunk.

"Leave that alone!" she cried.

James's grip tightened on her hand, preventing her from moving. From the corners of his eyes, he could see the front robber sight down the barrel of his gun at her.

"Now, you just sit quiet like a proper lady," he told Rina. "Go on, Davy."

James nodded to Rina and turned to face front again. She did likewise, but the height of her head betrayed her reluctance. A thunk behind him told James that the other thief had opened the lid of her trunk.

"Dresses," he called. "Too fancy to bother with, Nash. Couple of hair combs and a bunch of books."

"Throw it out," his partner ordered. "Now, if you two will just get down, we'll be on our way."

Get down? But that would mean he intended to make off with the wagon.

And the horses.

James went still. "You can't take the wagon. My family needs it."

"And we needs it more," Davy said, joining Nash at the front of the wagon. "I reckon those horses will fetch a pretty penny."

James felt as if they'd reached in and plucked out his

heart. Still, he smiled at them. "You might get a good price for them, if one wasn't lame and the other blind."

Rina frowned at him, but Davy leaned around his partner to stare at the horses. Lance raised his head, nostrils flaring, and Percy grumbled to himself.

"They don't look sick to me," Davy said, straightening.

"That's what I said," James agreed. "Right before their previous owner took my money and ran. You'll be doing me a favor by taking them off my hands."

"James," Rina said, shock vibrating through the word. "How can you say such things about Lance and Percy?"

"Lance and Percy!" Nash guffawed, belly quivering. "Figure on a woman to give her horses such prissy names."

His friend started laughing too.

James couldn't stand it. "For your information," he grit out, "*I* named my horses."

"Then they ought to be glad to go with fellows having more sense," Davy gibed. "Now get down."

James climbed down and came around for Rina, all the while trying to reason out something else he could do, something he could say to stop the thieves. Once he would have been rash enough to throw a punch or two, make a grab for a gun. But now all he could think about was the possibility of Rina getting hurt in the process.

And that was even more unthinkable than losing his horses.

In the end, he could only stand at the side of the road, Rina's trunk tumbled nearby, while Nash and Davy made off with the rifle, the wagon and Lance and Percy.

"Forgive me," she said.

James made himself shrug. "It's not your fault they happened upon us. I was the one who wanted to take the shortcut."

"You wouldn't have been anywhere near here but for me," she protested.

He strode over to her trunk. "Oh, you never know. I might have taken a hankering to wander." He bent and hefted one handle.

Rina darted forward as if to take it from him. "You can't mean to carry that!"

He gave it a tug to test the strength of the leather strap. "Just because I lost everything doesn't mean you have to." He dragged it a few feet, feeling it catch on every rock, each root. He lowered the trunk and eyed her.

"How would you feel about leaving the books?"

She closed the distance between them, face intent as her gaze met his. "I would rather leave the clothes. They at least are replaceable."

"Not out here," James warned.

As if to deny it, she bent and opened the lid. James leaned over, gazing down into the depths. Bright fabrics gleamed in the light.

"That's silk," he marveled, reaching down to finger a gown and then a shawl patterned with autumn leaves. "And the softest wool I ever felt."

"Cashmere," she said. "I will not miss it."

He jerked back. "Are you mad? We're lucky the robbers had no idea of the value or we'd probably be standing out here in our flannels!"

She straightened, chin coming up once more. "Nonsense. Our lives are far more important than mere cloth."

James crouched beside the trunk. "No argument there. But, Rina, I can't let you give this up."

She moved away from the trunk as if distancing herself from everything it represented. "That, sir, is not your decision to make."

Perhaps. But as he lifted one of her lovely gowns, something slid out into his hand. The miniature was a typical family portrait—father, mother, daughter— except the parents wore robes trimmed in ermine and heavy crowns encrusted with jewels on their heads. In the image Rina gazed out with sober eyes, as if well aware that she would one day rule a nation.

Who had pictures painted of themselves in costume? Was she really some sort of princess? It would certainly explain those airs of hers and why she'd bristled when he'd called her "your majesty." But a princess on the Mercer expedition, going to teach school on the White River? Impossible!

"Well, Mr. Wallin?" she asked, gaze on the path back. "Are you coming?"

James tucked the miniature into his waistcoat. "When we've dressed properly."

Rina's gaze swung back to him. "I was unaware formal attire was required to be stranded in the wilderness."

"And you claim to be a schoolteacher," he teased. He scooped up an armful of clothing and held it out to her.

Rina eyed it as if he'd offered her his brother's snake. "I will not change clothes in front of you."

James rose. "I wouldn't ask that of you. I want you to put on as much of this as you can over the clothing you're already wearing. You have no idea how cold it can get at night when you're wet and tired. We have a long way to walk before we find help, and I have no interest in either of us freezing along the way."

Rina couldn't believe how attached he was to her clothing. James would not listen to her arguments, draping dresses, shawls and jackets about her person as he talked. What was left he tied around himself or stuffed in his pockets. She could not imagine what the Fosgraves would have thought had they seen the pair of them.

"The lace is very becoming," she said as they started off the way they had come. They had agreed that their best course was to try to make it back to McKenzie's Corner by nightfall. Already the sun was dipping below the branches, the air cooling with a breeze from the west.

He flipped the flat black velvet hood back from his face, the white satin bow hugging his chin. "Why, thank you, ma'am. I predict it will set a new style for loggers around the world."

That forced a smile from her. "You are more determined to set a positive tone to our situation than a style," she marveled, lifting her heavy skirts to circle a stump. "I appreciate that."

"Does no good to complain," he replied, detouring around the next stump. "The trees can't hear you, and the animals don't care."

The mention of animals sobered her. "Are we likely to meet many creatures?"

He cast her a glance, serious even under a cloud of

lace. "I won't lie to you. We have maybe an hour left to walk before we have to find shelter for the night."

"Shelter." Rina seized on the word. "Then there are farmsteads out this way."

"Not many," he confessed. "And none along this stretch of road as far as I know. Our best bet if we can't find a cave is to shinny up a tree."

Rina nearly choked as she spread her skirts. "In these?"

"I'll help you," he promised. "We just have to get off the ground."

Somehow, the thought of climbing a tree made walking all the more difficult.

But walk she did, loaded down with clothing, until the path reached the road once more. At least, it reached where the road had been.

The river had been busy in their absence. Wide swaths of ground were gone, trees tilting precariously toward the rushing waters. She could not see the beginning of the road other than the wide spot where debris pooled, bobbing in circles before it was swept downstream again.

James pulled her away from it. "We'll have to go through the woods, meet the road farther back."

Rina glanced into the forest. There was no path to follow, no sense of any order. Thick firs rose into the sky, while their fallen brothers and sisters obscured the ground, sporting carpets of moss. Any kind of opening was filled with the sweeping fronds of ferns, lacy canopies dotted with tiny red berries and snaking prickly vines covered in white flowers.

"I cannot navigate that," she said.

"I can." James took her hand and led her forward.

"Step up on this log now. See? Just like promenading along the boardwalk."

No boardwalk she'd ever visited had limbs poking out at odd angles and mushrooms popping up below. James, however, was as sure-footed as a mule, guiding her along fallen logs, ducking under tilting branches, taking her ever deeper into the wilderness.

With her hand in his, she found she could not fear. Birds called overhead. Fir scented the air. Sunlight filtered down, anointing branches with gold. She'd always thought she'd visit a grand cathedral on her coronation, not wander through one in which the columns were made of wood and the branches seemed to support the roof of the sky.

Yet even as she glanced around in wonder, she noticed that James was not nearly so amused. He seemed to be seeking something, for every once in a while he'd stop, look up as if in consideration, then shake his head and lead her on. Finally, he pulled up short in an area with a group of narrow-leafed trees, brighter green against the backdrop of fir. Several grew close together, branches intermingling overhead.

"Give me those shawls," he said.

Rina unwound them from around her waist. "Why? What are you planning?"

He took them from her and draped them around his neck. "A blasphemy on this fine clothing, but a necessity, I fear. Stay close and see if you can gather some dry wood for a fire." He leaped up, caught a branch and pulled himself into the tree.

She knew she should do as he'd suggested and gather wood, but she couldn't seem to take her gaze away from him. He moved through the tree as if he were doing nothing more than climbing the stairs to bed. She'd seen acrobats perform at a circus once, with her family in the front box as befitted their station. Those men had soared about the ring like swallows darting over a river. James was no less graceful and sure of himself, and he had no net to catch him if he fell.

He must have brushed aside a branch, for sunlight speared her gaze, reminding her of their purpose. She looked down and cast about for fallen limbs they could use, all the while listening for any movements around her. By the time James jumped down beside her, she'd managed to scrape together a small pile of downed timber.

"That ought to last an hour or two," he said.

"An hour!" Rina dumped the last few twigs onto the others. "Is that all?"

"Well, you know how quickly a good fire burns," he said. When she didn't answer right away, he peered closer. "You do know how to start a fire, don't you?"

She refused to lie. "Not in the slightest. I was able to keep yours burning in the schoolroom, but I never learned to light one." She felt as if her confidence was fading with the sun. "Is it terribly difficult?"

His face turned serious, but she could see the twinkle in his eyes. "Extremely difficult," he said. "I'm amazed mankind survives. I don't suppose you brought any parlor matches."

Rina frowned. "I refuse to carry the things. They are entirely too easy to catch fire."

"And aren't we all thankful for that." James bent over the ground and began sweeping the dried needles together in a pile. "Good thing I still have my flint.

I'll start the fire, then you tend it while I see if I can find some food."

Rina stiffened. "You're leaving?"

"Not far and not for long," he promised, glancing up with a smile. "Now, watch so you'll know what to do next time."

She certainly hoped she wouldn't be stranded in the wilderness more than once. But she knew the ability to start a fire would come in handy on the White River. She'd seen footmen lay a coal fire, and a girl-of-all-work had usually kept the fires going in the boardinghouse. But she'd never realized there was such an art to it.

James laid the sticks she had gathered around his pile of needles as if constructing a log cabin. Fascinated, she watched as he struck his flint over the pile, then crouched and blew into the embers, lips pursed as if he meant to kiss the rising flames. At the thought, heat flushed up her, and she knew it had little to do with the warmth spreading from the fire.

"Now, a few pieces a little bigger," he said, straightening. He pointed. "That branch there and any that size will do."

She hurried to drag the branch over to him. He propped it against his glowing house and stood back. "That ought to do it. If it starts to go out, take a stick and poke it up."

She nodded. "I can do that."

James eyed her. "And don't get too close. We don't want to ruin any more of your clothes than we have to."

Again with the clothes. For a moment, back where they'd lost his precious horses, she'd thought she'd actually seen a tear in his eye at the idea of leaving her things behind. She'd been more concerned about sapping his strength than at the loss of her meager belongings. They only served to remind her of a time she'd sooner forget.

A person who never had been.

The person she was now guarded the fire as he disappeared into the darkening woods. He seemed to find her skills interesting, but she struggled to see their utility out here. She'd never have to calculate the political ramifications of introducing a grand duke to a cabinet member who was a mere mister. She had no fine house to decorate, no linen-draped table to set. As Mrs. Wallin had said, Rina might speak Italian, but the person who could answer her was rare.

A cool breeze darted through the clearing, setting the trees to whispering. Tiny things croaked and chirped, content with their lots. Rina cuddled her cloak closer.

Oh, Lord, I cannot help James now. Only You can see us through this.

Her fire popped, embers scattered and smoke billowed up. Was it going out? Batting away the gray cloud with one hand, she laid another log against the glow. The mound settled, crackling and hissing. The flames sputtered.

"No, no, no," she told the fire, panic starting to build. She nudged the log closer with her toe. "Come on! You must be hungry! Eat that!"

The smoke thickened, singeing her lungs and stinging her eyes. Blinking back tears, she ventured lower, pushing at the wood. "Come on!" she begged.

With another pop, an ember flew out to land on her

skirts. The silk flamed immediately, and she fell back from it with a cry.

"Roll!"

James was on her in an instant, driving her back from the fire, twisting her so her skirt was smothered against the ground. Heat pushed through her petticoats, then evaporated. She managed to catch her breath as she sat.

James knelt beside her, eyes wide. "Are you hurt?"

"I…I don't think so." Rina spread her skirts. In the center was a hole, blackened around the edges, to show the gray smoke stain on her petticoat. Her best day dress—utterly ruined!

James rocked back on his heels. "Thank the Lord! When I saw that spark flare, I thought you were going up in smoke instead of the fire!"

What if she had? If he hadn't returned just then, she might easily have been burned. The very thought set her hands to shaking, but she forced them against the ground to climb to her feet.

"Thank you for returning so soon." She glanced back at the traitorous fire, which was now no more than a smoldering ruin. "It nearly went out."

"Forget it," he said, and he gathered her close and held her a moment.

Oh, but that was what she needed, this strength, this belief in herself and the future. She wanted to wrap him around her like her shawl and hold him tight. No one had ever made her feel so safe.

But with night closing in, she was very much afraid this feeling of safety was only an illusion.

Chapter Thirteen

James held Rina close, his heart thundering painfully against his ribs. He'd managed to locate some food in the forest. It wasn't much, but it would see them through until morning. When he'd come out of the woods to see her skirts ablaze, he'd never known such fear.

Thank You, Lord, for sparing her!

She was the one to pull back. In the twilight, he could see her lips trembling a moment before she spoke. "What do we do now?"

Best to keep things light. He was sincerely concerned about their safety, but she didn't need to know that. With the main road out, miles lay between them and help, and he wasn't sure where to find shelter or water. Then there were the animals she'd asked about—cougars, wolves and bears. He'd have had a difficult time of it alone. Protecting Rina complicated matters threefold.

But he was not about to let her down.

"Now, we feast," he said. Glancing around, he spotted a downed tree not too far from where they'd laid the fire. He unwrapped the wool gown from his shoulders and draped it over the moss. "Won't you be seated, milady?"

She went to sit, arranging her skirts to hide the burn. The frown on her face didn't ease. "I dislike special treatment."

She might dislike it, but she required it. Any of his brothers would have known how to help. Ma and Beth would have had some idea of how to pitch in. The schoolteacher had a lot to learn.

"Humor me," he said before turning to the fire. He could still feel heat from it, so it hadn't gone out completely. Nudging the larger log with one foot, he saw the glow of coals inside.

"It simply would not cooperate," she said, exasperation lacing her polished tone. "Why did it go out?"

"Fire requires three things—fuel, heat and air. Deprive it of any, and it dies. Looks like it might have gotten just a bit too cozy." He crouched to fix the situation.

"Is that why you built the little house the way you did?" she asked. "To allow air to flow between the sticks?"

He nodded, intent on his work. "Pa taught us that. He said a fire had to be tended like your first love. Give it attention and care, and it will last."

"Beautifully put." She sighed. "And too true, I suspect."

James glanced up to grin at her. "You suspect? How long did your first love last, Rina?"

She fussed with her skirts again, twitching them this way and that as if their drape could not please her. "Less time than that fire, most likely." She cleared her throat. "What about you?"

"Oh, that's easy," He rocked back on his heels to survey the now brightly glowing fire. "From the day I first saw those steeldusts until now."

"I so regret I cost you your horses."

She sounded as if she might cry again. He couldn't have that. He felt as if her pain reached down to the secret place where he'd hidden his.

"I'll get them back," he said, rising. "As soon as we're settled. Pa didn't hold much with thieving, and neither do I."

"How long has he been gone?" she asked.

James dusted his hands off on his trousers, careful not to get any of her clothing dirtier than necessary. "Ten years. But I'll never forget him." The smoke must have gotten into his eyes, for they were tearing. He waved a hand as he turned. "Where are my manners? I promised you a feast." He strode to where he'd dropped the food he'd gathered, scooped it up and brought it to her.

"The finest victuals for your table, ma'am," he proclaimed. "The green leafy things are miner's lettuce, as fine a vegetable as you could want. These crooked little fellows are the roots of the young bracken fern—if you chew on them, they taste just like potatoes. And these are mushrooms."

"What's good about mushrooms?" she asked, picking up a thick stalk and eyeing the umbrella-like growth at the top.

"They don't stick in your teeth," he said.

She giggled, and gooseflesh pimpled his arms. This was more like it.

He perched on the log beside her as they ate and kept up a steady string of silly comments, all the while determining their next steps. He'd started building them a nest in the tree, but he still needed a way to help her reach it.

"It appears to be going out again," she said, frown aimed at the fire as if daring it to behave.

"It is, but by design," he replied, rising. "We can't stay down here all night to tend it."

She rose as well. "Why not? Fire would seem our best defense."

"A good defense," he qualified. "It's also a beacon— letting others know we're in the woods. The only people out this far are not the sort I would introduce to a lady."

"I see." She clasped her hands tightly in front of her, one hand cupping the other. It was a sure sign, he was coming to realize, that she was uncomfortable with the situation. "And after we sleep," she said, "how much farther must we walk to reach Mr. McKenzie's?"

"A ways," he qualified. He gestured to the now meager pile of food. "But we have food, strong legs and clever minds. We'll have no trouble making it back."

"You usually lie better than that."

He refused to let her see his fear. "Lie, ma'am? I try not to lie. I might color up a drab story or make a quip to bring a smile, but I rarely utter a falsehood."

She put her hands on her hips. "A truth that's told with bad intent beats all the lies you can invent."

"Now that," James said, "sounds like a school-marm."

Far too close to hand, something large pushed its way through the brush. She must have heard it, too, for suddenly she was right next to him.

"What was that?"

Fear raised her voice another octave, but there was no time for him to explain his plan.

"I need you to trust me," he said, taking her by the shoulders and pressing her back against the biggest tree. "I won't leave you, I promise. Stay here." He leaped and caught the lowest branch and hauled himself up into the tree.

He expected her to simply stand here while danger thundered closer? She wanted to run, to hide. How could she simply trust he knew what he was doing, that he'd be there to protect her when she needed him?

Because he'd been there every other time.

She straightened her shoulders and slowed her panicked breathing. James would make good on his promise; she had to believe that. And she had to take herself in hand and be alert to help his plans.

So she stayed against the tree, ears straining for any other sound from the woods. The croaks and chirps she'd heard earlier had gone silent, as if everything was intent on escaping the notice of something larger, more predatory. She could barely make out the shapes of the bushes and trees in the growing darkness. Were those eyes watching her? The breath of something hungry brushing her skirts?

"Grab this," James called, and something fell from above. She reached up and caught a loop of wool. It seemed he'd twisted her shawl together with other pieces of clothing to make a rope of sorts.

"Sit in it like a swing," James instructed.

The bushes to her right crackled as they parted to something massive. A smell came with it, like a wet dog that had played in the stables too long. When Clay

Howard had taught them aboard ship about making their way in the wild, he'd said that stench was the best way to know a bear was in the area. She yanked down on the sling and wiggled into the seat.

"Hold on," James said.

The sling edged up as the bear lumbered closer. The fur on its back brushed her skirts, and she sucked in a breath, but the beast headed for the log and the remains of their dinner.

The sling inched higher and higher still. In the light of the dying fire, she saw the creature's head turn, the blaze reflecting on its beady eyes as they fixed on her.

The sling jerked to a halt.

"Sorry," James said. "Caught on a branch. Give me a moment."

She didn't have a moment. The bear was turning, moving, heading her way. Glancing up, she made out a branch just above her. She reached up, grasped it and pulled.

The sling fell away, leaving her dangling.

Something bumped her boots. She didn't dare look down to see if it was the sling or a snout. If she could haul on the reins to slow a team of racing horses, surely she could pull herself over the branch. She drew in a breath and tried.

One shoulder made it up, but already she could feel her muscles straining. If only she could find purchase with her feet, but she was afraid to swing them lest she hit the bear and make it mad.

Mad enough to come up after them.

Fingers clawing at the bark, she started to slip.

Stronger arms wrapped around hers, helping her. In a moment, she was sitting on the branch.

Below them, the bear growled, the rumble vibrating along her nerves and setting them to tingling.

"We need to get a little higher," James urged her. He was standing against the tree, feet braced. "He's big enough that he won't chance following us on the lighter branches."

She wasn't so sure. Even now, the brute was sniffing around the base of the tree, as if intent on finding a way up. Beside her, James caught the next branch above them and pulled himself over it until his belly rested on the bark and his arms hung down. "Take my hands," he ordered.

Trying not to think about the bear, Rina slipped her hands into his. James slid over the branch, pulling her up as he went down. As her face passed his, he gave her a quick peck on the cheek.

"Sorry," he said as he landed below her. "Couldn't resist."

She perched on the branch and drew in a breath before glancing down. Then her breath left in a rush. James was standing on the branch, but the bear had reared up on its hind legs, putting its teeth level with James's knees.

"Jump!" Rina cried, scrambling to her feet.

Instead, James raised both hands beside his face and wiggled his fingers. "Yah! Get out of here, you old monster! Go!"

The bear dropped down.

Rina hugged the trunk as James climbed up beside her. "That was amazing," she told him. "You were so brave."

"Not so brave," he demurred with a shrug. "Bears

are big cowards, unless you surprise a sow and her cubs. Make enough noise, and they generally clear off."

Rina hazarded a glance down. The space below the tree seemed to be empty. No shadows moved around the fire. "Should we go back down?"

"Not tonight," James told her. "We'll sleep up here."

"Up here?" Rina straightened so fast she nearly lost her balance. James caught her arm and steadied her.

"See there how the trunk separates?" he said with a nod toward the center. "There's room for you on one branch and me on the other. We can use your clothing for padding and warmth. We'll be snug enough."

Entirely too snug. She could see that he had gone to great lengths to build them a safe place to spend the night. But while she might hope to live to see tomorrow, her future was very much in jeopardy.

What school would hire her when it became known that she'd spent the night alone with a man who was not a member of her family?

James felt rather pleased as he settled against the tree for the night. Rina was safely nestled nearby, tied to the branch with one of her shawls so she couldn't fall as she slept. He'd looped his belt over a branch for the same effect. Her cloak was draped over the top of them like a tent to keep off any rain. The entire setup was a masterpiece of ingenuity, if he said so himself. It would shelter them from the cold, catch any rain for drinking tomorrow and hide them from the curious gaze of passing predators. Not bad for the least talented member of the Wallin family. He laid his head back and smiled.

Until he heard the sniffle on the other side of the tree.

He shifted so he could see her body pressed against the branch. "Now, then, Rina," he murmured. "It will all come right. You'll see."

"I…I believe it might," she said, doubt evident in every word.

James sighed. "You picked the worst of us to get stranded with, you know. Now, if Drew was here, he'd swing his ax and cut a path straight through the trees to Seattle."

"*If* he'd brought his ax with him," she said, voice beginning to regain its usual tone. "And the robbers allowed him to keep it."

"And Simon," James continued undaunted, "why, he'd brook no nonsense and keep you walking all night to make it back faster."

"We'd have to sleep sometime," she protested.

James smiled in the dark. "Ah, but if John was here, he could probably figure out the distance to the nearest navigable stream and float you back to Seattle."

"Or wherever the stream let out on the Sound," she argued. "If we could even navigate as far as the Sound. I think your plan is the wisest."

That was a first. "I suppose time will tell," he allowed, pleased that she'd stopped crying at least.

"What about Levi?" she asked.

James frowned at her outline. "Levi?"

He heard a rustle as if she'd turned to look at him.

"Yes," she said. "You told me how your other brothers would have dealt with the situation. What about Levi?"

"Oh, that's easy." James laid back again. "Levi would have left everyone behind and set off on his own, as far from Seattle as he could get. That is, until Beth caught up with him and hauled him home."

She giggled. He loved that sound. It made him feel tremendously clever.

"Now, Ma," he said, warming to his theme, "would never have gotten stranded to begin with. She would have looked those robbers in the eyes and told them how *their* mothers would feel about such behavior."

She giggled again. "And Catherine?"

"She'd have dosed them with tonic water."

"A shame we neglected to bring any. What about your father?"

"He…" James swallowed. Try as he might, he couldn't joke about that. "He would have taken you safely to the White River. Pa didn't make many mistakes. Even in the end, it wasn't his fault he missed the widow-maker."

"Widow-maker?" All laughter had fled from her voice. "What's that?"

"Sometimes a big branch breaks loose on one of these trees." Why was it so hard to explain? He felt as if he'd gone hoarse. "It snaps partway through in a windstorm or gets snagged on another branch. When you start chopping or sawing at the tree, the vibration works the broken branch loose, and down it comes. If you're under it at the time, it can break your arm or leg or worse."

"And your father failed to see it?" She sounded surprised. No more so than the rest of them had been.

"No one saw it," he said, remembering. "It was just Pa, Drew, Simon and me on the logging team back then. John and Levi were too young to help. I was nearly too young myself, so Pa gave me a simple job.

I was supposed to be the lookout, the one who watched the tree and the area around it and warned the others of any danger. And I never saw that branch."

"You were just a boy," she murmured. "If your father and brothers missed it, you cannot blame yourself for failing to notice it."

"It was my job to notice!" His voice was rising, and he forced it to lower. "I was bored, so I started thinking about other things—a pocket watch I hoped to purchase, the ax I'd use one day. Next thing I knew, Pa was down, and all I could do was help Drew and Simon pull the branch off him."

His stomach tightened at the memory. Pa had lain there, so still, staring up at the sky, ordering Drew to take his place as head of the family. He had never spoken to James, never looked his way. And then, he'd simply gone. James had turned and retched.

He felt a hand on his foot now, soft, gentle.

"I know it must be difficult to imagine," she murmured, "but you are very fortunate. You grew up knowing your father, learning from him. You knew he loved you."

He'd thought Pa had loved him. James could remember Pa laughing at some of his jokes. Why hadn't Pa looked his way? Why hadn't Pa forgiven him for his mistake? Perhaps because what he'd done was unforgivable.

"How horrid and unfair that he was taken from you," she continued. "But I think his death hurts so much because of that love."

"But that's the thing about love," James said. "You can't control who gives it to you, how they respond, when they decide to leave. You have to give it not knowing whether it will ever be returned. It's a crazy thing."

"Perhaps, but I envy you. I cannot remember my real parents. I was adopted by a couple who had no other children."

How different from his life. And small wonder she seemed daunted by his large, boisterous family. "They must have wanted you if they adopted you," he pointed out.

"In some ways." Now her voice was growing as dim as her silhouette. "But being an only child, I never had sisters or brothers, cousins or aunts and uncles. It was just me and the Fosgraves until they were gone. That's why I hated to part with that pocket watch the thieves took. It is one of the last things I have from a happier time."

She sounded so sad, so lost, that he didn't press her on how they'd died. He knew how much it hurt to remember Pa's death. Perhaps they'd been an elderly couple. Perhaps they'd met with an accident like Pa. Whatever the reason for their loss, he felt her pain once more.

"You have a chance for another family," he told her. "There are plenty of fellows here around Seattle. One of them might strike your fancy. Next thing you know, you'll be married with children of your own."

"We should try to get some sleep," she said. "I fear tomorrow will be a long, difficult day. Thank you, James, for everything. I would have perished a dozen ways by now without your help."

"Pretty sure it only takes one way to perish," he teased her. "But you're welcome. It was my honor."

He heard the clothing rustle as she settled for the night.

But he couldn't settle. He'd meant what he'd said. It was his honor to protect her. He understood that now in ways he never had before Pa had died.

But beyond honor, he knew protection was also a debt he owed her. He'd brought her out here. He had to see her safely home.

But he knew he couldn't do that by himself. He'd joined his family every Sunday for worship services, singing hymns, listening to Drew or Simon or John read from the Bible. They seldom asked him to read; they were all too afraid he'd add something to the story or make a joke about the passage. He'd always thought God must have a sense of humor. After all, He'd created James. Perhaps that thought was why the prayer came more easily than usual.

Trying to atone isn't working out so well, Lord. I brought a schoolteacher, but she didn't stick. Now, we're the ones stuck, where only You know the directions. I wish You'd share them with me because I'm running out of ideas.

The sigh of the breeze was his only answer.

You don't have to talk to me. I figure I haven't earned that, either. But maybe, for Rina's sake, You could help us live to tell the tale.

The branches above him shifted with the breeze, brushing aside Rina's cloak for a moment, and he caught a clear glimpse of the sky. The North Star gleamed in the darkness.

James dug his nail into the bark, marking the compass. If that was north, then McKenzie's and Seattle lay just to the left. That's where he'd head tomorrow.

He could pray only to stay strong and focused for her, instead of failing her the way he had his father.

Chapter Fourteen

Rina wasn't sure when she fell asleep. One moment she was listening to James tell a story about trying to swim across Lake Union all the way to Mt. Rainier and pretending she didn't hear the rustles and creaks of the forest around her. The next moment, she was opening her eyes to sunlight shafting through the trees. She blinked, remembering where she was and how she'd gotten here. Turning carefully, she saw James a few feet away.

He was curled up as well as he might along the branch, fingers gripping the bark. Long bronzed lashes lay against his golden skin, his face soft with sleep. He'd removed her lace hood, and a day's worth of beard wreathed his mouth and speckled his chin.

Somewhere, a branch must have moved, for suddenly sunlight bathed his face. His eyes popped open, and his gaze met hers. He grinned, and something brightened inside her.

"Now, that's a fine sight to wake up to," he said, and she wasn't sure he meant the sun.

He helped her to the ground in the sling, then tossed

the clothes down to her. She was certain the Fosgraves would never have dreamed the use to which she and James had put the fine garments. Then again, maybe they would.

She'd very nearly told him about her parents last night, but she hadn't been able to convince herself that he'd understand. For everyone but her, royalty was something told in stories or read about in the newspaper or books. And she truly wasn't royalty, unless there really had been a king and queen wandering about America and forgetting their two-year-old princess in the process. Raised in such a family as the Wallins, how could James possibly understand her upbringing? He'd think her mad or as crooked as the Fosgraves.

So she avoided the topic of family that morning as they prepared to set off once more. She managed to comb out her hair with her fingers and repin it behind her head. Her cloak was heavy with dew, and she didn't relish wrapping it about her, but James took it from her before she could put it on. He'd laid out several leaves on the ground, their edges curling up toward the sun so they resembled little cups. Now he gripped the wool of her cloak and twisted, strong fingers wringing the material. Water pattered down on the leaves, filling them.

"You looked like you could use a stiff drink," he said as he shook out the cloak.

Smiling at his teasing and his ingenuity, Rina lifted a leaf and drank. The cool water cleared her throat and her head. When he'd finished drinking as well, she used the last drops to wash her hands and face.

"Now that's just gilding the lily," James accused her.

"We may not be able to find civilization," she countered, "but we can still be civilized."

He swept her a bow, one hand pointing toward a long fallen log, which must be the start of their path for the day. "Of course, my lady. This way, if you please."

With him smiling so broadly, it wasn't hard to feel encouraged. The sun was shining, brightening the green of the forest. Birds called from the woods and flittered through the trees ahead of them as if leading the way.

"Ah, perfect," James said, stopping by a broad, leafy plant and plucking off some of the reddish berries. "Try these."

Rina accepted his gift, lifted them to her nose and sniffed.

James raised a brow. "Do you think I'd poison you?"

She blushed. "No, of course not." She put some of the berries in her mouth and chewed. They had a sweet and sour taste, reminding her a bit of ripe oranges.

James was watching her. "Like them?"

She nodded, swallowing. "Yes, thank you."

He cocked his head. "No muscle spasms, stomach cramps?"

Rina nearly choked. "No. Should there be?"

He shrugged. "I have no idea. But if you didn't die, I figure I can eat them." He popped the remaining berries in his mouth.

"James Wallin…" she started, then she saw that telltale sparkle in his eyes. "Oh, you tease! You behave, or you'll be wearing those berries."

He flipped at the hood he had stuck back on his head. "Don't be silly. They wouldn't go well with lace."

Rina gave it up and laughed.

The downed tree led to an open, marshy area, which James was careful to skirt, pointing out the thick mud along the edges. A swarm of tiny flies chased them into the forest, where the bushes grew so dense that at times he had to shove his way through to wedge an opening for her. Brambles scratched her face and hands; branches tugged at her hair and skirts. Her half boots, which had never been all that sturdy to begin with, were starting to protest the hard work. She refused to complain. James had enough to concern him.

Though, as usual, he didn't appear in the least concerned. He strolled along, ducking under branches, detouring around bushes, keeping up a steady stream of nonsense she was certain was meant to distract her from their predicament. It nearly worked.

"You know," he said as the sun climbed higher, "I'm not too sure, but I think today is Sunday."

Rina thought back as she followed him around a massive fir that blocked their way. "I believe it is." Which meant Mr. Buckhorn had left the Crossing empty-handed. She couldn't help her sigh.

James must have heard it, for he straightened. "Now, then. No need for that. Weren't you the one who told me people didn't need a church building to worship?"

He had mistaken the reason for her sigh, but she decided not to correct him. "The Lord will forgive us for not worshiping in style, given our situation."

James stopped in his tracks. "I do nothing, madam, unless it is with style." Before she could comment, he glanced around so fast the lace fluttered about his face. He seized her hand. "Come on."

He had the maddest starts! Rina stumbled behind him as he led her into the forest. Suddenly he stopped again, grabbing her shoulders to turn her to the right. Twelve mighty cedars grew in a ring, the space in the center covered in needles so thick they resembled a scarlet carpet. Sunlight set the resinous air to sparkling. The forest fell silent around them, as if waiting.

"Amazing grace, how sweet the sound," James began, voice a warm tenor as he pulled off the hood and lifted his gaze heavenward. "That saved a wretch like me."

"I once was lost, but now I'm found," Rina sang, joining her soprano to the melody. "Was blind, but now I see."

And suddenly, she felt as if she could see. The light was so clear, the song so pure. The world might change around her, but she could choose to be who she was through it all. She didn't have to let anyone take that from her.

James's hand reached for hers, and she clasped it tightly. They finished the song together and stood for a moment, sunlight bathing their faces.

James lowered his head. "Now that," he said with a smile, "is worshiping in style."

She could not argue with him there. With a tug on her hand, he led her forth once more. The birds began to sing around them. Her fears fell away with each step. They were going to be all right. She could feel it. *Thank You, Lord!*

"Keep an eye out, now," he said after they'd paused to graze on a patch of mushrooms. "Look for a column of smoke, any sign of a trail. McKenzie's can't be the only homestead out this way. If we find one, we ought to be able to beg food and a ride."

"Beg?" She couldn't like that word. Her adopted parents had never begged, even for mercy. Of course, they'd just lied their way out of any scrape, which she thought no more heroic.

"In a matter of speaking," he assured her, dusting his hands off on his trousers. "We haven't much to pay with. We'll have to rely on the goodness of their hearts."

Just like the Fosgraves. "We shall offer them the clothes," Rina insisted. "I refuse to do anything to incur a debt."

He pulled up the last remaining fungi and stuffed them in a pocket. "You mentioned debts yesterday. You don't look like the sort to run up bills." He eyed her. "Wait, don't tell me. They were all to your milliner."

Rina shook her head. "The milliner was the least of my problems. My family had a tendency to live beyond their means. It is a philosophy I do not share."

"Me either," he replied, holding out his hand to help her up. "Right now, I just want to live."

So did she.

They kept walking, wandering a circuitous route through the woods to avoid marshes and cliffs, taking time to rest now and then, and to drink from swiftly flowing streams. The day warmed, until the layers of clothing felt considerably less comfortable. Once in a while she thought she could hear something in the bushes, but it always scuttled away without showing itself, for which she was thankful. But no smoke, no path and no sign of civilization greeted them.

James did not complain. She was fairly sure he slowed his pace to allow her to keep up. He'd have been much farther along if not for her. Talk about debt!

The sun was once more dipping to the west when

she spotted an outline through the trees. She grabbed James's arm with one hand and pointed with the other.

"Is that a house?"

James squinted. He hadn't replaced the hood, but the exertion of the day had plastered his hair to his head. "I think you're right. Come on!"

He towed her through the brush to where it opened onto a small clearing. The log cabin huddled in the center had clearly seen better days. The porch sagged to the muddy ground. Moss all but obscured the roof. But the windows were shuttered against the night, and the solid door was closed against the wind, iron latch slowly turning red with rust.

"Anyone home?" James called as they approached.

Rina wasn't surprised when no one answered.

Still, as if to make sure, James went from side to side, examining the cabin from every angle. Did he expect to see a friendly hand waving through a hole in the wall?

"Someone must have abandoned the claim," he said as he returned to her. "We should be able to stay here safely tonight." He cast about. "They must have had a water source."

"Let me look," Rina offered. "See if you can find a way in."

"That's easy." He backed off a little and took a run at the door, crashing into it with a jar that shook the house so hard Rina thought it might keel over. The door stayed shut. James stepped back, rubbing his shoulder.

"Perhaps use the latch?" she suggested.

With a rueful grin, he tried, and the door creaked open.

Rina was almost afraid to see what lay inside. James

left the door open, so light filtered past them as they peered in. The floor seemed solid, the planks dusty but without obvious holes. One wall boasted a stone hearth, but it didn't look as if the previous occupants had left anything else behind.

James glanced her way. "Well?"

"It will do," she answered.

Outside, they located a rusting pump with a pipe leading down into the ground. The first few yanks on the handle yielded nothing but dust. James gave the pump a good kick before backing away. "Useless."

"Perhaps it takes patience," Rina said, bending. She kept cranking the handle, up and down, up and down, until her arms ached. The spigot spat out something black and oily. That was enough to make her stop, but James brightened.

"Keep it up," he urged. He ran around to the closest corner of the house, where muddy water had pooled from the recent rain. Scooping up a handful, he ran back to the pump and dribbled the water into a valve on the top as Rina worked the handle. With a gurgle, water spilled out onto the ground.

"Hallelujah!" James declared. He seized Rina's hands and swung her around in a circle, boots splashing in the puddle left from the pump. "We have water!"

Strange how such a small success could make her giddy. She didn't want to let go, could barely tear her gaze from his. Still, Rina pulled away, forcing him to halt.

"We have water," she agreed, trying to catch her breath. "But we need more than that to make it through the night."

He backed away, holding up one finger. "You're

right. I'll find food. You start the fire." He tossed her his flint kit and dashed off into the brush.

The fire. She fingered the cool metal of the little box, remembering what had happened last night. How could he believe in her after that performance?

Still, she was certain she must have learned something from his demonstration. After taking a long drink from the pump, she lay the kit on the edge of the porch. Then she moved in a half circle around the door, keeping it in sight as she gathered fallen branches, twigs and dried fir cones. She brought it all into the house and piled it near the cold hearth.

Sitting with her skirts puddled around her, she built a mound of tinder in the center of the hearth, then overlapped the twigs in a square around it. She took a deep breath and held it as she scraped the flint from James's kit over the stone inside it. Tiny sparks like falling stars tumbled down, and spots of red warmed the pile. She bent closer and blew softly, hoping, praying. The spots widened, flared.

Rina sat back with a smile. "Just like tending your first love."

She kept the fire burning, adding larger branches around the sides as needed. She used one that still had needles on it to sweep out the worst of the dust on the floor. Then she laid out her now hopelessly rumpled clothes in two lines opposite the fire for beds.

As she stepped back to admire her handiwork, something crunched under her foot. Bending, she found an ivory thimble, cracked from the impact. Not much to show for a life. But then, could she say any better?

Her pleasure at her accomplishments rushed away like water in a sieve, and her concerns filled the void.

Lord, what am I to do? All I wanted was to teach. Even that will be denied me now if other school districts are anything like the White River one. Where will I go? How will I pay my way?

Despite her best efforts, tears were gathering once more. She sniffed them back. She had to find the convictions she'd felt earlier. Surely there was something she could do.

"Just like home," James proclaimed, coming through the door and closing it behind him. Through the cracks on the shutters the setting sun lit the room with a red glow. In James's grip, she could make out a long stick with something wiggling on the end of it. She turned her back and wiped at her tears before he could see them.

She needn't have bothered. She heard him pause, his voice sad. "Are you crying again?"

Rina refused to look at him. "Certainly not."

The stick thunked as he must have set it down. Then he moved to her side.

"I'm sorry, Rina," he said, peering up under her fingers. "You have every right to be concerned. I know I haven't found a way out of this yet, but I won't stop trying. I promise."

This time it wasn't hard to believe him. He liked to joke and tease, make light of most situations. But when it came to important matters, like his family's school and her safety, he took things seriously indeed.

"I know you will," she told him. "These last two days have merely made me wonder about my future."

He smiled. "Well, then. Rethinking the need to re-locate to the White River?"

He was so pleased with himself she might have thought he'd planned all this. "I fear there may not be a need to go anywhere. There will be some who claim I'm ruined. I spent the night alone with a man who is not of my family."

He snorted. "Pretty shortsighted of them. How else were you to survive?"

He didn't understand. "That is immaterial. My reputation will have been compromised. I'll be deemed unfit to teach."

"Because surviving would have affected your teaching skills," he said with a nod. "Oh, yes, I see the sense in that. You probably forgot how to add and subtract, much less speak properly." He leaned closer and lowered his voice. "I wouldn't be surprised if you started using double negatives."

"Be serious!" Rina scolded. "The notion may seem far-fetched to you, but I assure you my employers will take a different view."

"A demented one," he replied, straightening. "You were worth your weight in gold before, Rina. Nothing's changed."

She threw up her hands. "Everything's changed! If I lose my profession, I forfeit any chance of supporting myself."

He grinned at her. "Nothing to worry about there. If no one else will have you, you can always marry me."

"That isn't funny!" she insisted.

"No? Maybe I should try harder." He went down on one knee and raised his hands beseechingly. "Please,

Miss Fosgrave, I know I'll never be worthy of you, but since it seems you have nothing better to do, won't you marry me?"

He'd thought he'd been silly enough to win a smile from her. Anything would be better than the bleak look she'd worn when he'd brought back dinner. Instead, she blanched.

"No," she said, taking a step back. "Now, please, get up. If you cannot take your own life seriously, leave mine out of it." She turned and hurried to the piles of cloth, leaving him looking at her back.

James climbed to his feet. "I didn't mean to offend you. But I refuse to see tragedy and destruction everywhere I look. There's too much of that in this world, and I can't change most of it."

"Ignoring it won't make it go away," she told the wall.

"Groveling in it won't make it better," he countered. "At least a laugh and a joke make people smile. Usually."

She sniffed. "You must think I have no sense of humor. I do see you're trying to make light of a bad situation. I simply cannot think what to do. I never intended this to be my life. At times I feel as if I'm wearing someone else's skin."

James shuddered. "Well, that sounds hideous. So, what did you intend to do if not teach? Marry some wealthy society fellow?"

She sighed. When she spoke, her voice was subdued. "No. I thought I'd rule a nation."

"Really?" James wandered closer. Her head was down, her fingers rubbing over each other as if her thoughts tumbled just as quickly. "Which one? Because I personally have always felt Canada should be conquered."

She glanced over at him, and he was pleased to see a smile hovering at the corners of her mouth. "Not Canada. A tiny kingdom in Europe called Battenburgia."

James shrugged. "Sorry. My knowledge of geography pretty much ends on the East Coast."

"You would never have learned about it in any school," she said, dropping her hands. "It is a figment of my parents' imagination."

The pain radiated out of her. He wanted to gather her close, but he wasn't sure she'd let him. "I thought you said you were adopted."

"I was, but not through any formal process. Mr. and Mrs. Fosgrave apparently found me and took me with them. I made a good prop in their charade, you see."

All he could see was that she needed to let this pain out or it would destroy her. "Sounds like a good yarn," he said, making for the fireplace. "Why don't you tell me while I get this fish dressed for dinner?"

She turned with him. "Shouldn't someone keep watch?"

"No need," James assured her, lifting the makeshift spear he'd used to capture the fish from the stream a ways into the woods. "I don't see a bear working that latch. Besides, do you hear that peeping noise?"

She frowned, head cocked as if she were listening. "Yes."

"Those are frogs out by the stream. They'll sing up a storm until they hear something that scares them. And most everything that might hurt us terrifies them. So long as they chirp, we have nothing to worry about."

She seemed to accept that, for she moved closer. "How can I help with dinner?"

James pointed to the hearth. "You have smaller hands. See if you can pry that stone loose. I mean to use it for a fry pan."

She set to work, shoulders bunching, as if she put all her fear and frustration into the effort. Keeping his questions locked inside, James filleted and laid out the trout as best he could with the sharp end of the stick, stuffing the fish with the mushrooms he'd picked earlier in the day. He was itching to know more about the people who'd raised her, but she clearly disliked remembering. Yet he couldn't help thinking that he would finally understand her if he could understand them.

He waited until she had finished eating the food, picking at the white flesh with her nimble fingers.

"You never ate this good back home," he teased.

"The food might have been better," she answered, finishing the last mushroom, "but today's company is far to be preferred."

"Families can be trying," he commented, scraping the bones and skin into the fire. "Take mine. They can demand your time, your loyalty."

"And in exchange offer you love and devotion," she reminded him.

"And yours didn't?"

She dropped her gaze, and he feared for a moment he'd pushed too hard too soon. "Mine made me feel as if I were valued, loved," she admitted. "But then, it all turned to dust."

James slid closer to her, determined to help her release her concerns. "They up and die on you?"

"I wish it were that simple."

His breath tightened in his chest. "Dying isn't necessarily simple."

"But it's an end," she insisted, glancing up at him, face puckered. "It's over and done, and you can get on with your life."

Unless you caused the death. "So if your adopted parents didn't die, what happened to them?" he asked, taking her clasped hands in his own and holding them tight, trying to steady her.

As if she knew what he was doing, she sighed. "I fear you will think less of me."

James frowned. "Did you murder someone?"

Her head jerked up, eyes wide. "Of course not!"

"Then nothing you can say can change my admiration for you," James promised her.

She paused, head cocked. Did she doubt him still?

"Perhaps I haven't made myself clear," James said, sitting taller and giving her hands a squeeze. "You're one of the most clever, educated, refined ladies it has been my privilege to know. I doubt there's anything you couldn't accomplish if you set your mind to it."

She frowned.

"Rina?" he asked. "What have I said wrong now?"

She tugged away from his grip. "Shh! Listen! The frogs have gone silent!"

Chapter Fifteen

For a moment, the loudest sound Rina heard was the pounding of her heart. She'd been nervous enough about confessing her family's shortcomings to James, and then the forest had gone silent. What had happened to the frogs? Was danger even now creeping up on them?

James must have thought so, for he put his hands on her shoulders and pushed her closer to the plank floor.

"Stay down," he warned. Releasing her, he crawled across the floor on all fours, braced his back against the wall and raised himself level with the window to peer through the cracks on the shutters.

"Is it a cougar?" she whispered.

He shook his head. "Worse. It's walking on two legs and headed toward the door."

Rina scrambled to her feet as James crossed to her side. Putting her protectively behind him, he faced the door, fists raised.

Someone knocked.

James glanced back at her with a frown, and Rina

knew they were thinking the same thing. Would an outlaw knock politely?

"Beg pardon," a familiar voice called through the crack. "I'm not here for trouble. I'm looking for my brother."

James strode to the door and whipped it open.

"Can't a man get a moment to himself?" he demanded.

Simon Wallin seemed to sag at the sight of James. He put a long-fingered hand on his brother's shoulder. "You know our family. We tend to go after strays." His gaze traveled past James to touch Rina. "And Miss Fosgrave, too. How…convenient."

Rina felt her cheeks heating as James ushered his brother into the room. James might not take her plight seriously, but she had no doubt his practical older brother would see things differently.

"How did you find us?" James asked, waving Simon to a spot by the fire.

Simon settled his tall frame down on the worn planks beside Rina, unslinging a leather pack from his shoulder and unbuttoning his wool coat in the warmth. Underneath he wore the trousers and plaid cotton shirt over flannel she'd seen on all the brothers at Wallin Landing, but his boots were muddy and his long face looked tired.

"We expected you back from the Crossing yesterday," he told James, who joined them by the fire, sinking onto the plank floor to sit cross-legged. "When you didn't return, I set off for McKenzie's, thinking I'd meet you."

Rina frowned. "You walked all the way from Wallin Landing to McKenzie's Corner in one day?"

James seemed to be counting the rocks in the chimney.

"A man afoot can go places a wagon and team can't," Simon said. "Speaking of which, where are the wagon and team?"

"Stolen." James nearly growled the word. As he went on to explain the situation to his brother, Rina stared at the leaping flames. It had taken half a day to drive from Wallin Landing to Seattle and most of the second day to reach McKenzie's Corner. Certainly roads curved around obstacles a person might more easily overcome, but she could not help wondering whether James had purposely chosen a more circuitous route just to delay her and give him more time to wear her down.

It shouldn't matter to her now. As soon as she reached Seattle, she would have to write to the White River supervisor to explain her delay. Questions would be asked. She was fairly sure in the end he would withdraw his offer of employment. Yet she could not shake the idea that James might have lied to her, just like her parents had.

"We'll have to spend the night here," Simon said when James finished. "We'll never make McKenzie's in the dark. I was lucky to smell the smoke from the fire, or I might have missed you." He turned to Rina. "How are you faring in all this, Miss Fosgrave?"

"She's been amazing," James answered for her, eyes brightening with his smile. "A real asset."

Now that was a lie. She knew she'd been more hindrance than help.

"That's good to hear," Simon replied, though his gaze remained on Rina as if he too doubted James's word. "My brother can use all the help he can get."

James rolled his eyes. "I did all right."

Simon nodded thoughtfully. "I'd say you did exceptionally well. You lost your team and the family's wagon, stranded yourself and Miss Fosgrave in the wilderness, threatened her reputation and managed to miss McKenzie's not once but twice if the trail I followed was yours."

Rina stared at James. "We missed McKenzie's?"

James raised his hands as if surrendering. "I didn't know! I was trying to get us safely through this mess."

"With an emphasis on mess," Simon said. "Not many men could achieve all that in the matter of a few days."

"I aim to please," James quipped, eyes narrowing.

Despite her misgivings, Rina bristled on James's behalf. Surely he hadn't intended to strand them like this. His life had been in jeopardy, as well. He'd eaten little food, walked for miles. He couldn't have chosen all that. She had to let go of this mistrust! Besides, Simon hadn't been with them. He didn't know how hard James had had to work to find paths she could travel.

"Your brother also found us food and shelter for the last two nights," she informed Simon, "protected us from ravenous predators and kept us moving toward civilization. I have no doubt I would have perished but for him."

Perhaps it was his position near the fire, but she thought James's cheeks were turning pink.

"Sounds like you had no need for my rescue, then," Simon replied. "I hope you'll allow me to follow you back to Seattle. I might get lost without my brother's tracking skills."

She could hear the sarcasm behind the words. Why was he being so unkind?

James evidently was resigned to how his brother treated him, for he waved a hand. "Be my guest. I'm sure Rina won't mind the extra escort."

Under other conditions, she would have been overjoyed. And she was pleased to hear that Seattle wasn't so far away. But as James and Simon discussed options and plans, the first emotion to wash over her was disappointment.

What was wrong with her? They were safe. They were almost home. With Simon's help, tomorrow would be far less dangerous. She should be over the moon with relief.

But, for a moment, she'd wished Simon had never found them just so she could spend more time alone with James.

Simon insisted that he and James sleep on the ruined porch, leaving Rina the privacy of the cabin. She wasn't sure who slept worse—them on their bumpy bed or her with her thorny thoughts. She was thankful for a moment to change out of her damaged gown and into a thoroughly rumpled but at least whole dress of matte blue satin.

They set off in the morning, following Simon's trail back through the woods. He went first, with Rina right behind and James bringing up the rear. Knowing they could reach town by nightfall, Rina had managed to convince James to leave the clothes behind, so they made a fairly conventional group except for the tattered nature of her once-fine gown.

"Ma can loan you one of her dresses," James said from behind her as if he'd noticed her lifting the sagging skirts out of her way. "It might be a little long and loose, but Beth can fix it."

He seemed to assume she was returning to Wallin Landing. "I could not impose on your family's generosity, Mr. Wallin," she said.

She heard him blow out a breath. "If I'm not James by now, I shudder to think what I'd have to do to earn the honor."

"Perhaps behave with sense and responsibility?" Simon suggested, reminding Rina he could hear everything they discussed. James must have had second thoughts as well, for he said little the rest of the morning.

The sun was high in the sky when they broke from the trees onto the main road into Seattle. A passing farmer offered them a ride in his wagon the rest of the way. Rina sat next to James in the wagon bed, with Simon across from them, as the equipage bumped its way west. As if he knew Rina feared the questions that might be asked, Simon engaged the farmer in conversation.

James hitched himself closer to her. Without her hood to shield his face, his skin had reddened in the sunlight. It made his eyes look all the more blue.

"So what will you do when we reach Seattle?" he asked.

Rina sighed, picking at the frayed edge of her sleeve. "Write to the school and await their decision. After that, I'm unsure."

"We'd welcome you back," he said.

She wasn't so certain. "Your mother and sister-in-law might have other ideas."

"Doubtful," he said with a grin. "They'd understand the situation. After all, you were with me."

Did he mean that as an absolution or an excuse? "Then there's the matter of Mr. Rankin," she reminded him.

James straightened, look darkening. "You leave him to me."

She would have preferred to fight her own battles, although she was willing to concede that she might not have the wherewithal to take on a bully the likes of Scout's father. Yet even as she considered allowing James to address the issue, she knew Rankin's presence wasn't the only thing scaring her away from Wallin Landing.

But she was tired of hiding her nature and her past. After all they had been through, James at least deserved to know the truth.

"When we reach Seattle, we should talk," she told him. "Before I feel comfortable returning to Wallin Landing, there are some things you should know about me."

James pressed a hand to his heart and spoiled his serious look with a wink. "Why, Rina, have you been toying with my affections?"

She only wished that was the problem.

She wasn't sure where to go when the farmer stopped in front of one of Seattle's mercantiles. She felt as if every gaze was turned her way, frowning at her disheveled state. Undeterred, Simon went inside to see about horses for hire.

James took her hand. "I know what you need," he promised, and he tugged her down the block for the Brown Church.

The quiet of the sanctuary slipped over her as they entered. She felt as if her worries were slipping away as well. She entered one of the box pews and sat, spreading her stiff skirts about her, lifting her gaze to the interlocking beams of the ceiling. They reminded her of the chapel James had found among the cedars.

"Be right back," he promised before disappearing through a side door.

Rina took a deep breath and bowed her head. *Thank You, Lord, for returning us to Seattle, for keeping us safe. I don't know Your will from here, but I hope You'll show me.*

The sound of footsteps made her raise her head. James was returning with Mr. Bagley in tow. One look at the minister's kindly lined face, and Rina felt tears forming.

"There now, Miss Fosgrave," he said, sitting beside her on the pew and taking her hand in his warm grip. "You have been through a great deal it seems, but the Lord has delivered you, and for that we are all grateful."

Rina nodded, unable to form the words pressing against her lips.

"She was worried no one would hire her after this," James said. "I told her that was nonsense."

Mr. Bagley eyed him a moment before returning his attention to Rina. "I can understand why you might be concerned, my dear."

"If for no other reason than that you were forced to throw in your lot with the likes of me," James put in.

Mr. Bagley frowned as if he could not like the interruption. She supposed few would go so far as to interfere with the renowned minister's declarations.

"Nonetheless," he continued, "I fear you are correct that some may see your sojourn in the wilderness as unseemly."

Rina sagged. It was one thing to wonder; it was another to hear her fears confirmed. "How can I prove my innocence?"

"I told her she can teach at Wallin Landing," James said.

Mr. Bagley nodded. "That might suffice, for now. But as more and more families move out that way, there may be problems. Will they want their children taught by what they consider a fallen woman?"

Rina cringed.

James straightened. "Fallen woman? I may not have your learning, Mr. Bagley, but I seem to recall a story about casting the first stone. Most folks came to Seattle because of trouble back home. They didn't fit in or they wanted something more. Miss Fosgrave's no different, and I won't have her judged for it."

He was so determined, so fierce in his defense of her, that she felt her spine straightening. "You're right, James. I've done nothing wrong."

James nodded, laying a hand on her shoulder in support.

Mr. Bagley squeezed her hand. "Indeed you haven't, Miss Fosgrave. Any wrongdoing could be laid at Mr. Wallin's door. He was your escort. It was his responsibility to see you safely to the White River. I understand he is your betrothed." He turned to James, feathered brows coming thundering down, and James stepped back under the force of it.

"If you were any kind of gentleman, sir," Mr. Bagley

scolded, "you would marry this young woman immediately and give her the shelter of your name."

James's first thought was that Mr. Bagley had gone mad. Even Rina was staring at the fellow as if she suspected as much.

"You forget, sir," James said. "Folks around here don't think all that highly of my name."

The minister rose to look him in the eye. For a little fellow, he could sure puff himself up when he wanted. Now his chest stuck out of his black wool suit, making the brass buttons on his plain blue waistcoat stand out.

"Nothing of the sort," he declared. "The name of Wallin is highly respected in these parts. Your father helped build this church. Your brother Andrew donated lumber for the parsonage."

"I've no argument my father and brother earned your respect," James allowed. "But I haven't. I'm the joker, the clown, the one you can't rely on. Miss Fosgrave can do better."

Bagley looked ready to argue, but Rina rose. "I disagree, but that is neither here nor there. The fact of the matter is that I was never certain our engagement would last. I think it best not to marry, and this matter has only strengthened my convictions."

Mr. Bagley aimed his potent frown her way. "But it is every young lady's duty to marry, particularly here, where your civilized influence is so badly needed."

James could see the fire building behind Rina's eyes as her convictions gathered steam. Best to head this one off before she started something she would later regret. No one fought Mr. Bagley and won.

"Oh, nothing much could civilize me," James assured him. "No offense meant, Miss Fosgrave."

She inclined her head, as regal as a queen granting a pardon. "None taken, Mr. Wallin. After all, if my sole purpose in life was to civilize man, then I would do better to marry someone thoroughly uncivilized, like Mr. Rankin."

She'd made a joke. He could see the gleam in those clear eyes, daring him to laugh. James wanted to grab her by the shoulders and spin her around with glee.

Mr. Bagley, however, appeared to be considering the matter, for he stroked his whiskered chin with his fingers. "Young Scout could certainly use a mother. I am uncertain how well his father would take to a woman's influence, but I could approach him about the matter if you like."

Rina looked as if she was having trouble breathing by the way her mouth opened and closed, eyes going wide in disbelief that the man would take her suggestion seriously.

James held out his hand to help her from the pew. "No need. He's well known to my family. I'm sure Ma would be delighted to broker a marriage, if that's what Miss Fosgrave wants."

Mr. Bagley nodded thoughtfully. Rina was shaking her head violently as she exited the pew. Then she turned to the minister and put on a smile.

"Thank you for your help, Mr. Bagley. We should be going."

He nodded again, but James thought he was less sure of her actions this time. "You are welcome to stay with Mrs. Bagley and me while you determine your next steps," he offered.

"How very kind," she said. "But I believe I know what to do now." Hand on James's arm, she nearly dragged him from the church.

Outside, she drew in a deep breath of the brine-scented air as if she'd suddenly found freedom after years of incarceration.

"That went well," James quipped.

She released her hold on him. "I appreciate his concern on my behalf, but I cannot espouse his views."

James grinned. "There were a whole lot of spouses being proposed from what I heard. Rankin. Me. I'm surprised someone didn't suggest Doc Maynard. Folks say he had two wives, for he neglected to legally divorce the first before marrying the second. What's one more?"

Rina shook her head as they started back for the mercantile. "How could anyone think I'd entertain marriage to Rankin, even for a moment?" She shuddered.

"Goes to show you the good reverend just doesn't understand you," James commiserated, stuffing his hands into the pockets of his trousers. "I knew you were after Simon the moment he laid eyes on you."

Rina glared at him. "That's enough of that, as well. I have no intentions of going after any Wallin gentleman."

"Fair warning," James replied. "Beth won't have you. She's sweet on the deputy sheriff."

"Stop that!" Rina scolded. "I need you to be serious for once." She stopped on the corner and drew him back against the wooden wall of the building, face firm, voice firmer.

"It seems my best choice is to return to Wallin

Landing and teach," she said, gaze lifting to his. "But before I do that, you need to know something about me."

This was it. He was finally going to hear the secret she'd guarded so carefully. James stood straighter. "I'm listening."

She took another deep breath, but this time he thought in resolution. "Remember what I told you last night, about the kingdom of Battenburgia?" she asked.

"You said there was no such place," James supplied.

She nodded. "The Fosgraves made me believe it was real. They made everyone they met believe in it. And they pretended they were its exiled rulers."

James smiled. "Now, that's some fine talking."

She would not relent. "It was not admirable, I assure you. They solicited loans of money and gifts of clothing and jewels, with the idea that someday the donors would be repaid, with influence if nothing else. They lied. And they made me into a liar as well."

Her face was tightening, as if she was waiting for him to agree, to walk away from her in disgust. He couldn't see things the way she did.

"Did you know the stories were lies?" he asked.

She frowned. "No. I believed the fables."

He shrugged. "Then I'm sorry, ma'am, but you're not a liar. Liars tell falsehoods for a purpose—to gain something good or avoid something bad. You just passed along what you believed to be true."

She was staring at him. "But they stole money from innocent people. Failed to pay their bills at dozens of establishments."

"They did," James said. "You didn't."

"They raised me," she protested. "I benefited from their actions."

"And my Ma and Drew raised me," he said. "I don't see anyone blaming me for anything they have done."

She sighed. "But you turned out fine."

James made a point of looking her up and down. "So did you. Mighty fine."

She shook her head. "How can I believe you when you take nothing seriously?"

James took her hand and gave it a squeeze. "Most likely you can't. But you can believe Ma and Catherine. I say we head for home and ask them whether they'll have you back. And I'm pretty sure I know the answer, Princess Alexandrina."

Chapter Sixteen

Simon managed to hire a wagon and team to take them on to Wallin Landing, promising the owner that he would return the set the next day. He insisted on driving, relegating James to the back of the wagon. Rina would have been content to join him, but James led her around to the front.

"It's a more comfortable ride up here," he told her with a smile. His nod gave her fair warning before he lifted her onto the bench. "Besides, it's befitting your station. You're still a princess in my book."

It was the first time in a long time that she felt honored to be given the title.

"All set, Miss Fosgrave?" Simon asked as she arranged her thoroughly dusty skirts with fingers that persisted in trembling at James's touch.

Rina glanced back to where James was climbing into the wagon bed. "Give your brother a moment."

"I give him entirely too many moments," Simon said, but he waited to slap the reins until James was seated in the bed of the wagon.

Rina had never paid Simon much attention, being

focused on James or Catherine and Mrs. Wallin when she'd been at the Landing before. Now, she studied him as he maneuvered the wagon out of town.

He was taller than James, his head above hers as the trees closed around them. His hair was a shade lighter and a few inches shorter than James's, but just as straight. His eyes were much paler, a light translucent green that lacked the depth of James's midnight blue. Every chiseled line of his long face and angle of his lean body said he held himself in tight control.

All in all, he was a handsome man, but she couldn't imagine him wearing her clothing so she wouldn't be deprived of it, dancing with Deerlund at McKenzie's Corner or wiggling his fingers and shouting to scare away a bear. And she wasn't impressed with how he handled the team, directing their every movement rather than giving them their heads. Perhaps it was because he wasn't used to them, but she had a feeling Simon preferred to be the one in charge.

James, however, lounged in the bed of the wagon, back braced against one side, gaze off among the trees they passed, as if nothing could concern him. Catching her gaze on him, he winked, and Rina's cheeks heated.

"I was thinking," he announced, raising himself a little. "We should go back for your trunk. You might need those books for teaching."

Rina had wondered the same thing. "How difficult would that be?"

"Far too difficult afoot," Simon answered beside her. "A shame we don't have a wagon. I doubt you could carry it otherwise."

"Oh, you'd be surprised," Rina said with a smile to James, remembering his attempts to do just that.

He grinned. "I managed a few yards anyway."

"Even Drew couldn't carry it all the way back to the Landing," his brother insisted. "A horse would help, but we seem to have misplaced those, as well."

James's grin faded. Was his brother trying to make him feel guilty?

"I would not call theft misplacement," Rina informed Simon, swiveling to face him. "We were at a distinct disadvantage."

"One you might have avoided if you'd traveled more populated roads," he pointed out, guiding the horses around a set of stumps.

"Is there such a thing as a populated road near Seattle?" Rina challenged him.

A noise from behind her told her James was trying not to laugh.

"Perhaps not," Simon allowed, hands tightening on the reins. "But my brother could have found a more direct route that might have afforded you some protection from thieves."

He would not let the matter go. "Oh, I would not be so sure," Rina told him. "In my experience, thieves prefer a certain level of populace. The more people, the easier to find a victim."

"I'd listen to her," James piped up. "She knows a thing or two about thieves."

Simon frowned. "Perhaps she wouldn't if you hadn't introduced her to the concept."

He had no idea who had raised her. "This was only my most recent brush with criminals," she assured him. "I know what to look for now, in villains and in heroes. You will never convince me that your brother acted anything less than heroic."

"If you count falling out of trees and eating bark as heroic," James qualified.

Simon did not laugh at his jest.

"It seems we have a difference of opinion, ma'am," he said. "Or perhaps I merely have a greater familiarity with my brother."

"You may have known your brother longer, sir," Rina answered him. "But I imagine you've never had to call on his strength as I have. And if you don't stop sawing at those poor horses' mouths, I will insist on taking the reins from you."

Simon's brows shot up, but he eased back on his hold.

"Don't you find her candor refreshing?" James asked, reaching up to thump his brother on the back. "She begins to remind me of you."

By the scowl on Simon's face, he did not take that as a compliment.

He did, however, manage to be kind to the horses and James during the remaining time it took to reach the Landing. But though Simon was pleasant, worry dug its claws into Rina's chest. Her hands fisted in her lap, fingers tightening around each other. What would she do if Mrs. Wallin and Catherine didn't agree with James? As far as she could tell, no one looked at the world like James did!

Then they were coming out of the trees, the clearing opening up around them. Everything was just as she'd left it. She wasn't sure why she'd expected it to look different, to feel different. Just the sight of the cabin, barn and schoolhouse made breathing easier as Simon pulled the wagon up before the house.

James jumped down and came around to assist

Rina. She leaned into his strength, took courage from the admiration in his gaze.

"Welcome home," he said as he deposited her on the ground.

Home. She'd never called any place that over the years, always thinking that her true home lay in a tiny kingdom beyond the sea. Was she wrong to hope this could be her home now?

The sound of the wagon must have alerted the house, for Beth and Mrs. Wallin came out onto the porch.

"You found him!" Beth proclaimed, clapping her hands before her pink gingham gown. Her delight brightened her smile and sparkled in her deep blue eyes. "And Miss Fosgrave, too! Catherine will be so happy when she gets back from dosing Mr. Rankin."

Just the name sobered Rina as Mrs. Wallin hurried forward to meet her at the edge of the boardwalk.

"Oh, but look at you!" she cried, taking Rina's hands, her green eyes wide. "You poor dear! Come inside now. Let's set you to rights."

Before Rina could protest, Mrs. Wallin pulled her up on the boardwalk, and Beth took her arm to escort her into the cabin. The last sight she had was of James waving farewell with a sad smile that said he thought he might never see her again.

Mrs. Wallin and Beth insisted on taking Rina upstairs, where she found two rooms, one on either side of the stone fireplace. Both appeared to be used as bedchambers, for the one Mrs. Wallin entered had a large bed across the back and a smaller one near the stairs.

"Now, you just sit there," Mrs. Wallin said, pressing Rina down on the quilt-covered bed. "Let Beth and me do the work."

She wasn't sure what work there was to be done, but Mrs. Wallin hurried over to a chest by the log wall while Beth went to fetch an ivory-backed brush from a table by the smaller bed.

"May I?" she asked Rina, holding up the brush.

Rina nodded, and Beth set to work letting down Rina's hair and giving it a good brushing. She'd forgotten how good a brush felt skimming through her hair. She closed her eyes a moment, feeling tense muscles relaxing, thoughts drifting away.

"What happened?" Beth asked. "Was the White River so horrid?"

Time for confessions. Rina opened her eyes to find Beth and Mrs. Wallin watching her as if hanging on every word.

"We never reached the White River," Rina told them. She went on to explain their adventures in the wilderness as well as her past, expecting to see dismay and judgment. But whereas Mrs. Wallin and Beth exclaimed over the robbery and the bear, and Beth's eyes grew wistful at Rina's upbringing, they seemed more concerned about the loss of her books and clothes.

"I'm not sure which distresses me more," Beth said, going to put the brush away. "It's hard to find books out here, but I've never seen anything like your dresses, Miss Fosgrave. They're fit for a queen, and now I know why."

"They certainly cannot serve me well out here," Rina said. Truth be told, she'd have liked nothing better than to throw away everything she'd worn, from the ruined dress to her sweat-dampened chemise, but she knew she couldn't afford to replace them, especially here in Seattle. "Now this gown is all I have. I must find some way to refurbish it."

"I'll help you," Beth offered, returning to her side, eagerness evident in the way her fingers fluttered. "I know lots of ways to turn a seam and add some embellishments to hide stains and such. I'll show you."

"Now, then," her mother said, bringing Rina a red-and-green plaid cotton gown she'd taken from the chest. "Our Rina hasn't said she'll be staying with us, Beth. Perhaps she still wants to make for the White River while James finishes his claim." She eyed Rina over the gown.

Rina accepted it from her with a nod of thanks. Now was the time for complete honesty. "The White River school board may not want me to come any longer. They may think my reputation has been damaged. James and I only intended to remain engaged until I reached my new school. We felt that agreement was the best way to protect me on the journey. We never planned on marrying."

Beth clapped her hands over her mouth as if suddenly realizing the enormity of the situation.

Mrs. Wallin tsked. "Nothing is more important to a lady than her reputation," she said with a look of warning to her daughter. "Once lost, it's nearly impossible to regain. But you needn't worry, Miss Fosgrave. I know our school isn't the position you'd hoped for, but we'd still be honored to have you."

Rina drew in a breath. "Truly?"

"Truly," Mrs. Wallin said with a smile. "I'm sure Catherine will feel the same way." She stepped back. "Now, Beth and I will leave you to yourself. I'm sure you'd like a moment of privacy to change." Her smile hardened. "And I'd like a few choice words with my son."

James helped Simon stable the horses for the night. Something about seeing strange geldings standing in Lance and Percy's stalls made the barn feel foreign. It was as if he'd lost part of his family.

"Fickle beasts," Simon complained, closing the stall door behind him as he and James exited into the main aisle of the barn. "How can you favor them?"

James shook his head as they started for the house. "What you see as fussiness, I see as personality."

"Personality," Simon scoffed, stepping out into the sunlight. "Give me an ox any day. Dependable, predictable…"

"Plodding, brainless," James countered, stride matching his.

"Sturdy, useful," Simon insisted.

"Positively boring," James finished, bumping his shoulder against his brother's. "Come on, admit it. You miss Lance and Percy."

Simon eyed him as they reached the cabin. "It really doesn't matter how I feel about your horses. You lost them, James, and the fact is that none of us can afford to replace them, even if we could find two of their quality near Seattle. You better get used to boring oxen, brother, because that's all we'll have for quite some time."

He climbed up on the boardwalk and went through the door into the house, but his words brought James to a halt. He'd been so busy trying to survive, he really hadn't considered the finality of it until now.

He'd lost Lance and Percy.

Emotions flared inside him—guilt and remorse and anger. He wanted to shout at the sky, slam his fist into a wall. What had he been thinking to take that route? He'd cost his family a wagon and himself his horses, and for what? Rina still wasn't willing to commit to teaching at Wallin Landing. He'd failed again.

The door popped open, and his mother marched out onto the boardwalk. She stopped a few feet from James, hands grasping the apron covering her green wool gown. "What are you doing moping out here?" she demanded. "There's work to be done!"

James saluted. "Yes, sir, General Wallin. What are your orders, sir?"

She dropped the apron to shake a finger at him. "Enough of your nonsense, young man. What I want is a son who understands his duty."

Would she light into him about Pa's death at last? He'd been expecting it for ten years now. Every other time he'd disappointed her, he'd been able to turn aside her wrath with a quip before she could go too far. By the fire in her green eyes now, he'd have to do some fast talking this time.

"Oh, but it's always a pleasure to do my duty toward you, Ma," he said, dropping his gaze. "I think I saw some wild roses by the road as we came in. Let me pick you a bushel."

She caught his arm before he could escape. "Don't you set one foot off this porch, James Thaddeus Wallin."

All three names? Oh, but he was in trouble. "Whatever you want," he assured her. "But staying on the porch will make eating dinner a little hard."

She gave his arm a shake. "As if you deserve dinner after what you've done."

Here it came. He might as well meet it head on. James straightened, gaze rising to hers.

"I'm sorry, Ma. I know it was wrong. I didn't intend for it to happen. I looked away for a moment, and the deed was done."

"That's the worst excuse I ever heard," she informed him, foot tapping below her skirts.

He cringed. "I know. There is no excuse for what I've done."

She nodded. "That's more like it. Humility never hurt anyone. The question is, what do you intend to do about it?"

James threw up his hands. "What can I do? He's dead!"

His mother blanched, taking a step back from him. "Dead? Who's dead? Oh, what have you done?"

James blinked, hands falling. "Nothing. I… What are we talking about?"

"Our dear Rina," his mother said, face scrunching in obvious confusion. "What else?"

James drew in a breath, determined not to open the wound any further. "Of course you would be concerned about Rina. But she's back at Wallin Landing where she belongs. I for one think that's cause for celebration."

His mother frowned. "I'm not prepared to celebrate just yet. I'm still trying to figure out what just happened. You thought I was talking about something else. What?"

James shook his head. "It doesn't matter."

Once more his mother put a hand to his arm, but

this time it was kind. Her gaze softened as she met his gaze. "It matters to you. Therefore, it matters to me."

James swallowed. Why not confess? At least he'd know it was over. Or just beginning.

"I never told you how sorry I was that Pa died," he said, holding himself still. "I should have seen that branch, should have warned him, but I didn't. I hope you can forgive me."

His mother's face melted, and he felt his heart breaking with her sorrow. She reached up and touched his cheek.

"Dear boy, there's nothing to forgive. Living out here, accidents happen. I'm just so thankful the Lord has seen fit to allow all my boys to grow into fine men."

His usual grin felt a little shaky. "You didn't sound like you thought I was such a fine fellow a few moments ago."

"I've always thought you were a fine fellow," she insisted. "Who else can make me laugh when I'm ready to cry?"

"If I have helped in any way," James told her, "I'm honored."

"You are a great blessing to this family, James," she said, pulling back her hand. "But you must see the problem with Rina now. Given what happened out in the woods, her reputation is ruined."

James made a face. "The only things that are ruined are her dresses. Anyone with any sense would know I wouldn't take advantage of a woman stranded in the wilderness. And I was too busy trying to stay alive and find our way home to succumb to her charms."

"I would expect nothing less of you," his mother

assured him. "But others may think differently. From where I sit, you were the cause of her troubles. You must fix them."

He was afraid he knew where this was going. Catherine had been determined to match him and Rina. It would be just like his mother to want to play along.

"I did fix the matter," James said, moving around her for the door. "I brought Rina here and gave her back her position as schoolteacher. That should be sufficient."

"James Wallin."

His mother's tone pulled him up short, and he turned to look at her. This time, her face was sad, her bow of a mouth drooping.

"I raised you better than this," she said.

The familiar guilt reached out for him, but this time he knew it was false. He was fully prepared to protect Rina from every predator, any slander. But marriage? That was an entirely different matter.

"She doesn't want to marry me, Ma," he said. "I asked."

She frowned as if she couldn't have heard him properly. "You proposed marriage?"

"On bended knee, with hands outstretched," James promised.

She narrowed her eyes. "In all sincerity?"

Well, he had been aiming more for Rina's smile than her acceptance. He wasn't sure what he'd have done if she had agreed to marry him. He didn't know if he could talk himself out of that.

"Leave be, woman," he told his mother. "She has more sense than to tie herself to the likes of me."

His mother drew herself up, eyes flashing fire once

more. "And what's wrong with you? If you ask me, she should count herself lucky to marry any of my sons!"

"Then trot out Simon or John," James said, turning for the door once more. "Because the last person Rina Fosgrave should marry is me."

Chapter Seventeen

Rina had never felt so fussed over in her life, even when she'd thought she was a princess. Under her parents' watchful gazes, she'd been feted by financiers and courted by congressmen. But she'd never had an entire family prepared to drop everything just to make sure she was comfortable.

She had barely come downstairs in her borrowed gown before Simon ushered her to his mother's bentwood rocker by the hearth, insisting that she needed to rest. John brought her a book to read. Levi dragged over a bench so she could prop up her feet. Catherine, who had returned from her nursing duties, checked Rina's pulse and temperature, as if certain she must have overexerted herself.

James, watching from near the table, seemed to find it all amusing. He kept tilting his head to see around whoever was hovering over her at the moment, offering winks or rolling his eyes at each petition. She had to fight to keep from laughing with him, fearing she might offend his family.

He didn't come near her, until Drew offered to carry her across the clearing to the schoolroom.

"If there's any carrying to be done," James said, pushing off the wall and intercepting his brother, "I'll be doing it. Miss Fosgrave and I have an understanding, if you recall."

He had to stop saying that! He and Rina had agreed to honor their engagement until she reached her new school. Surely they had no need to further it now. Before she could explain, the men exchanged glances and Catherine straightened. Mrs. Wallin's frown said she feared he was telling tales again.

Beth had no such concerns. "Oh, how wonderful!" she cried with a happy skip. "Let me plan the wedding! I have lots of ideas left from Catherine's."

Oh, no. "It is not that kind of understanding," Rina hurried to explain as James closed the distance between them. "And I have no need for anyone to carry me anywhere."

Beth's face puckered, and the others looked deflated.

"Still," Catherine said, rising from beside Rina as if to give James her spot, "it wouldn't hurt to take things easy for a day or two. I suggest we serve you supper in bed."

Arms outstretched, James paused.

"Good idea," Mrs. Wallin said. "Beth, loan our Rina a nightgown, one of your flannels. We'll settle her in now and bring the meal over when it's ready."

James straightened with a shrug. But Rina could see the laughter in his eyes as his mother and sister-in-law led her out of the cabin.

"I'm not an invalid," she protested as they crossed the clearing for the schoolhouse.

"And we'd like to ensure you don't become one," Catherine replied, looking determined.

My, but she could be a force of nature. "I'll be fine," Rina tried again as they climbed up into the schoolhouse. "I just need a good night's sleep. I'm fully prepared to start teaching tomorrow."

"Oh, good!" Beth said, hurrying to catch up with them, nightgown draping her arms. "I was wondering about past participles. Are they terribly difficult to conjugate?"

"I insist that you rest tomorrow," Catherine said with a look to Beth. The nurse opened the door to the teacher's quarters and guided Rina inside. "We owe you that much at least."

In Rina's mind, she was the one who owed the Wallins something, if only thanks for their continued kindness. Indeed, the room looked as if they'd fully expected her back at any time. The quilt still draped the bed, fresh paper and ink waited on the table, and Beth's precious hope chest sat with its carved top open, ready to receive her clothing once more. A shame she had almost nothing to put into it except her hope.

But the ladies set to work as if the room had been derelict for years. Catherine dusted off the table and chair; Mrs. Wallin started a fire.

"I can do that," Rina suggested.

James's mother merely smiled at her. "Of course you could. I just like doing for my family."

Something tugged at her heart. "Mrs. Wallin, I told you—James and I are no longer engaged."

Her eyes, though green, still held the same light

Rina had seen so many times in James's. "Perhaps not at the moment."

Rina blinked. Turning, she glanced around the room again. Catherine was closing the trunk. Beth had just finished arranging a selection of *Godey's* magazines she must have brought over in the interim for Rina's reading pleasure.

"You knew I'd be back," Rina realized.

The others stilled, exchanged glances. Rina stepped forward, conviction growing. "You knew! Did you intend to see me stranded, forced to marry James to save my reputation?"

Catherine held up her hands as if to appease. "No, Rina, of course not."

"We simply know James," Beth added.

"And we saw the spark between the two of you," Mrs. Wallin concluded. "We were certain he could convince you to return to us."

Rina felt as if the air had thickened. "So that was his charter—to do all he could to make me return. And I thought he actually cared."

Mrs. Wallin's face crumpled, but Beth was the first one to reach Rina's side. "Of course he cares!" she cried, taking up one of Rina's cold hands. "I know my brother, Miss Fosgrave. He's a joker, he's a tease. He'll take any dark situation and show you there's still light to be found in the world. I've seen him flirt at barn raisings, flatter ladies at church. I've never seen him look at anyone the way he looks at you."

She shouldn't believe the tales. They were putting their own interests before hers, just like the Fosgraves. Yet, she'd thought she'd seen the same look in James's eyes. Could it be true? Was she meant to stay here, at Wallin Landing, with him?

Catherine stepped forward. "Please don't fault us for our hopes, Rina. James is a fine man, and we'd all like to see him married to a fine woman."

"And I can think of no one finer than our new schoolteacher," Mrs. Wallin said with a nod.

Rina felt a laugh rising. "I don't know what to believe."

"Just believe in the future," Catherine said, laying out the nightgown Beth had brought from the house. "You are exactly what we need at the Lake Union school, Rina." She fluttered her fingers, and Mrs. Wallin and Beth went out into the schoolroom so Catherine could help Rina change into the nightgown.

The clean flannel warmed against her skin, but still she struggled to understand her feelings. Catherine must have sensed the tumult, for she said little until Mrs. Wallin and Beth returned.

Rina felt like a child again as they ushered her into bed, and she wasn't altogether pleased by the memories. "I truly am fine," she tried once more.

Catherine pulled the covers up around her. "A little rest never hurt anyone. You have had an eventful few days."

"And likely to have more," Mrs. Wallin said, gown lifted to protect her hands from a stone she must have heated in the fireplace.

Rina forced herself to settle back against the pillow. "I suppose you're right."

"Although you will only have Beth and Levi to teach for now," Mrs. Wallin warned as she slipped the stone between the sheets and warmth radiated up

Rina's legs. "I doubt that detestable Mr. Rankin will allow Scout a moment's freedom."

Rankin. She would have to face him sooner or later. Rina glanced at Catherine, who had perched on the bed next to her. "James said you might be able to convince Mr. Rankin to allow his son to attend school."

Catherine's lips thinned. "I did what I could. He seems to think we're trying to turn his son against him."

"He isn't far off," Mrs. Wallin said, straightening. "As if anyone would want to grow up to be like him. Young Scout could do so much more. Has he no ambitions for the boy?"

"None beyond his own," Catherine said with a shake of her head. "I find it very odd, but there it is. I'm sorry, Rina."

"It was nothing you did," Rina said. "I should have realized a father might resent his son changing his name."

"I like the name Thomas," Beth said, sitting on the other side of the bed. "It suited him more than Scout. That's not a name—it's a job."

The fact slammed into her, and Rina stiffened. "Yes it is, Beth. Why didn't I see that before?"

Catherine frowned. "What is it, Rina?"

She was almost afraid to voice her theory lest she be proven wrong yet again. "From what I understand," she said, glancing at the ladies around her, "Mr. Rankin's work is rather, well, unsavory. I imagine he must be vigilant to keep the law from finding out too much."

"Very vigilant," Catherine agreed with an arch look. "He absolutely detests Deputy McCormick."

"And you would know how silly that is if you had

ever met Deputy McCormick," Beth put in with a shake of her head. "He's wonderful."

Her mother frowned her into silence.

"I doubt Mr. Rankin shares your views," Rina told Beth. "In fact, I'm certain he doesn't. Don't you see? He isn't concerned about Scout learning something. He's concerned that if Scout is in school and not playing lookout, the law might learn something about Mr. Rankin!"

Mrs. Wallin and Catherine nodded as if they quite agreed.

"And that's why he doesn't want the school to grow," Mrs. Wallin mused. "The more families come this way, the more likely some are to object to his business."

"So he'll keep trying to close the school?" Beth asked, looking from one to the other, hands clasped before her.

Rina's smile grew with her confidence. "Oh, I think we can change his mind. You leave things to me. I suddenly find I have a great desire to discuss matters with Mr. Rankin."

Beth bit her lower lip as if she wasn't so sure of the advisability of that approach, but Rina had no more doubts. Rankin might be a bully, but she thought he might back down if the tables were turned.

They left her a short while later, promising to return with soup. As soon as Rina heard the schoolhouse door close, she climbed out of bed. Catherine seemed to think lying about was restful, but with so much on her mind, Rina felt as if she might explode if she didn't do something.

Throwing her cloak about her shoulders for extra warmth, she sat at the table and planned her lesson for the following day. It felt good to be purposeful, productive. She could do this. If she could survive the wild, she could do anything.

You made me see that, Father. Thank You. I know I can rely on Your strength, but I'm grateful to know that You've given me strength as well.

The wind must have been rising, for she thought she heard a branch scratch at the window. When the sound came again, she narrowed her eyes and rose. By the time the third scratch rasped out, she had her hand on the shutter.

"Not this time, Levi Wallin," she said, yanking open the wood. "You go home before I inform your mother!"

On the other side of the glass panes, James put his hand on his heart. "Rina. I never took you for a tell-tale."

Rina chuckled as she unlatched the window and swung it open. Night had fallen on the Landing, and the moon was rising, touching his hair with silver. "What are you doing?"

"Everyone is so worried about your reputation I didn't dare come through the front door." He lifted a cloth bag up onto the sill. "And if I know Catherine she'll feed you nothing but gruel and calf's foot jelly. I thought you deserved better."

Rina took the sack and opened it. Inside lay a thick slice of strawberry pie, the red juice staining the bottom of the sack. "James Wallin, I could kiss you."

"Yes, please," he said and puckered his lips.

Rina shook her head with a smile. "It was a joke."

James threw up his hands. "How could you joke about a subject like that? Do you take nothing seriously?"

"Apparently more than you," she retorted. She set the bag down carefully, then frowned at him. "But I don't understand. If I'm to do nothing but rusticate in bed, why do you get to wander free? You faced as much hardship as I did. More, in my opinion."

James cocked his head. "Because I'm a strapping fellow and you're a delicate flower?"

Rina slapped his fingers where they rested on the sill. James pulled them back with a theatrical yelp.

"Because my family likes you more than they like me?" he suggested, rubbing his fingers.

"Nonsense," she said. "I'd say it's the other way around. Your family has faith in you that they lack in me."

"You'll never make me believe that," he said. Then he glanced toward the house. "I better go before they see me. They seem determined to force you to marry me, and I won't have it." He heaved himself up and pressed a kiss to her lips before dropping down and disappearing into the night.

Rina shut the window and latched the shutter over it. There he went again, stealing kisses at the same time he avoided any thought of marriage. Once she would have scolded him for the former and agreed with him on the latter.

She drew in a breath as she turned from the window. Now, she wasn't so sure. She couldn't deny she enjoyed his wit, his kiss. But there was so much more to James Wallin than she'd dreamed when he'd arrived in his fancy suit with his fancier horses at the boardinghouse.

It was time to be honest with herself. She hadn't left Wallin Landing the first time because she was afraid of Scout's father or lacked conviction over her ability to teach. She'd left because she was afraid of falling in love with a charmer like James.

She was afraid of his banter, his unswerving belief in himself. She was afraid to rely on him as she had relied on her parents, only to find that there was nothing of substance behind them. She'd run away just like her parents had to escape a commitment. She was through running.

She no longer doubted James. She knew what lay behind his glib facade—strength, determination and an unwillingness to ever fail those he loved. He felt his father's death keenly, blamed himself for it. But that hadn't stopped him from seeing life as an opportunity waiting to unfold, an adventure. He'd made her realize that she didn't have to look backward. She just needed to move forward.

How could she not love him for that? How could she not love him for him?

He didn't want to marry. She refused to join his family in pressuring him. But perhaps, with proximity and shared goals, they might grow even closer. Perhaps one day he'd go down on his knee and ask her to marry him again.

And then, perhaps, she might find the courage to say yes.

James walked back from the schoolhouse with a smile on his face. When Rina argued with him like that, giving as good as she got, he knew she was going to be all right. That bleak look had left her face at last. She seemed to have found the confidence that had drawn him to her from the beginning. He had no doubt she would lead the school into the future. He'd done his duty.

I hope you're proud, Pa. I hope You're proud, Father.

John was waiting for him on the porch. The downturn of his green eyes, so like their mother's, told James his brother didn't appreciate what he had to do now. James wasn't surprised his family had chosen his second youngest brother to deliver bad news. John's short, red-gold hair and strong chin made him look serious and concerned. His easygoing nature and studious pursuits made him everyone's confessor and confidante.

"A shame about your horses," he said as James stepped up on the porch. "We'll not see their like again."

Something settled inside him, like a log burned through in the fire. "No, we won't."

John rubbed the back of his neck. "The others are over at Simon's ready to talk to you about it all."

James shook his head. "Let's get it over with."

Drew was pacing the floor of the cabin when they entered. His older brother was a man to look up to, both in height and in accomplishments. Drew was sturdy; Drew was strong; Drew never wavered in any course of action, except when he had been trying to decide whether to court Catherine. But then, James supposed, love made even men like Drew a little crazy. His brother glanced up at James and inclined his head in greeting.

Simon's cabin was the perfect place to be interrogated. From the unadorned wood furniture to the bare wood floor, there was little warm about it aside from the stone hearth along one wall. Simon pushed off from it as John closed the door behind him and James, leaving Levi sitting on the floor by the fire.

"We have a problem," Simon announced. "And I want to know what you intend to do about it, James."

With a grimace at the confrontation, John went to take a seat on a bench along the opposite wall.

"It isn't just his problem," Drew said, voice a deep rumble as he stopped in the middle of the floor. "The wagon is gone, and that affects us all. We need it to bring in the crops."

"Fetch supplies from town," John added.

"Escape this place once in a while," Levi said.

"I know the position I've put you in," James told them. "You can have all my wages from logging to pay for another wagon. It may take a while, but…"

"Not good enough," Simon said, eyes narrowing and shoulders bunching.

If John was the confessor, Simon was the accuser. Nothing James did ever satisfied him. James raised his chin and met his brother's gaze. This was his problem. He knew that. And he would fix it.

"Simon." Drew frowned him into silence before turning to James. "I appreciate your offer, James, and I accept it. In the meantime, however, we need to think about alternatives."

"I suppose I can use the oxen behind the plow when we don't need them for hauling logs," Simon allowed, though grudgingly.

"We might be able to rig some kind of skid," John mused. "I don't think it will make it all the way to town, but we could use it to carry things around here."

"See what you can do," Drew said. "And as for

going to town, it looks like we'll be relying on neighbors for supplies and the mail or walking."

Levi stiffened. "That will take most of a day!"

"If you have another idea, I'd be glad to hear it," Drew said.

Simon shook his head. "So that's it? James gets off scot-free?"

"What would you prefer, Simon?" James asked. "Stretch me on the rack? Pillory me and throw cabbages? Sad waste of vegetables if you ask me."

"No one asked you," Simon retorted.

John grimaced. "He lost his horses, Simon. And he is losing his pay for weeks."

"Months, probably," James corrected him. "Seeing as how I count for so little."

"You said it," Simon challenged.

Drew stepped forward. "Enough. What's done is done. We know what we must do from here. This discussion is over." He started for the door and held it open. "Levi."

Their youngest brother uncurled to stand. "Coming."

John, who generally stayed with Simon, rose as well. "You want company tonight, James?"

Simon frowned at him as if he felt John was choosing sides. James appreciated John's vote of confidence, but the entire confrontation raised too many memories to feel comfortable sharing them.

"Not particularly," he told his younger brother. "Save your concerns for Simon. He needs company." He turned and left before he said something they'd all come to regret.

But his cabin felt colder than Simon's and not just

because he didn't take the time to kindle a fire before falling onto his pallet. The forest around the house was silent, the house stuffy, his mother's quilt heavy about his frame. It was as if the very air stood in judgment of him.

Had he accomplished nothing of worth for his family over the years? He'd helped his brothers with the logging, done anything Ma asked of him. He'd built this house, had nearly proved up the claim enough to take permanent possession of his acreage. But anyone might have done all that. It was nothing special, nothing unique, nothing to make up for what he'd cost his family.

First Pa, and now the wagon and horses.

He tried to think of anything he'd done to contribute more than his share, to think beyond his own needs, and all he could find was that he'd brought Rina to teach.

But even there, had he been right? He'd used every tactic at his disposal to convince her to come back with him. In the end, she'd returned because she felt she had no other choice. He'd focused on the school, on making up for his father's death. He'd told himself he was doing her a favor.

He imagined the couple who had adopted her had thought the same thing. Why not pick up an orphan, a lost child with no other hope for the future? Pretend she was theirs, pretend she was a princess. What a grand upbringing.

They'd ended up hurting her with their tall tales. Was he any better?

And when she came to the same realization, would she ever forgive him for the role he'd played in her life?

Chapter Eighteen

Rina rang the bell just before eight a day later. She had used the intervening time to work with Beth on cleaning and mending her dress and washing her underthings. While she'd seen James at meals, he'd been unaccountably quiet, and she wasn't sure why. The rest of the family seemed pleased to have her back and school opening again.

Now Beth hurried across the clearing at the sound of the bell as she had before, pink gingham skirts flapping. Rina wasn't surprised to see Levi following at a more sedate pace, as if making sure he didn't reach the schoolhouse one second sooner than necessary. She didn't wait for him. Instead, she let Beth in, strode to the front of the room and waved to the instructions on the board.

"First one who finishes copying this down wins a helping of your mother's apple bread," she told Beth, who promptly bent her golden-haired head over her slate and started writing.

When Levi let himself in a few moments later, Rina pointed at the slate resting on the nearest bench. "You better hurry, Mr. Wallin," she said, toe tapping under the skirts of her blue dress. "Your sister is already two lines ahead of you."

Levi slung a leg over the bench and grabbed his slate, fingers flying with the chalk. The two finished at almost the same time, and Rina declared their efforts a tie. Her students were happily consuming their reward when she noticed a movement at the back of the room. Had Mr. Rankin arrived so soon with his threats? Squaring her shoulders, she turned to face the door.

Scout stood there, bare feet dirty against the boards, trousers frayed at the ends. His deep brown eyes looked heavy, as if he hadn't slept in some time. "Can I come, too?"

Rina smiled at him. "We would not have been a school without you, Thomas. Your slate is waiting."

Smile blossoming, he hurried into the room. Rina watched as he took a seat near Levi, who handed him the last of the apple bread.

"And me?"

She started at the deep voice and turned to find a large man ducking through the door to follow Scout. He had broad shoulders and thick fingers, and his neck was nearly the size of her waist. Whipping the battered hat from his grizzled head and gripping it with both hands as if he feared someone might take it from him, he nodded respectfully at Rina.

"Young Thomas here was telling me that you don't mind helping folks understand things," he said, venturing closer. His nearly black eyes shone with a light she had seldom seen. "Never did learn to read or write, but I'd account myself fortunate to be able to sign my name instead of an X."

This was definitely not the type of student she'd hoped to teach, yet how could she ignore such a need? "You are very welcome," Rina assured him, gesturing him toward a bench. "Mister…"

"Hennessy, ma'am. Just Hennessy." He slipped onto one of the benches, which tilted up with his weight. Beth handed him a slate with a smile.

"And would you be having room for us, too?"

Once more Rina turned. Three more men clustered in the doorway. At her nod, they crowded into the school, the red and green of their flannel shirts brightening the room. Each claimed to have been encouraged by Scout to visit the school.

One wanted to learn to add and subtract to make sure his employer was paying him what he was owed. Another sought to understand measurements so he could work at one of the mercantiles. The third yearned to be able to read the Bible he'd been given when he'd been baptized a few weeks ago. Rina assured them all they were welcome and found them seats and slates.

The last through the door was a young woman a few years older than Beth. Though her dress of red gingham looked like that of nearly every other frontier lady Rina had seen in Seattle, her dark hair and dusky skin proclaimed her native heritage.

"The cook at the Occidental said she'd teach me to bake fancy things," she confessed to Rina, hands folded calmly in front of her white apron, "but I have to know how to read a recipe out of a book and cut the amounts in half or double and triple them. Can you teach me that kind of ciphering?"

Rina might never have cooked a meal in her life, but she knew how to manipulate fractions. "Yes, I can," she said. "Please, join us."

They all settled in, and Rina moved among them, explaining, encouraging, leaving one working on a problem while she explained a solution to another. She was bending to check one of her new student's work when she felt eyes on her.

Glancing up, she saw that James was standing in the doorway. He was dressed for logging, cotton shirt showing red flannel at his wrists and throat, loose trousers topping thick-soled boots. His gaze, however, was almost wistful, as if she'd done something so amazing he could only stand in awe.

She straightened with a smile of welcome, then motioned him in. "Don't just stand there, Mr. Wallin," she teased him. "Make yourself useful."

His brows shot up as if he was surprised by her request, then he snapped a salute and crossed to her side.

"Corporal Wallin reporting for duty, ma'am," he assured her. "What do you need?"

"At the moment, a second pair of hands." The abilities of her students varied so widely, there was little she could do with them as a group. But James proved to be a good listener for the readers, correcting their mistakes with a joke that won smiles and making a game out of pronouncing difficult words. She focused on the math studies, explaining rudimentary multiplication and division by using the remains of the apple bread as an example. She was just about to bring the students back together when she felt the floor tremble.

"For a schoolteacher," Benjamin Rankin said, boots

thudding against the boards as he entered, "you sure don't learn fast."

His shoulders were hunched in his dusty coat, hands fisted at his waist. Scout turned white and hunkered behind Levi as if trying to disappear. James rose and positioned himself next to Rina.

"Let me deal with him," he murmured. "I promised you that when you said you'd return."

"I can do this," Rina replied. "Just stay near."

By the way he widened his stance, she knew he was going nowhere until she was safe.

"I thought I scared you away," Mr. Rankin said, coming to a stop a few feet from them.

"It turns out I don't scare as easily as I thought," she replied, keeping her head up and her breath even.

He leered, the smell of onions wafting over her. "Then I reckon I'll just have to try harder," he said, raising his fists higher, "especially seeing as how Mr. Wallin here forgot to bring his gun this time."

He made it sound as if James drew his courage with his weapon. As if to disprove that, James raised his own fists.

Mr. Hennessy rose as well, putting himself between Rina and Mr. Rankin. "I don't know your game, Rankin," he said, "but you got no call to be troubling our teacher."

"Your teacher?" Around Mr. Hennessy's arm, Rina could see Mr. Rankin scowling at him. "Since when did you have a child in school?"

"He don't have a child." One of the other men stood and came around to Rina's other side. "And neither do I. But that might change if a lady was to see that I'm a fellow who can read and write and speak proper."

The other men also rose, nodding. So did Beth and Anna, Rina's native student. Levi was nearly the last on his feet, exposing Scout, who scurried up as well.

"Education is a good thing, Pa," he said, voice squeaking. "I don't rightly see how you can be against it."

"You," his father snarled. "Get home. Now."

Scout started to move, but Rina held up her hand. This was her opportunity, and she wasn't about to waste it.

"Allow me one more lesson before you take Scout home, Mr. Rankin," she told him. "A history lesson, if you will. You see, where I come from in Massachusetts, education is compulsory."

The gathering of his heavy brow told her he had no idea what the word meant. Rina tried again. "Going to school is required. By law."

Mr. Rankin's brow cleared. "Never heard of that law here."

"It could be made at any time," she assured him. "In fact, as the teacher for the Lake Union School, I recommend that attendance here be required. What do you say, Mr. Wallin? You are on the school board, are you not?"

James did his best to look serious, but she could see the telltale twinkle in his eyes. "I am indeed, Miss Fosgrave. And your suggestion seems very wise. There should be a law about attending school. And laws, as we all know, are enforced by the sheriff."

He was playing along perfectly. Already she could see that Mr. Rankin had paled.

"Indeed," Rina said, inclining her head. "One school I know has the deputy sheriff play truant officer. He goes to the home of any student who misses class and asks the parents about problems that might be preventing attendance."

Mr. Rankin stilled. "Deputy McCormick? Out here on a regular basis?"

"I think it's a wonderful idea," Beth put in.

"I'm afraid it would be a terrible imposition," Rina told her before facing her former tormentor once more. "Don't you think his time would be better spent catching criminals, Mr. Rankin?"

Scout's father tugged at his collar as if he were having trouble breathing. "Oh, certainly. No need to trouble him about a school."

Rina smiled. "I'm glad to hear you say that. If every parent was as conscientious as you are, we wouldn't need a truant officer. I know Scout is eager to attend."

"Yes, ma'am," Scout said, then he glanced at his father. "If I don't have chores for Pa, that is."

His father reached out and cuffed him. "Didn't you hear your teacher, boy? You attend every day for as long as she wants, or I'll tan your hide."

Scout scuttled back, nodding. "Yes, sir."

Mr. Rankin nodded as well. "Good. I'll leave you to it, then. Ma'am." He turned and strode from the room as if he expected the law to be on his tail right then.

James grabbed Rina and spun her around. "Yeehaw! You did it, Rina! You faced him down!"

Laughter bubbled up from deep inside her, flowing out like water from a spring.

"Bravest thing I ever saw, ma'am," Mr. Hennessy agreed as James set her on her feet.

Rina giggled. She knew it wasn't the most authoritative sound, but she couldn't help it. She grinned with

James a moment, sharing his joy, his pride. She'd rid the school of Rankin's interference and won his son a chance at an education. She'd made a difference.

Thank You, Lord!

The rest of her students were laughing and cheering, as well. Rina let them whoop it up for a few moments, then adjusted the drape of her skirt and straightened. "Now then, that is entirely enough frivolity, class. We have lessons to learn."

"I think you taught them the finest lesson of all," James said. "You can't let fear stop you from what you were meant to do."

Rina nodded as the others quickly returned to their work.

"I don't know what this frivolity thing is," she heard Scout murmur to Levi, "but she sure don't hold with it."

James nudged Rina. "Is that a fact, ma'am? You don't hold with frivolity?"

"That," Rina said, sharing his smile, "depends on who's offering it, Mr. Wallin."

James left Rina with her doting students and strolled back across the clearing. He'd never been more proud to know someone. She'd faced down her fears, both in teaching older students and in wrestling with Rankin. Whatever happened between her and James in the future, he could not doubt that Rina would find her way.

Now he needed to see if there was anything more he could do for his brothers. He'd asked Drew to spare him today just so he could make sure Rina felt comfortable resuming her role as teacher. Simon's frown as James had left them logging had said he thought James was shirking his duty. Maybe James just saw duty a little differently than his older brother did.

He was on his way toward the woods when he saw Rankin sitting on the stone lip of the pond they used to water the stock. What was that old codger still doing here?

"You sweet on the schoolteacher?" Rankin asked, rising from his seat as James detoured to meet him.

"Don't you have anything better to do?" James asked, stopping in front of him. "A claim to work? Loans to collect? Innocents to harass?"

"I have a moment," Rankin said. He nodded over James's shoulder toward the schoolhouse. "How long will she stay?"

For the rest of her life, he hoped. "As long as she's needed."

He nodded, sucking his teeth. "Folks seem to like her. Never thought I'd see Hennessy in a school."

Neither had James, but he didn't think Rankin was here to discuss the finer points of education. "What's this about?" James demanded.

Rankin focused on James, eyes narrowing in his flabby face. "I didn't much like her suggestion. We don't need the sheriff or his deputy out this way."

So Rina's gambit was still troubling him. It was no idle jest. McCormick was itching to get the drop on Rankin. If Rina suggested that he visit more often, he would.

"Deputy McCormick isn't needed so long as every student is free to come and learn," James allowed.

"Good," Rankin said with a nod. "Good. It seems we're in agreement."

"Stranger things have happened," James replied.

Rankin gazed up at James out of the corners of his eyes. "And to show there are no hard feelings, I'll do you a favor."

Rankin's favors always came with debts. "I want nothing from you," James said, holding up his hands and backing away.

"What's this, another robbery?" Simon drawled, coming out of the wood with his ax over his shoulder. The darker stains around the neck and arms of his cotton shirt told James his older brother hadn't stinted on his efforts that day. "My, but you have poor luck, James."

James lowered his hands as Rankin turned to eye the older Wallin. He jerked a thumb over his shoulder at James. "Your brother here doesn't want to hear my news. Maybe you'll think differently."

Simon came abreast of them and lowered his ax so that the handle rested across his palms. Anyone else would have been intimidated by the move, but Rankin drew himself up as if ready for trouble.

"We don't peddle gossip," Simon said, eyeing him as if he were a bug that had crawled onto his lunch.

"Oh, you might change your mind when you hear this." He glanced between Simon and James as if to make sure he had their attention. "Those thieves who took your horses? They were seen not too far from here the other day."

James's heart jerked, but he was careful not to show Rankin or Simon that he cared. Either could make too much of it. "Imagine that."

Simon frowned at him before turning to Rankin. "Where?"

"Fellow I know ran across them on the other side

of the lake," Rankin admitted, "camping near that old Indian outpost just about opposite my place."

He glanced at James as if expecting him to leap up and dash off right then. James wasn't about to give him, or his brother, the satisfaction. "I don't suppose they still had the horses and our wagon?" he asked, glancing up to watch a gull soar past as if he didn't care about the answer either way.

"He mentioned seeing the horses specifically," Rankin said, beginning to sound testy. "Not too many horses like that around these parts. Seems they're too good to sell, even when a man has bills to pay."

Even Rankin understood their value. James could barely stand there, knowing Lance and Percy were close enough to rescue. Yet he couldn't help thinking that Rankin was a little too eager to help the Wallins.

"Bills to pay or debts to pay?" James asked, lowering his gaze to meet Rankin's. "How much do the thieves owe you, Rankin?"

Simon stiffened. "You knew those men?"

Rankin waved a hand. "Everyone shows up at my tables sooner or later, with the exception of you fellows. And let's just say those horse thieves are behind on their payments and not likely to be accommodating about paying up. You see you meet Deputy McCormick, and I'll call it even."

"Done," James said before Simon could do more than open his mouth.

"Wait a minute…" Simon started.

Rankin stuck out his hand. "Good doing business with you."

"We don't do business with you," Simon said, but

James took the miscreant's hand and shook it. Then he turned to head for the main cabin.

All James needed was Pa's rifle, which hung on a hook by the back door. Drew had carved the family two dugout canoes a few years ago. They were hidden under some brush by the edge of the lake and used for the occasional fishing trip into deeper water. He'd take one across the lake, hunt down those robbers and rescue his horses and wagon.

He was a little surprised to find Simon pacing him. "You're not going after those men."

"Sure I am," James said, climbing up on the porch and taking down the rifle. It was a special piece with seven rounds in the chamber. Bless Levi for keeping it fully loaded.

"You've made it abundantly clear that this is my problem, Simon," he said, slinging the gun over his shoulder. "You ought to be happy I intend to fix it."

Simon grabbed his arm, drawing him up short. "There are two of them and only one of you."

"Grossly unfair, I know," James said. "I'll try to give them a warning so they have time to draw their guns."

Simon's eyes looked like two chips of green ice. "This isn't funny."

"I think it's hilarious, you worried about me," James said. "Never thought I'd see that in my lifetime."

Simon dropped his hold. "I worry about you all the time. Why do you think I went looking for you when you didn't come home on time?"

"I figured you were following Drew's orders, as usual."

He knew it irked Simon to have been raised under

Drew's thumb, and the red that washed into his brother's face proved he wasn't beyond caring even now that they were grown. "If you won't listen to me," Simon threatened, "maybe you'll listen to him."

"Why set a precedent?" James countered, turning for the shore.

He heard Simon stop behind him. "Catherine might have something to say about this."

For once, the reaction of his determined sister-in-law could not sway him. He knew what he was doing was right. This was his chance to make amends. To make a difference for his family.

"Then by all means," James slung over his shoulder, "go tell her."

"What about Rina?" Simon said. "Are you willing to leave her behind, too?"

James stopped, feeling as if his brother had thrown a rope that tugged him home. "She'll understand," James said. "More than you do."

"You're right there," Simon said. "I've never understood you."

James glanced back to where his brother stood on the path, stiff with concern. "Don't worry, Simon. If everything goes right, I'll have the wagon back to you before dark."

"And if everything goes wrong?" Simon challenged.

James smiled. "You won't have to worry about me failing the family again."

Chapter Nineteen

Rina was making notes at her desk when Simon burst through the door. Mr. Hennessy, who had stayed after class to clean off the blackboard for her, looked up with a frown as the tall logger strode up the center aisle of the school.

"You have to stop James," Simon said, coming to a halt in front of Rina's desk.

Rina raised her brows and set down her pencil. "I sincerely doubt anyone can stop your brother when he's set his mind on something," she told Simon.

He ran a hand back through his hair, and it suddenly struck her that she had never seen Simon discomposed before. Now his eyes were wide enough that she could see the expanse of green clearly, and his breathing was ragged even though she doubted he could have run very far.

"You don't understand," he grit out. "He's going after those horse thieves alone."

Fear pushed her to her feet. "What? He could be killed!"

Simon stepped aside and motioned her to the door. "Agreed. Go tell him that, for he won't listen to me."

Rina swept around the desk and hurried for the door, Simon falling into step behind her. But when she reached the porch and scanned the clearing, she caught no sign of James.

Simon directed her around the main house to a path that led down toward the lake. "He'll take one of the dugouts," he explained, shoving aside a branch that had dipped low over the track. "Rankin said the thieves were camped across the lake."

"And you believed him?" Rina challenged, lifting her skirts so she could move faster over the uneven ground.

"James did," Simon qualified. He crossed in front of her to help her over a large puddle. "He's determined to rescue those horses."

"Of course he is," Rina scolded. "You must know what they mean to him."

Simon shook his head as he stepped back from her. "They're big and powerful, and everyone remarks on them whenever he takes them into town. That's no reason to risk his life."

Rina frowned at him. Did his brother truly not understand what Lance and Percy meant to James? She was beginning to realize from James's conversation that he considered himself the least important of his talented family. She had a feeling that everything he did—from his tailored suits to his etched-silver gun—was to convince himself he was worthwhile. Of course he would want to make up for losing the horses and the wagon, believing that he had failed his family again.

She could easily have throttled the person who had put such nonsense in his head.

And she wouldn't have been surprised if he wasn't walking beside her now.

They came out on the lake. The water stretched blue before them, lapping against the pebbled shore. At the very end, Mt. Rainer rose in snow-capped majesty, as if standing guardian. Yet still she couldn't spy James.

Simon's head turned from left to right as he surveyed the lake. Then he pointed. "There."

Rina could just make out a craft far across the water. The sun caught on the gold-brown hair of the boat's only occupant.

"James!" she cried, but her call drifted away on the breeze.

"He'll never hear you," Simon said. He turned to glance around the shore, then strode up to a group of bushes and shoved inside them.

"What are you doing?" Rina asked, following him. "Shouldn't we find a way to go after him?"

Simon reemerged, dragging a small boat. It looked as if someone had taken a log, scraped off the bark and hollowed out the center to allow a few people to sit inside it.

"I am going after him," he said, pulling the boat down to the water, where the end began to float. "You're going back to the house and alerting the family."

Perhaps she should. It would be safe, quick. But she refused to take the easy way out when James might be in danger. She shook her head. "Let me come with you."

One foot in the boat, Simon straightened to eye her. "You'll only slow me down."

"Perhaps someone should slow you," she told him. "Perhaps we should both take a moment to think. James is after the horses and wagon. He seems to know where to go. Do we?"

She could almost see the thoughts shifting behind Simon's light green eyes. "Only a general direction. I'll take John with me. He's our best tracker."

Rina cocked her head. "And what will you do if you locate the thieves before James does? If they disposed of the horses and wagon, how will you recognize them before they rob you, too? Only James and I have seen them."

Simon puffed out a breath. "All right, Miss Fosgrave. You win. I'll take you and John with me. But not dressed like that. You'll never fit in the boat."

Rina glanced down at her full-skirted gown. "I fear this is all I currently own, Mr. Wallin."

He bent and tugged the boat up out of the reach of the waves. "Then it's a good thing I have a large family, ma'am. Surely we'll have something more useful for you to wear if I'm to take you into the deep woods."

On the east side of Lake Union, James drew the dugout up onto the shore and stowed it under a blackberry bush. He doubted too many people would happen upon it, but he didn't want to lose any more of his family's property.

Adjusting the gun strap over his shoulder, he set off through the woods. His plan was simple—locate the outlaws' camp, get the drop on them and make off with Lance and Percy. Without the horses, the two thieves wouldn't be able to move the wagon far. While they might get away temporarily, James could come back with Deputy McCormick and harness the horses to drive the wagon home while the lawman hunted down the robbers.

This side of the lake was more sparsely populated. He knew a wagon road led north toward outlying settlements. Given the forest's untamed nature, the wagon was pretty much constrained to that road. All he had to do was find it.

That proved easier than he'd thought. He'd only gone a mile into the woods, tracking directly east from the water by keeping the sun at his back, when he reached the road. Just wide enough for a wagon, the track threaded through the fir, cedar and thick stands of alder. Pressed into the mud was the long line of iron-bound wheels and the hoofprints of horses. No one else he knew in these parts used horses to pull their wagons. It had to be his team. He headed north, keeping an eye out for movement and an ear open for the creak of the wagon.

The sun was dipping toward home when he located the camp. He heard the voices first, whining, complaining. Then he caught the scent of cooking fish. Apparently the thieves didn't feel the need to hide their presence. They had reason to believe they were alone out here. But they were wrong.

Unslinging Pa's rifle, he crept closer.

They'd set up camp in a clearing just off the road where a stream ran down to the lake. Davy was crouched beside a fire, cooking a trout on a stick, while Nash brought back another armload of firewood. Their bedrolls were laid under the wagon for protection, guns propped in easy reach against the wheels.

But what made James's heart start beating faster was the sight of Lance and Percy. His horses were standing under a fir, their halters tied high on a branch so they couldn't even lower their heads past their knees to graze on the greenery clustered below them. Their matted manes and tails told of their treatment. Had the thieves even bothered to feed them? Water them? He felt as if someone had shoved a burning coal down his throat.

Suddenly, Percy raised his head, nostrils twitching and ears coming forward. He shifted, tugged on the halter as if testing its strength. The wind was blowing in from the lake, so James should have been upwind of them. Had the horse still managed to sense James's presence?

Now Lance stamped his feet, jerking against the halter, as if trying to turn his head and look in James's direction. James wanted to reach out, soothe the horses, but he knew that would have to wait. First he had to take care of those thieves.

He glanced back at the fire and frowned. Davy was still crouched by the fire, licking oil from his thick fingers. Where was Nash?

He heard the double click of a rifle cocking behind him.

"Put down the gun," Nash said. "Now."

He'd never turn in time to shoot before he was shot. But to surrender Pa's rifle on top of the horses and wagon?

"Let me walk away," James said, "and I won't tell the sheriff."

"Now, why don't I believe you?" Nash sneered. "Seems like those horses mean a lot to you. Haven't found a fellow yet who's willing to take them off our hands, and a few even tried to chase us down for them. Everyone knows they belong to a fellow named James Wallin."

"He sounds like an upstanding gentleman," James said.

The cold metal of the gun barrel touched his skin. "He sounds like a pain in the neck. Now, drop your gun and march. It's time we figured out what to do about all of you."

James set down the rifle and rose, hands up. Nash bent just far enough to scoop up Pa's gun, then walked James into camp and directed him toward the tree where Lance and Percy were tied. Percy nickered in greeting, straining at the halter.

Davy scrambled to his feet at the sight of James. "Did he bring the law?"

"Not that I can tell," Nash replied, handing Davy Pa's rifle. "Cover him while I do the honors."

Davy raised the gun and sighted down it at James's chest. His partner crossed to James's side and eyed him a moment.

"Maybe we best make sure you don't have any other weapons on you," Nash said, eyes narrowed as if he didn't trust James for a second. "Keep those arms up."

Fingers laced behind his head, James stood as the outlaw patted his arms, his chest.

"I should warn you I'm ticklish," he said.

Nash didn't respond to the joke. His poking and prodding had yielded a thunk, and he dipped into James's pocket and drew out the miniature.

James lunged for it. "Give me that!"

Nash shoved him back.

Immediately, Lance and Percy shifted, buffeting Nash on either side. He swatted them back with his free hand.

"Stupid critters," he complained, tucking the miniature away. "I'll just keep this little trinket as a remembrance of our time together. I figure you owe me something for bothering with them. Now, sit!"

James considered shoving past him for the lake, but if Davy was any kind of shot, the outlaw could pick him off before he reached the water. So he sat on the roots of the tree while Nash bound his arms back around it.

Percy took a bite at the thief as he rose, but Nash twisted away before the horse could do more than snag his sleeve.

"I'm sorry I ever laid eyes on you," he told Percy.

"I'm sure they feel the same way about you," James said as Nash headed back for the fire. He tugged at the rope, but it held tight. Both horses lowered their heads to blow in his face.

"I'm happy to see you, too, boys," James murmured to them. "But we're in a real fix now."

Davy seemed to think so, as well. "Maybe we should just shoot them all," he said, face pale in the fading light. "Get rid of the evidence in the lake."

Nash nodded. "Might be a good idea. Looky what I found." He pulled out the miniature and handed it to his partner before bending to retrieve the last of the fish.

James felt ill. "Do what you want with me, but let them go."

Nash snorted, straightening. "They're dead either way. They wouldn't last a day out here alone. We already had to chase off a catamount that was drooling over them."

Davy had been studying the miniature. Now he slipped it into his pocket and raised his head. "Then let's leave them all. I can't take this no more."

As if Lance and Percy knew the robbers had reached their limit, both horses raised their heads and bugled, stomping at the ground, thrashing against their ties. James had to press himself back against the tree to keep from being trampled.

Davy clapped his hands over his ears. "Make them stop!"

Nash snapped up Pa's rifle and aimed it at the horses.

"Don't!" James cried. Breath coming fast, he lowered his voice and tried to catch Lance's eye.

"Easy," James called. "Easy, gents. There now. Quiet."

At the sound of his voice, they settled. Lance lowered his head and blew a breath against James's hair. Percy snorted in annoyance at the thieves.

Nash eyed James. "Well look at that, Davy. They listen to him well enough."

He turned to his partner. "I can see we've been trying to sell to the wrong folks. None of these farmers is ever going to take a chance on them horses. They all know the beasts belong to this fellow. We need to find men like us, who won't care where the horses came from."

Davy nodded slowly. "All right, but what about him?"

Nash glanced James's way. "We'll take him along to keep the horses biddable until we can find a buyer. He won't risk us shooting them."

With a sinking feeling, James knew Nash was right.

"And then what?" Davy pressed.

"Then," Nash said, fingers tightening on the gun, "we leave him in the deep woods for the catamounts to play with."

Chapter Twenty

Rifles slung over their shoulders, Simon and John jumped out of the second dugout, their boots splashing in the clear waters of Lake Union as they hauled the boat ashore with Rina clutching the side. She hadn't been sure of the craft when she'd first seen it, but it had borne them safely across the lake to the area where Simon was certain James had landed. As the men released it, she rose and stepped out, half boots crunching on the pebbles and dried moss that littered the area.

She hadn't been sure of her attire, either. Both the White River school and the Fosgraves would have been shocked by the outfit Beth had put together for her.

"You can't wander around in the woods in a dress," the girl had said, rummaging around in various chests upstairs at the Wallin main cabin.

"I did before," Rina had pointed out.

Beth had raised her head and her brows. "And look how well that turned out."

She had insisted on something more practical. So now Levi's trousers were cinched at Rina's waist with her leather belt and puddled over her half boots.

James's dress shirt was tucked into the trousers, sleeves rolled up at the wrist. With her cloak slung about her shoulders, she thought she looked more like the outlaws they hunted than the schoolteacher she had once dreamed of becoming.

A dream that had come true because of James.

She drew in a deep breath of the moist air. He had to be safe. Oh, he could be so bold, so rash, but this time, just this time, he had to have thought things through.

Protect him, Lord! He's trying to do what's right. Surely You honor that!

John left Simon to hide the boat from prying eyes and went to study the edge of the forest. Rina knew he was looking for any sign that James had passed this way. Simon stowed the boat under an overhanging bush, then returned to Rina's side.

"No sign of the other dugout," he commented, eyes narrowing as he scanned the shoreline. "James must have hidden it."

Rina frowned at him. "You sound surprised."

"I am," he said. "It's not like him to think ahead."

He was always so hard on his brother. "He thought ahead," Rina informed him, pulling her cloak a little closer in the cool air as she waited for John to give them the signal to move out. "He planned this so he wouldn't endanger anyone else in the family. He likely reasoned that they were his horses, so it was his duty to find them."

John motioned to them, and Simon started out for the trees. "You assume he thinks about his duty," he said.

"No, Mr. Wallin," Rina replied, pacing him. "I don't assume. I know James thinks about his duty. Perhaps he would confide in you more if you stopped picking at him incessantly."

Simon stiffened, but John clapped a hand to his brother's shoulder as Simon and Rina drew abreast.

"It's in Simon's nature to pick," he told Rina with a smile to soften his words. "He prefers that things progress in an orderly fashion. Nothing ever truly satisfies him unless it's perfect."

"There actually isn't such a thing as perfection," Simon said, but John poked a finger in his chest.

"See? You couldn't even let my statement stand."

"Because it isn't accurate," Simon protested. "I don't expect the world to be perfect."

"No," Rina said. "Just James, it seems."

John chuckled at the look on Simon's face, then hurried to lead them into the woods.

Following James's path was fairly easy. He had not been attempting to cover his trail, and he seemed to know where he was heading. The trail led unerringly through the woods, always toward the east. The sun was low on the horizon, lengthening their shadows and slanting through the woods with a reddish light that made it look as if a fire was chasing them forward. The trousers felt odd against her legs, and she had to stop herself from reaching for skirts that weren't there every time she climbed over a log or ducked under a low-hanging branch.

She was glad when, a short while later, they came out on a wagon road, winding its way north.

"Hoofprints," John said, pointing to the shapes in the muddy track. "Those have to belong to James's horses."

"And that one to James," Rina said, nodding at the outline of a boot.

Simon glanced up at the sky. "We don't have much light left. Keep moving."

"I'll go ahead, scout the way," John offered, breaking into a jog. He disappeared around a bend in the road.

"You're wrong, you know," Simon told Rina as they followed at a brisk walk. "I do not expect James to be perfect. No one is perfect. Our father was the finest man I've ever known, and even he made mistakes."

Rina knew he must be thinking about the widowmaker. "How awful that you all had to see him die. I know you must feel his loss keenly, even as James does."

"Pa's death hurt us all," he said, voice hard and eyes once more narrowed. "James no more than the rest of us."

"And there you would be wrong," Rina said, shaking mud off one of her boots. "James feels it more. He blames himself."

Simon jerked to a stop on the road. "Did he tell you that?"

"Yes," Rina said, raising her chin. "And I think you blame him, as well."

He shook his head, hands tightening on the gun strap about his chest. "I never said that."

"Not in so many words," Rina allowed. "But John is right. You tell him by word and deed that you doubt his choices, his actions. Believing that, how could he not think you blame him for failing to see the branch?"

Simon's look went out into the trees, but she thought he saw another clearing from ten years ago.

"None of us saw that branch," he said, voice softening. "James's job was to look out for danger, but he couldn't have seen the widow-maker from where Pa had stationed him."

Rina kept her gaze on him. "So it wasn't James's fault."

"Not at all." His look came back to meet hers, and sorrow darkened the green. "No one blames James."

"Except James himself," Rina realized.

"I don't argue with him because of Pa," Simon continued, starting forward once more. "I argue because I don't understand some of his choices since Pa died. He makes everything into a joke."

"He makes light of the world because he cannot dwell on the dark," Rina explained, lengthening her stride to keep up with him.

Simon cast her a glance as if he wasn't so sure of her interpretation. "He wastes money on fancy clothes no one but us will see, and he bought horses better suited to race than to pull a plow."

"When you think no one else believes in you, you have to take steps to believe in yourself," Rina countered.

Simon gave her a hand to help her over a particularly rough patch. "And then he appointed a school-teacher who had no experience teaching."

"A terrible fault to be sure, believing in someone," she said, landing on the other side. "I was certain it was the wrong choice, too, until I met James."

Simon sighed. "Perhaps I don't know my brother as well as I thought. Thank you for telling me this. If we find James, I'll talk to him."

"*When* we find James," she corrected him, "I will hold you to your promise."

They came around the bend to find John waiting in the brush as little ways along. Finger to his lips, he motioned them forward with his free hand.

"There's a camp just into the woods," he murmured when they reached him. "The horses are tied to a tree, and so is James."

Rina's breath felt tight. "Can we set them all free?"

"Not easily," John assured her. "I only caught sight of two men, but their guns are close to hand. I doubt we could get the drop on them."

"Can we circle around?" Simon asked. "Free James at least?"

"There isn't a lot of brush between here and there," John answered. "Too great a chance they'd see us."

"Unless someone distracted them," Rina said. "People rarely see what they don't expect."

It was something Mr. Fosgrave had said once, and she'd only realized the truth of it when he'd confessed. It was her choice whether she followed in his footsteps or embraced who she truly was, a woman who was not above a bit of whimsy, who no longer feared to reach for the future and the man she loved.

Simon and John were staring at her as if they guessed what she was about to suggest.

"No," John started, but Simon put a hand on his arm to stop him.

"A distraction might work," he said, gaze on Rina. "What did you have in mind, Miss Fosgrave?"

Rina swallowed, fear gathering around her like her cloak. She knew she must put it aside for James's sake.

You've taught me so much the last few days, Father.
Help me use it to good purpose now.

"I intend to give them an engagement they would
never expect on the frontier," she said. "Find me a
good-sized stick, and I'll explain."

James's arms sagged. He'd been rubbing the rope
along the rough bark for an hour if the dimming light
was any indication, but still the rope stayed tight. All
the while his mind had been turning over his predicament, seeking another way out. Nothing had seemed
likely of success.

He should have asked his brothers for help, but he'd
wanted to prove that he could solve the problem he'd
created. He owed them that, at least. Now he was likely
to lose everything—the horses, the wagon, his life.

And Rina.

He rested his head against the bark and closed his
eyes. That was the greatest loss—the chance to grow
closer to her. She brought out the best in him, made
him want to be the hero instead of the clown. She made
him believe he could succeed, could make a difference, if only for her.

And he loved her for it.

He'd held her back from the first, fearing just this
reaction. He hadn't wanted to fall in love, to risk his
heart, to risk a loss as great as when Ma had lost Pa.
Yet what had Ma gained? Love and a family and memories to sustain her. Surely loving Rina could bring all
that and more. Winning her was worth the risk.

Lord, protect her. I knew I was falling in love, but
I couldn't find the courage to tell her. I thought I had
to be more than I am. Now I know she is all I need

save You. Forgive me for failing again, her and my family and You.

From deep inside, a verse floated up, remembered from family worship years ago. He could hear his father's deep voice, so like Drew's, reading from the leather-bound tome.

Judge not, and ye shall not be judged; condemn not, and ye shall not be condemned; forgive, and ye shall be forgiven. Give, and it will be given unto you, a good measure, pressed down and shaken together, and running over.

For the last ten years, he'd waited for someone to call his bluff, tell him how he'd failed—Drew, Ma, Simon, God. But they never had. Perhaps they'd never seen the need. They'd given him the good measure of their love and friendship. Perhaps they didn't blame him.

Perhaps the person whose forgiveness he needed was his own.

A flurry of movement forced his eyes open. Davy had climbed to his feet and was pointing his gun toward the road.

"Someone's coming."

Nash rose as well, weapon at the ready.

Rina glided out of the woods. Her silky hair fell past her shoulders in a curtain of gold. Her cloak flowed past her lithe figure outlined in a pair of trousers and... his dress shirt? Her gaze was serene, her steps steady, as if she walked down the hall of a castle. His call of warning died away. She was simply magnificent.

The outlaws seemed just as mesmerized, for they stood openmouthed until she was only a few feet away from the fire. The light flickered about her, making her seem even more unreal. Her gaze was clear as she looked from one thief to the other. Percy nickered a greeting, and Lance bobbed his head as if doing her homage.

"Ain't that the woman he had with him afore?" Davy muttered to his partner.

Nash nodded, aiming at her. "You ain't getting the horses or your man, missus."

She planted her staff in the moss as if claiming the area for president and country. "I think you'll find you are mistaken, sir," she said, voice echoing in the woods. "You have no idea whose wrath you have incurred. I am the Princess Alexandrina Eugenia of the Kingdom of Battenburgia, and I demand that you release my royal escort at once." She swung the staff and pointed to James.

James wanted to shout with delight at her confidence, but he knew that would only ruin her presentation. He kept his head down and eyed the outlaws through his lashes.

Nash and Davy were staring at her.

"Never heard of a princess in the woods," Nash said, but James could hear doubt in his voice.

"Never seen a woman dressed like that afore neither," Davy murmured to him. "And remember all them fancy dresses she had with her?"

Something tugged at James's bonds, and he stiffened.

"Hold still," Simon whispered from behind him. "I'll have you free in a moment."

So that was the plan. Simon intended to cut him loose, and Rina was the distraction. While he applauded her bravery, he didn't like her making herself a target. The outlaws could only take so much before they reacted, badly. But perhaps he could help convince her audience of her ruse.

"Don't humble yourself for my sake, your highness," he called. "I'm not worth your trouble."

Rina inclined her head regally in his direction as if acknowledging her superior position. "I refuse to see one of my loyal servants mistreated," she said. Now the staff, which she held like a scepter, swung toward the outlaws. "By stealing what is mine, you have committed an act of war against a sovereign nation. Surrender now, or face retribution."

Nash and Davy exchanged glances. James could see sweat on their brows even as he felt the strands of the rope parting.

"She's telling tales," Nash said, turning to Rina once more. "If you're a princess, where's your crown?"

Rina regarded him as if he were mud that speckled her slipper. "No princess wears her jewels around thieves."

Davy started, then nudged Nash with his boot. "I knew I seen her afore."

"You already said," Nash grumbled. "She was with him in the woods."

"No," Davy said with a shake of his head. "She was in that picture!" He lowered his gun to dig out the miniature and shove it at Nash.

Rina took a step forward. "That's mine!"

Would she give herself away? James strained at the rope and felt it give a little more. He had to protect her.

Nash glanced between the miniature and her, eyes narrowed. "So you're a princess, eh? What about your army, then? Don't princesses usually have a whole flock of fellows to do their bidding?"

She seemed to recall her role, for she lifted her staff as if summoning her loyal subjects right then. "Sir John of the Vale," she called. "Are you in position?"

The bushes to the north rattled as if a regiment awaited her word. "Aye, your highness!"

So John was in on it, too. Another strand parted, then the rope went slack. What had happened to Simon?

"Sir Simon de Mont," she called again. "Are you ready, as well?"

"I and all my retainers are at your service, your highness," Simon called from a little ways away.

Davy dropped his gun and held up his hands.

Nash backed away, gun trained on Rina. "Don't shoot, or I'll kill your princess."

James wrenched at the rope. He had to reach Nash before that gun went off.

Rina didn't betray the least fear. "You," she spat out, head high and eyes blazing, "wouldn't dare. Every law officer in America, Canada and the Continent would hunt you down." She strode forward, staff outstretched. "Now, kneel!"

Nash knelt.

The last strand snapped, and James pulled the rope from his body even as he scrambled to his feet.

"Sir John, Sir Simon," Rina called. "Secure the road and then tie up these men. I grow tired of their presence." Turning, she motioned to James with her staff. With her back to the outlaws, James was the only one who could see the laughter in her gaze.

"Come along, Mr. Wallin," she said, mouth twitching as if she fought a smile. "The Kingdom of Battenburgia has further need of your services, and so do I."

Chapter Twenty-One

"**Y**ou should have seen her," John crowed to the rest of the family the moment they returned to Wallin Landing. "She had those thieves cowering from the moment she walked out of the woods."

"Our Miss Fosgrave has a presence," Beth bragged.

"So I said from the beginning," Catherine agreed.

As the rest of the Wallins crowded around John to hear the story, Rina slipped away. She knew how the tale ended. They had loaded the horse thieves into the wagon, and Simon had driven them back to Seattle after dropping off James, John and Rina and picking up Levi as a guard. John and Drew had plans to go after the dugouts in the light of day.

James had made sure to retrieve the miniature from Nash and return it to Rina before Simon or John saw what it portrayed. "This is yours," he murmured. "Only you have the right to share it."

She had tucked it into her cloak for safekeeping. Someday, she'd confide the whole story to the other Wallins. Right now, however, the only voice she wanted to hear was James's.

He had hung back on the porch when they'd entered the main house as if unsure of his welcome. She'd hoped the conversation she'd overheard on the way back might have changed his outlook. True to his word, Simon had spoken to James about the death of their father and assured James he did not blame him.

"Though I may never see life as you do," Simon had admitted. "Something to joke about."

James had clapped him on the shoulder. "Don't worry about that, Simon. You're serious enough for the both of us."

Now she found him leaning against one of the porch supports, gaze out into the starlight.

"Everything all right?" she asked.

In answer, he slipped an arm around her waist and drew her close. Her head rested on his chest as they stood, listening to the sounds of the night—the low of the oxen, the coo of a dove, the whisper of the wind through the trees. For a moment, she thought his heart beat in time with hers.

He reached for her hand, threaded their fingers together. "Thank you for talking to Simon."

Rina studied the shadows of their hands. "How did you know Simon and I had talked?"

"He seemed to see things differently. You have that same effect on your students. And me."

Oh, but she hoped so. "Then why did you stay out here?"

She felt him shrug. "It was your moment. You deserved to shine without any jokes or any of my family worrying about me."

"They worry about you because they love you," she told him.

"I'm beginning to believe that now. I had some time to think there at the outlaws' camp. I've always craved forgiveness, when I already had it. I was the one who had to let it go, to believe. I didn't fail them."

Rina gave him a squeeze. "You couldn't fail them. You care too much."

She felt his head brush hers. "I do care, Rina. About them. About Lance and Percy. About you."

Rina gazed up at him. He was a darker shape against the night, but she could hear the awe in his voice, the same awe she'd seen on his face when she'd walked into the clearing and demanded the outlaws set him free.

"I'm not a princess, James," she said. "I'm a schoolteacher, and that's enough for me."

He gave their joined hands a swing. "Do you want nothing else from life, Rina? A home of your own, marriage?"

Hope blossomed inside her. "Only with the right man. But the man I love has yet to ask me properly."

He pulled back. "Ask you properly? I went down on bended knee, woman!"

Of course he would assume she meant him, the rogue! "That's how you propose to a princess you admire," she said, heart beating faster. "How do you propose to a lady you love?"

In answer, he bent his head and kissed her, softly, gently. The sweet pressure of his lips set her to trembling. When he pulled back, she could feel him gazing down at her.

"Alexandrina Eugenia Fosgrave," he intoned, "dear Rina, I don't care if you're a princess royal or a penniless schoolteacher. I love you. I am only my best when

I am with you. And so I offer you all that I am or ever will be. Will you marry me?"

Tears were warming her eyes, but she didn't care. "Now that," she said, "was a proper proposal. Yes, James, I will marry you. You make me laugh, and you made me believe in myself when I wasn't even sure who I was anymore. How could I fail to fall in love with you?"

"It's a mystery, ma'am," he said, laughter spoiling his serious tone. He held her close and kissed her again, and, for the first time in a long time, Rina knew she was right where she belonged.

* * * * *

Dear Reader,

Thank you for reading *Frontier Engagement*, the third in my Frontier Bachelor series. I've always had a soft spot in my heart for rogues and rebels, and James Wallin is a little bit of both. I knew nothing less than a princess would do for him. And he was perfect for Rina, who needed a little frivolity in her life! If you enjoyed the story, please consider leaving a review on a major retailer site or reader site like Goodreads.

And if you'd like an excuse for frivolity, join me at my blog at nineteenteen.com, say hello on Facebook at facebook.com/authorreginascott, or visit my website at reginascott.com, where you can sign up to receive an alert when the next book is out.

Blessings!

Regina Scott

COMING NEXT MONTH FROM
Love Inspired® Historical

Available September 1, 2015

WOLF CREEK WIDOW
by Penny Richards

Still healing from emotional—and physical—wounds left by her late husband, widow Meg Thomerson turns to Ace Allen for help running her business. Promising to remain at her side while she recovers, can he also mend her bruised heart?

HIS PRECIOUS INHERITANCE
by Dorothy Clark

Newspaper editor Charles Thornberg is an expert at running a business, not raising a toddler. He desperately needs reporter Clarice Gordon's help caring for his little brother...and learning how to become a father—and husband.

A HOME FOR HIS FAMILY
by Jan Drexler

Cowboy Nate Colby journeys west for a fresh start with his orphaned nieces and nephew. Maybe fellow newcomer and beautiful schoolmarm Sarah MacFarland will be the missing piece to their fractured family...

THE MATCHMAKER'S MATCH
by Jessica Nelson

Lady Amelia Baxley is known for finding perfect love matches—for everyone except for herself. She agrees to help Lord Spencer Ashwhite find a wife...but can she follow through after she begins falling for the reformed rake?

LIHCNM0815

REQUEST YOUR FREE BOOKS!

2 FREE INSPIRATIONAL NOVELS
PLUS 2 *FREE* MYSTERY GIFTS

Love Inspired® HISTORICAL

YES! Please send me 2 FREE Love Inspired® Historical novels and my 2 FREE mystery gifts (gifts are worth about $10). After receiving them, if I don't wish to receive any more books, I can return the shipping statement marked "cancel." If I don't cancel, I will receive 4 brand-new novels every month and be billed just $4.99 per book in the U.S. or $5.49 per book in Canada. That's a saving of at least 17% off the cover price. It's quite a bargain! Shipping and handling is just 50¢ per book in the U.S. and 75¢ per book in Canada.* I understand that accepting the 2 free books and gifts places me under no obligation to buy anything. I can always return a shipment and cancel at any time. Even if I never buy another book, the two free books and gifts are mine to keep forever.

102/302 IDN GH6Z

Name _____ (PLEASE PRINT) _____

Address _____ Apt. # _____

City _____ State/Prov. _____ Zip/Postal Code _____

Signature (if under 18, a parent or guardian must sign)

Mail to the Reader Service:
IN U.S.A.: P.O. Box 1867, Buffalo, NY 14240-1867
IN CANADA: P.O. Box 609, Fort Erie, Ontario L2A 5X3

Want to try two free books from another series?
Call 1-800-873-8635 or visit www.ReaderService.com.

* Terms and prices subject to change without notice. Prices do not include applicable taxes. Sales tax applicable in N.Y. Canadian residents will be charged applicable taxes. Offer not valid in Quebec. This offer is limited to one order per household. Not valid for current subscribers to Love Inspired Historical books. All orders subject to credit approval. Credit or debit balances in a customer's account(s) may be offset by any other outstanding balance owed by or to the customer. Please allow 4 to 6 weeks for delivery. Offer available while quantities last.

Your Privacy—The Reader Service is committed to protecting your privacy. Our Privacy Policy is available online at www.ReaderService.com or upon request from the Reader Service.

We make a portion of our mailing list available to reputable third parties that offer products we believe may interest you. If you prefer that we not exchange your name with third parties, or if you wish to clarify or modify your communication preferences, please visit us at www.ReaderService.com/consumerchoice or write to us at Reader Service Preference Service, P.O. Box 9062, Buffalo, NY 14240-9062. Include your complete name and address.

LIH15

SPECIAL EXCERPT FROM

Love Inspired® HISTORICAL

Still healing from emotional—and physical—wounds left by her late husband, widow Meg Thomerson turns to Ace Allen for help running her business. Promising to remain at her side while she recovers, can he also mend her bruised heart?

Read on for a sneak preview of
WOLF CREEK WIDOW,
available in September 2015 from
Love Inspired Historical!

"Look at me, Meg," he said in that deep voice. "Who do you see?"

"What?" She frowned, unsure of what he was doing and wondering at the sorrow reflected in his eyes.

"Who do you see standing here?"

What did he want from her? she wondered in confusion. "I see you," she said at last. "Ace Allen."

"If you never believe anything else about me, you can believe that I would never deliberately harm a hair on your head."

His statement was much the same as what he'd said the day before in the woods. It seemed Ace was determined that she knew he was no threat to her.

"Elton used to stand in the doorway like that a lot. For just a moment when I looked up I saw him, not you. I…I'm s-sorry."

"I'm not Elton, Meg."

His voice held an urgency she didn't understand. "I know that."

"Do you?" he persisted. "Look at me. Do I look like Elton?"

"No," she murmured. Elton hadn't been nearly as tall, and unlike Ace he'd been almost too good-looking to be masculine. She'd once heard him called pretty. No one would ever think of Ace Allen as pretty. Striking, surely. Magnificent, maybe. Pretty, never.

"No, and I don't act like him. Can you see that? Do you believe it?"

Still confused, but knowing somehow that her answer was of utmost importance, she whispered, "Yes."

He nodded, and the torment in his eyes faded. "You have nothing to be sorry for, Meg Thomerson. That's something else you can be certain of, so never think it again." With that, he turned and left her alone with her thoughts and a lot of questions.

Don't miss
WOLF CREEK WIDOW by Penny Richards,
available September 2015 wherever
Love Inspired® Historical books and ebooks are sold.

OCT 28 2019 //

Love Inspired

Love the Love Inspired book you just read?

Your opinion matters.

Review this book on your favorite
book site, review site, blog or your own
social media properties and share your
opinion with other readers!